SAN FRANCISCO NOIR

EDITED BY PETER MARAVELIS

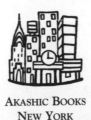

AKASHIC BOOKS
NEW YORK

Series concept by Tim McLoughlin and Johnny Temple

Published by Akashic Books
©2005 Peter Maravelis

San Francisco map by Sohrab Habibion

ISBN-13: 978-1-888451-91-7
ISBN-10: 1-888451-91-2
Library of Congress Control Number: 2005925465
All rights reserved
Third printing
Printed in Canada

Akashic Books
PO Box 1456
New York, NY 10009
Akashic7@aol.com
www.akashicbooks.com

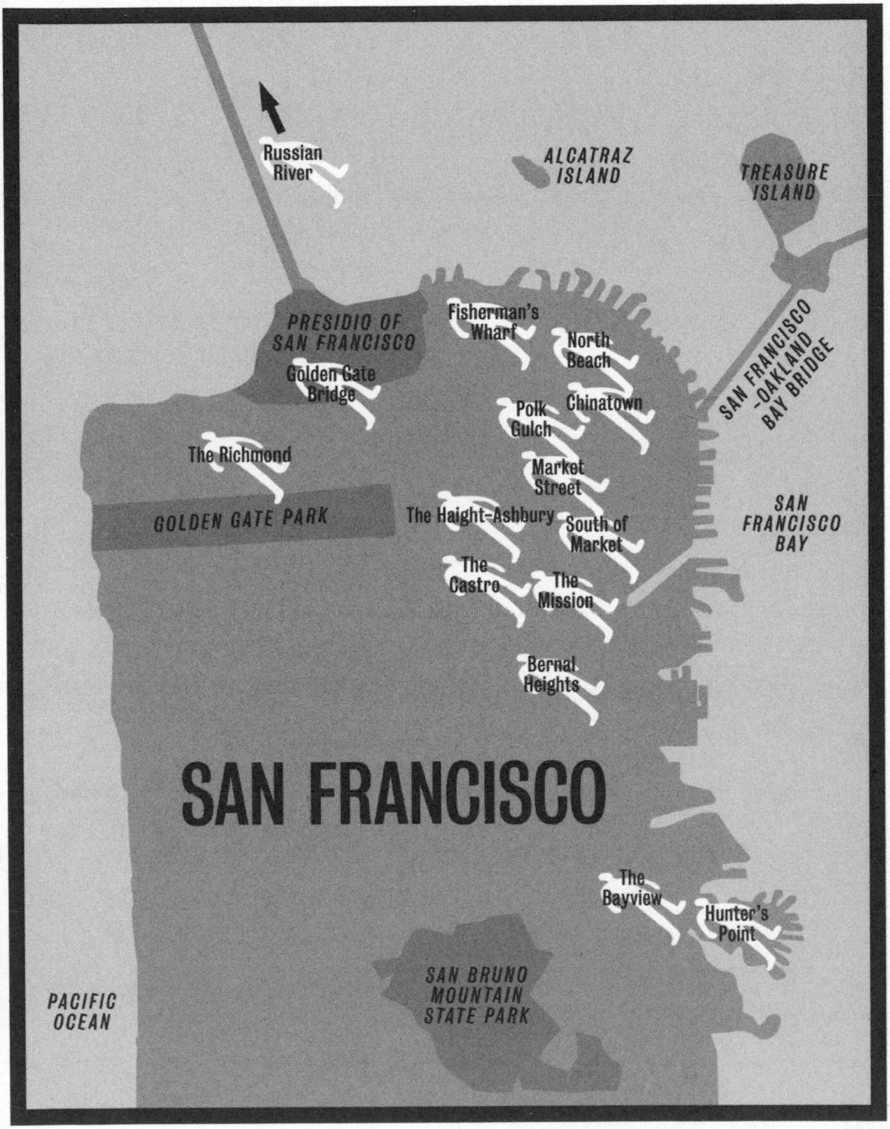
Russian River
ALCATRAZ ISLAND
TREASURE ISLAND
PRESIDIO OF SAN FRANCISCO
Fisherman's Wharf
North Beach
Golden Gate Bridge
Polk Gulch
Chinatown
SAN FRANCISCO -OAKLAND BAY BRIDGE
The Richmond
Market Street
GOLDEN GATE PARK
The Haight-Ashbury
South of Market
SAN FRANCISCO BAY
The Castro
The Mission
Bernal Heights
SAN FRANCISCO
The Bayview
Hunter's Point
SAN BRUNO MOUNTAIN STATE PARK
PACIFIC OCEAN

*It's an odd thing, but anyone who disappears
is said to be seen in San Francisco.*
—Oscar Wilde

TABLE OF CONTENTS

INTRODUCTION
A Geography of Transgression

Recently strolling through the narrow back alleys of Chinatown, I chanced upon an elderly Asian man playing a Chinese double-stringed violin known as an erhu. He was performing an eerie and atonal rendition of "Auld Lang Syne." I noticed a faint smile upon his lips as his fingers moved effortlessly up and down the neck of his delicate instrument. His sweet and ominous music followed me down the crooked cobblestone paths as I made my way to work that day.

Since then, I have repeatedly sighted him throughout North Beach and Chinatown. He always performs the same song in the same strange manner. It appears to be the only tune in his repertoire. The melody has become so embedded upon my psyche that it now serves as the de facto soundtrack for my walks through the city.

A few days ago, I caught yet another glimpse of the erhu-playing man. This time, he was performing a couple yards away from a scraggly and comatose guy doubled-up on the ground adjacent to a bus shelter. Next to the unconscious fellow was a paper coffee cup containing a scant number of dirty coins and a weakly scrawled sign pleading for a handout. Directly above him stood a billboard that read: *Is your business due for termination?* The ad was paid for by an organization calling itself Nevada Rescue. It displayed a photo of a middle-aged white man's beleaguered face, covered in bruises.

The billboard was referring to the recent downturn in the SF economy, encouraging the soon-to-be-disenfranchised to "jump ship" and join the burgeoning labor camps of Nevada. I asked the musician if he could play me a different tune. He smiled without reply.

San Francisco is a city shaped by protean forces. The fusion of terrain, weather, and seismic phenomena has produced an exquisitely volatile ecology. Hazardously steep hills lead into lush garden communities engulfed by banks of fog that roll through with regularity. The salty ocean air eats away at beachfront bungalows while constant tremors loosen the foundations of the most well-reinforced buildings. Skyscrapers built atop landfill haunt the dreams of jaded FEMA administrators, while insects the size of thumbnails threaten to crush local agribusiness. An eroding coastline offers even the staunchest of non-Buddhists a sobering meditation upon impermanence. These perilous conditions punctuate life on the edge of a continent. The divine travels on a collision course with the dangerous.

The city has also been shaped by dreams. Since its birth in the 1700s, immigrants have flocked to San Francisco in the hope of reinventing their lives. From the Gold Rush of the 1840s to the dot-com madness of the late twentieth century, the city has experienced successive waves of newcomers that have radically altered its profile. A myriad of social universes have come into being, quite often bleeding into each other's orbit. This has resulted in a rich cross-pollination of cultures. It has also led to tragic consequences. From "be-ins" to lynchings, San Franciscans have long had to live with a dialectic revolving around tolerance and backlash.

* * *

The operating motive behind this anthology has been to breach a certain literary canon. Crime fiction is the scalpel used to reveal San Francisco's pathological character. The contributors perform a brutal examination of the passions that govern life in the city. We offer tales that draw their breath from the obscured recesses of collective history.

Since the end of World War II there has been an ever-increasing rate of homelessness and displacement among the city's populace. This has been coupled with a privatization of public space that has largely erased the last structures of historic relevance. Some of the key questions that we hope to pose are: What happens when the history of a city begins to disappear? What happens to literature when it feeds upon the ruins of amnesia?

Bitterness becomes our poetry. We intend to poison you with its beauty.

San Francisco Noir brings together a stellar cast of writers to help expose the psychogeography of a city. Hidden and repressed memories are a focal point, as some of the best local writers, inside and out of the genre of crime fiction, weave tales that speak of the elemental motifs that surface in everyday life. These hard-biting stories explore San Francisco's shadowy nether regions in their sinister splendor. From inner-city boroughs like the Mission to the outlands of the Richmond, the authors investigate a broad cross section of the town. Landscape, historicity, and ethnicity are the backdrops as desperation, transgression, and madness fuel tales that offer a uniquely chthonic view of San Francisco.

Like nineteenth-century Frenchman Comte de Lautréamont's surrealist anti-hero, Maldoror, the characters that populate our collection traverse a landscape that is compelling and infernal. Sex-crazed bag-men, framed public officials, disillusioned prostitutes, psychotic kidnapping victims, and desperate ex-cons inhabit a realm where actions are governed by an algebra of desire. Beauty and treachery walk hand in hand. Welcome to a peninsula of broken dreams, shattered lives, and deadly liaisons. These are depictions of San Francisco the local visitors' bureau hopes will recede along with our fading memories. Meanwhile, the man with the violin continues to play his tune. We hope you'll enjoy the fare.

Peter Maravelis
San Francisco, July 2005

PART I

Edge City

THE PRISON

BY DOMENIC STANSBERRY

North Beach

I t was 1946, and Alcatraz was burning. I had just got back into town and stood in the crowd along the seawall, looking out toward the island. The riot at the prison had been going on for several days, and now a fire had broken out and smoke plumed out over the bay. There were all kinds of rumors running through the crowd. The prisoners had taken over. Warden Johnston was dead. Capone's gang had seized a patrol boat and a group of escapees had landed down at Baker Beach. The radio contradicted these reports, but from the seawall you could see that a marine flotilla had surrounded Alcatraz Island and helicopters were pouring tracer fire into the prison. The police had the wharf cordoned off but it didn't prevent the crowds from gathering. The off-duty sailors and Presidio boys mixing with the peace-time johnnies. The office girls and Chinese skirts. The Sicilians with their noses like giant fish.

In the crowd were people I knew from the old days. Some of them met my eyes, some didn't. My old friend Johnny Maglie stood in a group maybe ten yards away. He gave me a nod, but it wasn't him I was looking at. There was a woman, maybe twenty-five years old, black hair, wearing a red cardigan. Her name was Anne but I didn't know this yet. Her eyes met mine and I felt something fall apart inside me.

* * *

My father had given me a gun before I left Reno. He had been a figure in North Beach before the war—an editor, a man with opinions, and he used to carry a little German revolver in his vest pocket. The gun had been confiscated after Pearl Harbor, but he'd gotten himself another somewhere along the way and pressed it into my hand in the train station. A gallant, meaningless gesture.

"Take this," he said.

"I don't need a gun."

"You may be a war hero," he said, "but there are people in North Beach who hate me. Who have always hated me. They will go after you."

I humored the old man and took the gun. Truth was, he was ill. He and Sal Fusco had sent me to borrow some money from a crab fisherman by the name of Giovanni Pellicano. More than that, though, my father wanted me to talk with my mother. He wanted me to bring her on the train back to Reno.

Johnny Maglie broke away from his little group—the ex-soldiers with their chests out and the office janes up on their tiptoes, trying to get a glimpse of the prison. Maglie was a civilian now, looking good in his hat, his white shirt, his creases. My old friend extended his hand and I thought about my father's gun in my pocket.

I have impulses sometimes, ugly thoughts.

Maybe it was the three years I'd spent in the Pacific. Or maybe it was just something inside me. Still inside me.

Either way, I imagined myself sticking the gun in my old friend's stomach and pulling the trigger.

"So you're back in town," said Maglie.

"Yeah, I'm back."

Maglie put his arm around me. He and I had grown up

together, just down the street. We had both served in the Pacific theater, though in different divisions. He had served out the campaign, but I'd come back in '44—after I was wounded the second time around, taking some shrapnel in my chest. This was my first time back to The Beach. Johnny knew the reason I had stayed away, I figured, but it wasn't something we were going to talk about.

"We fought the Japs, we win the goddamn war—but it looks like the criminals are going to come back and storm the city."

I had liked Maglie once, but I didn't know how I felt about him anymore.

"You going to stick around town for a while?"

"Haven't decided," I said.

"How's your mom?"

"Good."

He didn't mention my father. No one mentioned my father.

"You know," he stuttered, and I saw in his face the mix of shame and awkwardness that I'd seen more than once in the faces of the people who'd known my family—who'd moved in the same circles. And that included just about everybody in The Beach. Some of them, of course, played it the other way now. They held their noses up, they smirked. "You know," he said, "I was getting some papers drawn up yesterday—down at Uncle's place—and your name came up . . ."

He stopped then. Maybe it was because he saw my expression at the mention of his uncle, the judge. Or maybe it was because the cops were herding us away, or because a blonde in Maglie's group gave a glance in his direction.

"Join us," he said. "We're going to Fontana's."

I was going to say no. And probably I should have. But the girl in the red cardigan was a member of their group.

For twenty years, my father had run the Italian-language paper, *Il Carnevale*. He had offices down at Columbus, and all the Italian *culturatti* used to stop by when they came through the city. Enrico Caruso. The great Marconi. Even Vittorio Mussolini, the aviator.

My father had been a public man. Fridays, to the opera. Saturdays, to Cavelli's Books—to stand on the sidewalk and listen to Il Duce's radio address. On Tuesdays, he visited the Salesian school. The young boys dressed in the uniforms of the Faciso Giovanile, and my father gave them lectures on the beauty of the Italian language.

I signed up in December, '41.

A few weeks later my father's office was raided. His paper was shut down. Hearings were held. My father and a dozen others were sent to a detention camp in Montana. My mother did not put this news in her letters. Sometime in '43 the case was reviewed and my father was released, provided he did not take up residence in a state contiguous to the Pacific Ocean. When I came home, with my wounds and my letters of commendation, my stateside commander suggested it might a good idea, all things considered, if I too stayed away from the waterfront.

But none of this is worth mentioning. Anyway, I am an old man now and there are times I don't know what day it is, what year. Or maybe I just don't care. I look up at the television, and that man in the nice suit, he could be Mussolini. He could be Stalin. He could be Missouri Harry, with his show-me smile and his atomic bomb. This hospital, there are a million old men like me, a million stories. They wave their hands.

They tell how they hit it big, played their cards, made all the right decisions. If they made a mistake, it wasn't their fault; it was that asshole down the block. Myself, I say nothing. I smell their shit. Some people get punished. Some of us, we get away with murder.

"You on leave?"

Anne had black hair and gray eyes and one of those big smiles that drew you in. There was something a bit off about her face, a skewed symmetry—a nose flat at the bridge, thin lips, a smile that was wide and crooked. The way she looked at you, she was brash and demure at the same time. A sales-man's daughter, maybe. She regarded me with her head tilted, looking up. Amused, wry. Something irrepressible in her eyes. Or almost irrepressible.

"No, no," I said. "I've been out of the service for a while now."

She glanced at my hand, checking for the ring. I wasn't wearing one—but she was. It was on the engagement finger, which she tucked away when she saw me looking. What this meant, exactly, I didn't know. Some of the girls wore engage-ment rings the whole time their fiancés were overseas, then dumped the guy the instant he strolled off the boat. Anne didn't look like that type, but you never knew.

As for me, like I said, I wasn't wearing any kind of ring—in spite of Julia Fusco, back in Reno. We weren't married, but . . .

"I grew up here."

"In The Beach?"

"Yes."

She smiled at that—like she had known the answer, just looking.

"And you?"

"I've been out East for a while," she said. "But I grew up here, too."

"But not in The Beach?" I asked, though I knew the answer, the same way she had known about me.

"No, no. Dolores Heights."

The area out there in the Mission was mostly Irish those days, though there were still some German families up in the Heights. Entrepreneurs. Jews. Here before the Italians, before the Irish. Back when the ships still came around the horn.

"Where did you serve?"

I averted my eyes, and she didn't pursue it. Maybe because I had that melancholy look that says *don't ask any more.* I glanced at a guy dancing in front of the juke with his girlfriend, and I thought of my gun and had another one of my ugly moments. I took a drink because that helped sometimes. It helped me push the thoughts away. The place was loud and raucous. Maglie and his blonde were sitting across from me, chatting it up, but I couldn't hear a word. One of the other girls said something, and Anne laughed. I laughed too, just for the hell of it.

I took another drink.

Fontana's had changed. It had used to be only Italians came here, and you didn't see a woman without her family. But that wasn't true anymore. Or at least it wasn't true this night. The place had a fevered air, like there was something people were trying to catch onto. Or maybe it was just the jailbreak.

Maglie came over to my side and put his arm around my shoulders once again. He had always been like this. One drink and he was all sentimental.

"People don't know it," he said. "Even round the neighborhood, they don't know it. But Jojo here, he did more than his share. Out there in the Pacific."

"People don't want to hear about this," I said. There was an edge in my voice, maybe a little more than there should have been.

"No," said Maglie. "But they should know."

I knew what Maglie was doing. Trying to make it up to me in some way. Letting me know that whatever happened to my father, in that hearing, it wasn't his idea. And to prove it, I could play the hero in front of this girl from The Heights with her cardigan and her pearls and that ring on her finger.

I turned to Anne.

"You?" I asked. "Where were you during the war?"

She gave me a little bit of her story then. About how she had been studying back East when the war broke out. Halfway through the war, she'd graduated and gotten a job with the VA, in a hospital, on the administrative side. But now that job was done—they'd given it to a returning soldier—and she was back home.

The jukebox was still playing.

"You want to dance?"

She was a little bit taller than me, but I didn't mind this. Sinatra was crooning on the juke. I wanted to hold her closer, but I feared she'd feel the gun in my pocket. Then I decided I didn't care.

I glanced at the ring on her finger, and she saw me looking.

"Where is he?" I asked.

"Berlin."

I didn't say anything. Frank went on crooning. Some of my father's friends, I remembered them talking about the Berlin of the old days. About the cabarets and the big-mouthed blondes with husky voices who made the bulge in their pants grow like Pinocchio's nose.

"He, my fiancé—he's a lieutenant," she said. "And there's the reconstruction. He thought it was important, not just to win the war. Not just to defeat them. But to build it back."

"He's an idealist."

"Yes."

I wondered how come she had fallen for him. I wondered if she had known him long. Or if it had been one of those things where you meet somebody and you can't escape. You fall in a whirlwind.

At that moment, inside Alcatraz, Bernie Coy and five other convicts were pinned down in the cellblock. None of us in the bar knew that yet, or even knew their names. If you wanted to know what was going on inside Alcatraz, the best you could do was climb up a rooftop and listen to the radio— but it was too far to see, and the radio was filtered by the military. Anyway, prison officials weren't talking. They were too busy to talk. Later, though, it came out how Bernie Coy was the brains. He knew the guards' routines. He'd managed to crow apart the bars and lead a handful of prisoners into the gun room. He and his buddies had clubbed the guards, taken their keys, and headed down the hall to the main yard; but the last door in the long line of doors would not open. The keys were not on the ring. They had all the ammunition in the world, but they could not get past that door. Now they were pinned down, cornered by the fire on one side and the guards on the other. So they fought, the way men in a foxhole fight. Our boys in Normandy. The Japanese in those bloody caves. The floodlights swept the shore and the tracer bullets lit the sky, and they fought the way desperate men fight, creeping forward on their bellies.

Sinatra was winding it up now, and I pulled Anne a little closer. Then I noticed a man watching us. He was sitting at the same table as Maglie and the rest. He was still watching when Anne and I walked back.

He put his arm around Anne, and they seemed to know each other better than I would like.

"This is Davey." Anne said.

"Mike's best friend," he said.

I didn't get it at first, and then I did. Mike was Anne's fiancé, and Davey was keeping his eye out.

Davey had blue eyes and yellow hair. When he spoke, first thing, I thought he was a Brit, but I was wrong.

"London?" I asked.

"No, California," he smiled. "Palo Alto. Educated abroad."

He had served with Anne's fiancé over in Germany. But unlike Mike, he had not re-enlisted. Apparently he was not quite so idealistic.

"Part of my duties, far as my best friend," he said, "are to make sure nothing happens to Anne."

The Brit laughed then. Or he was still the Brit to me. A big man, with a big laugh, hard to dislike, but I can't say I cared for him. He joined our group anyway. We ate then and we drank. We had antipasti. We had crabs and shrimp. We had mussels and linguini. Every once in a while someone would come in from the street with news. *At the Yacht Harbor now . . . three men in a rowboat . . . the marines are inside, cell-to-cell, shooting them in their cots.* At some point, Ellen Pagione, Fontana's sister-in-law, came out of the kitchen to make a fuss over me.

"I had no idea you were back in town." She pressed her cheek against mine. "This boy is my favorite," she said. "My goddamn favorite."

Part of me liked the attention, I admit, but another part, I knew better. Ellen Pagione had never liked my father. Maybe she didn't approve of what had happened to him, though, and felt bad. Or maybe she had pointed a finger herself. Either way, she loved me now. Everyone in North Beach, we loved one another now.

Anne smiled. Girl that she was, she believed the whole thing.

A little while later, she leaned toward me. She was a little in her cups maybe. Her cheeks were flush.

"I want to take you home."

Then she looked away. I wondered if I'd heard correctly. The table was noisy. Then the Brit raised his glass, and everyone was laughing.

After dinner, Johnny Maglie grabbed me at the bar. I was shaking inside, I'm not sure why. Johnny wanted to buy me a beer, and I went along, though I knew I'd had enough. There comes a time, whatever the drink is holding under, it comes back up all of a sudden and there's nothing you can do. At the moment, I didn't care. I caught a glimpse of Anne. Some of the others had left, but she was still at the table. So was the Brit.

"How's your mom?" It was the same question Johnny had asked before, out on the street, but maybe he'd forgotten.

"She's got her dignity," I said.

"That's right. Your mama. She's always got her head up." He was a little drunk and a smirk showed on his face.

I knew what people said about my mother. Or I could

guess, anyway. She was a Northern Italian, like my father, from Genoa. Refinement was important to her. We were not wealthy, but this wasn't the point. My father had only been a newspaperman, but it had been a newspaper of ideas, and the *prominenti* had respected him. Or so we had thought. My mother had tried for a little while to live in Montana, outside the camp where he was imprisoned, but it had been too remote, too brutal. So she had gone back to North Beach and lived with her sister. Now the war was over, and the restrictions had been lifted, but my father would not return. He had been disgraced, after all. And the people who could have helped him then—the people to whom he had catered, people like Judge Molinari, Johnny Maglie's uncle—they had done nothing for him. Worse than nothing.

"Are you going to stay in The Beach?" Johnny asked.

I didn't answer. My father worked in one of the casinos in Reno now, dealing cards. He lived in a clapboard house with Sal Fusco and Sal's daughter, Julia. Julia took care of them both.

About two months ago something had happened between Julia and me. It was the kind of thing that happens sometimes. To be honest, I didn't feel much toward her other than loyalty.

"So what are you going to do?"

I glanced toward Anne. The Brit had slid closer and was going on in that big-chested way of his.

"I don't know."

But I did know. There was a little roadhouse on the edge of Reno with some slots and card tables. Sal Fusco wanted my father and I to go into business with him. To get the loan, all I had to do was shake hands with Pellicano, the crab fisherman. But my father, I knew, did not really care about the roadhouse. All he wanted was for my mother to come to Reno.

I had spoken to my mother just hours before.

"If this is what you want, I will do it," she said.

"It's not for me. It's for him."

"Your father can come back here. The war is over."

"He has his pride."

"We all have our shame. You get used to it. At least here, I can wear my mink to the opera."

"There is no opera anymore."

"There will be again soon," she said. "But if this is what you want, I will go to Reno. If this is what my son wants . . ."

I understood something then. She blamed my father. Someone needed to take blame, and he was the one. And part of me, I understood. Part of me didn't want to go back to Reno either.

"It's what I want," I said.

Johnny Maglie looked at me with those big eyes of his. He wanted something from me. Like Ellen Pagione wanted. Like my father wanted. Like Julia Fusco. For a minute, I hated them all.

"I know how you used to talk about going into law," Johnny said. "Before all this business."

"Before all what business?"

"Before the war . . ." he stammered. "That's all I meant. I know you wanted to be an attorney."

"Everything's changed."

"My uncle—he said he would write a letter for you. Not just any school. Stanford. Columbia. His recommendation, it carries weight."

I would be lying if I said I didn't feel a rush of excitement—that I didn't sense a door opening and a chance to walk into another life.

"Is it because he feels guilty?" I asked. "Because of what happened to my father? He was at the hearing, wasn't he?"

Johnny looked at me blankly, as if he didn't understand.

"I saw Jake yesterday."

Jake was Judge Molinari's boy. He was a sweet-faced kid. His father's pride and joy. He'd done his tour in Sicily and distinguished himself, from what I heard.

"How's he doing?"

"Getting married."

"Good for him."

Back at the table, the Brit raised another glass. Beside him, Anne was beautiful. The way the Brit was looking at her, I didn't guess he was thinking about his buddy overseas.

I was born circa 1921. The records aren't exact. It doesn't matter. Like I said, there are times, these days, when I can't place the current date either. It is 1998, maybe. Or 2008. The nurse who takes care of me—who scoots me up off my ass and empties my bedpan—she was born in Saigon, just before the fall. 1971, I think. French Vietnamese, but the French part doesn't matter here in the States. Either way, she doesn't give a fuck about me. Outside the sunlight is white, and I glimpse the airplanes descending. We have a new airport, a new convention center. Every place, these days, has a new convention center. Every place you go, there are airplanes descending and signs advertising a casino on the edge of town.

I close my eyes. The Brit gets up all of a sudden, goes out into the night. I see Anne alone at the table. I see my father dealing cards in Reno. I see Julia Fusco in my father's kitchen, fingers on her swollen belly.

My kid. My son.

A few days ago, for recreation, they wheeled us to the convention center. We could have been anywhere. Chicago. Toronto. I spotted a couple in the hotel bar, and it didn't take a genius to see what was going on.

You can try to fuck your way out. You can work the slot. You can run down the long hall but in the end the door is locked and you are on your belly, crawling through smoke.

No one escapes.

The nurse comes, rolls me over.

Go to sleep, she says. *Go to fucking sleep.*

"I was on Guam." Anne and I were outside now, just the two of us. The evening was all but over. "The Japanese were on top of the hill. A machine-gun nest."

One of the marine choppers was overhead now, working in a widening gyre. The wind had shifted and you could smell the smoke from the prison.

"Is it hard?"

"What?"

"The memories?"

"Of the war, you mean."

"Yes, the war."

I didn't know what to say. "A lot of people on both sides," I made a vague gesture. "Us or them. Sometimes, the difference, I don't know." I felt the confusion inside of me. I saw the dead Japs in their nest. "I don't know what pulls people through."

She looked at me then. She smiled. "Love."

"What?"

She was a little shier now. "Something greater than themselves. A dedication to that. To someone they love. Or to something."

"To an idea?"

"Yes," she said. "An idea."

What she said, it didn't explain anything, not really, but it was the kind of thing people were saying those days—in the aftermath of all the killing. I felt myself falling for it, just like you fall for the girl in the movie. For a moment, she wasn't Anne anymore, the girl from The Heights. She was something else, her face sculpted out of light.

She smiled.

"I'm old-fashioned," she said. "Why don't you get me a taxi?"

Then I had an idea. I didn't have to go to Reno. I could just walk up Columbus with Anne. We could catch a taxi. And we could keep going. Not out to Dolores Heights, or Liberty Heights, or wherever it was she lived. But beyond the neighborhoods . . . beyond the city . . . out through the darkened fields . . . carried along on a river of light.

Then from behind came a loud voice. It belonged to the Brit and it boomed right through me.

"Anne," he said. "I have gotten us a taxi."

I felt her studying me, reading my face. I felt her hand on my back. The Brit opened the taxi door.

My legs were shaking as I headed down the alley. I could hear the copters still, and the sirens along the waterfront. As I walked deeper into the neighborhood, I heard the old sounds too. An aria from an open window. Old men neighing. Goats on a hillside. I was drunk. At some point I had taken my father's gun out of my pocket. It was a beautiful little gun. I could have gotten into the taxi, I supposed. Or I could find Anne tomorrow. But I knew that wasn't going to happen. I had other responsibilities. I hadn't been in The Beach for a while, and I was disoriented. The alley was familiar and not familiar. Rome, maybe. Calabria. An alley of tradesmen, maybe an accountant or two, in the offices over the street. I saw a figure ahead, coming out of a door, and I recognized the corner. Judge Molinari had his office upstairs. Had for years. But this was a younger man. He turned to lock the door. Go the other way, I thought. Don't come toward me. But on he came. Jake Molinari, the judge's son. With the war behind him and a bride waiting. I hadn't planned to be here, but here I was. There are things you don't escape. In the dark, he was smiling to himself. Or I thought he was. He raised his eyes. He saw me. He saw the gun in my hand and his mouth opened. I thought of my father and Julia Fusco, and I shot him. He fell against the alley wall. Then all I could see was Anne. Her face was a blinding light. A flash in the desert. The man lay at my feet now. I shot him again.

At the top of the hill, I paused to look back. I knew how it was but I looked anyway. The sky over the bay was red. Alcatraz was still burning.

IT CAN HAPPEN
BY DAVID CORBETT
Hunter's Point

Pilgrim watched as, just outside his bedroom door, Lorene handed Robert fifty dollars and told him she wanted to visit personal with her ex-husband for a spell. Robert was Pilgrim's nurse. He'd been a wrestler in college—you had to be strong to heft a paralyzed man in and out of bed—and worked sometimes now as a bouncer on his off-hours.

Robert glanced back toward the bedroom for approval and Pilgrim gave his nod. The big man pocketed the money, donned his hat, and walked out the door in his whites, not bothering with his coat despite the cold.

Pilgrim liked that about Robert—his strength, his vigor, his indifference to life's little bothers. Maybe "liked" wasn't quite the word. Envied.

He lay back in bed and waited for Lorene to rejoin him. His room was the largest in the cramped, dreary house and bare except for the $20,000 wheelchair gathering dust in the corner, the large-screen TV he was so very tired of watching, an armchair for visitors with a single lamp beside it. And the centerpiece—the mechanical bed, a hospital model, tilted up so he didn't just lie flat all day.

Lorene took up position bedside and crossed her arms. She was a pretty, short, ample, strong woman. "Don't make me go off on you."

Pilgrim tilted his head to see her, eyes glazed. Every ten minutes or so, someone needed to wipe the fluid away. It was a new problem, the tear ducts. Three years now since the accident, reduced to deadweight from the neck down, followed by organs failing, musty skin, powdery hair, his body in a slow but inexorable race with his mind to the grave. He was forty-three years old.

In a scratchy whisper, he said, "I got my eyes and ears out there."

"Corella?" Their daughter. *Corella the Giver*, Lorene called her, not kindly.

"You been buying things," he said.

"Furniture a crime now?"

"Things you can't afford, not by the wildest stretch—"

"Ain't your business, Pilgrim. My home, we're talkin' about." She pressed her finger against her breastbone. "Mine."

Lorene lived in a renovated Queen Anne Victorian in the Excelsior district of San Francisco, hardly an exclusive area but grand next to Hunter's Point, where Pilgrim remained, living in the same house he'd lived in on a warehouseman's salary, barely more than a shack.

Pilgrim bought the Excelsior house after his accident, when he came into money through the legal settlement. He was broadsided by a semi when his brakes failed, a design defect on his lightweight pickup. Lorene stood by him till the money came through, then filed for divorce, saying she was still young. She needed a real husband.

Actually, the word she used was "functional."

The divorce was uglier than some, less so than most. The major compromise concerned the Victorian. He gave her a living estate—it was her residence till she died—but it stayed in his name. He needed that. Lorene would have her lovers, the men would come and go, but he'd still have that cord, connecting them—his love, her guilt. His money, her wants.

He got $12,000 a month from the annuity the truck manufacturer set up. Half of that went to pay Lorene's mortgage, the rest got eaten up by medical bills, twenty-four-hour care, medicine, food, utilities. He had no choice but to stay here in this ugly, decrepit, shameful house.

"Know your problem, Pilgrim? You don't get out. Dust off that damn wheelchair and—"

"Catch pneumonia."

"Wrap your damn self up."

"Who is he, Lorene?"

She cocked her head. "Who you mean?"

"The man in the house I pay for."

Lorene put her hands on her hips and rocked a little, back and forth. "No. No, Pilgrim. You and me, we got an understanding. I don't know what Corella's been saying—"

"I know you got men. That's not the point here. You take this one in?"

"You got no say, Pilgrim."

"Even folks at Corella's church know about him. *Reverend Williams*, he calls himself. Slick as a frog's ass."

"I ain't listening to this."

"All AIDS this and Africa that. But he's running from trouble in Florida somewhere, down around Tampa."

"That's church gossip, Pilgrim. Raymont never even *been* to Tampa."

"Now you spending money hand over fist. That where it's coming from, Lorene? Phony charity, pass the basket? *Raymont?* No. That wouldn't pay the freight, way I hear you redone that house. What you up to, Lorene? You know I'll find out."

Finally, fear darkened her eyes. He wanted to ask her: What do you expect? Take away a man's body, he still has his heart. Mess with his heart, though, there's nothing left but the hate. And the hate builds.

"Pilgrim, you do me an injustice when you make accusations like that." The words came out with a sad, lukewarm pity. She sighed, slipped off her shoes, motored the bed down till he lay flat, then climbed on, straddling him. "This what you after? Then say so." She took a Kleenex from the box on the bed and wiped his puddled eyes, then stroked his face with her fingers, her skin cool against his. She cupped his cheek in her palm and leaned down to kiss him. "Why do you doubt my feelings, Pilgrim?"

"Send him away, Lorene."

"Pilgrim, you gotta let—"

"I'll forgive everything—I don't care what you've done to get the money or how much it is—but you gotta send him away. For good."

Lorene got down off the bed, slipped her shoes back on, and straightened her skirt. "One of these days, Pilgrim— before you die—you're gonna have to accept that I'm not to blame for what happened to you. And what you want from me, and what I'm able to give, are two entirely different things."

Robert returned to find Lorene gone. How long she leave Mr. Baxter alone? he wondered, chastising himself. He checked his watch, barely half an hour since he'd left but that was plenty of time to have an accident. And he ain't gonna blame her, hell no. That witch got the man's paralyzed dick wrapped around her little finger tight as a yo-yo. He's gonna lay blame on me.

That was pretty much the routine between them. Bitch

rant scream, beg snivel thank. Return to beginning and start again. Even so, Robert knew he had the makings of a good thing here. He didn't want it jeopardized. Mr. Baxter wasn't long for this life, every day something else went wrong, more and more, faster and faster. The man relied on Robert for all those sad, pathetic, humiliating little tasks no one else would bother with. If Robert played it right, made himself trusted and dependable—the final friend—there could be a little something on the back end worth waiting for.

Everybody working in-home care knew a story. One woman Robert knew personally had tended an old man down in Hillsborough, famously wealthy, and he scribbled on a napkin two days before he passed that she was to get $40,000 from his estate. The family fought it, of course—they were already inheriting millions, but that's white people for you—claiming she'd had undue influence over his weakened mind. The point was, though, it can happen. Long as you don't let the family hoodwink you.

Venturing into the bedroom doorway, Robert discovered Pilgrim trembling. His breathing was ragged.

"Mr. Baxter, you all right?" Edging closer, he saw more tears streaking down the older man's face than leakage could explain. "Good Lord, Mr. Baxter? What did that woman do?"

Pilgrim hissed, "Call my lawyer."

Marguerite Johnstone had gone to law school to escape Hunter's Point but still had clients in the neighborhood—wills and trusts, conservatorships, probate contests, for those who could afford them. She sat parked at the curb outside Pilgrim's house, waiting a moment behind the wheel, checking to make sure she had the address right.

The place was small and square with peeling paint and a

flat, tar-paper roof. In back, a makeshift carport had all but collapsed from dry rot. Weeds had claimed the yard from the grass and grew waist high. How in God's name, she thought, can a man worth three-quarters of a million dollars live in a dump like this?

It sat at the corner of Fitch and Crisp—"Fish & Chips," they used to call it when she lived up the hill on Jerrold—the last residence before the shabby warehouses and noxious body shops rimming the old shipyard. The Redevelopment Agency had big plans for new housing nearby but plans had never been the problem in this part of town. The problem was following through. And if any locals, meaning black folks, actually got a chance to live in what the city finally built up there, it would constitute an act of God. Meanwhile, the only construction actually underway was for the light rail, and that was lagging, millions over budget, years behind schedule, the muddy trench down Third Street all anyone could point to and say: *There's where the money went.*

The rest of the neighborhood consisted of bland, crumbling little two-story houses painted tacky colors, with iron bars on the windows. At least they looked lived in. There were families here, holding out, waiting for something better to come—where else could they go? And with the new white mayor coming down all the time, making a show of how he cared, people had a right to think maybe now, finally, things would turn around. But come sunset the hoodrats still crawled out, mayor or no mayor, claiming their corners. Making trade. Marguerite made a mental note to wrap things up and get out before dark.

Robert led the lawyer through the bedroom door and Pilgrim sized her up. A tall, freckled, coffee-skinned woman with her hair pulled back and tied with a bow, glasses, frumpy suit, and flats. Be nicer-looking if she made an effort, he thought.

"Nice to meet you," he said. "You come well recommended. This here's my daughter."

Corella sat at the end of the bed, dressed in black, down to the socks and shoes, her hair short like a man's. His other daughter, Cynthia, was the pretty one, but she wasn't Lorene's child. Cynthia lived with her mother far away—St. Louis, the last anybody heard.

Corella would never move away. She was Daddy's little princess, homely like him.

Marguerite extended her hand. "Pleasure."

"Obliged," Corella said.

Pilgrim shooed both Robert and his daughter from the room. Robert went quick, Corella less so. Clingy, that was the word he wanted. But bitter. He waited for the door to close.

"I got the feeling," he said, "way your voice sounded over the phone—"

"You were right, there are problems." Marguerite removed a thin stack of papers from her briefcase, copies of documents she'd discovered at the County Recorder. "With the Excelsior property."

She explained what she'd found. Six months earlier, the IRS had filed tax liens for over $300,000 in back taxes against a Raymont Williams—who came with a generous assortment of aliases. Soon after that, Lorene, who worked at a local credit union, recorded the first of three powers-of-attorney, forging Pilgrim's signature and getting a notary at the credit union to validate it. Then, acting as Pilgrim's surrogate under the power-of-attorney, she took out a loan for $120,000, same amount as the oldest of the tax liens, securing it with the Excelsior property.

But no release of lien was ever recorded. Apparently, when Lorene realized how easily she could phony up a loan, she got the fever. The IRS could wait for its money. Two more loans followed for increasingly shameless sums from hard-money lenders. The house was now leveraged to the hilt, the total indebtedness over $600,000, and that was just principal. Worse, though Lorene had made a token effort to cover her tracks, keep up with the payments, she'd already slipped into default.

"Expects me to come to the rescue," Pilgrim guessed.

"It's that or lose the house to foreclosure," Marguerite said.

"All that happen in just six months?" Pilgrim chided himself for not seeing it sooner. Hadn't even known about this Raymont fool till recent. Why hadn't Corella told him? She went to see her mother from time to time—not often, they didn't get on, but often enough. Daddy's homely, clingy, bitter little princess was playing both sides. But she'd pay. Everyone would pay.

Marguerite said, "You've got a very strong case against the notary, pretty strong against the lenders, though the last two are a step above loan sharks. I don't know what Lorene told them—"

"Woman can charm a stump."

"But they'll want their money. They'll know they can't go against Lorene or this Raymont individual for recovery. And they could say they had a right to rely on the notary and turn on her, but her pockets most likely aren't that deep either. So they'll come after you. And my guess is they won't be nice about it."

"How you figure?"

"It'll suit their purposes to stick with Lorene and her

story, at least for a while. She'll say she had your full authority to do what she did and now you're just reneging out of jealousy. It's not an argument that'll carry the day, not in the end, but the whole thing could get so drawn out and ugly they could grind you down, force a settlement that still leaves you holding a pretty sizable bag."

"Maybe I'll just walk away from the house."

"If you're okay with that, why not do it now? Save yourself my legal fees."

Pilgrim cackled. "You don't want my money?"

"Not as much as some other people do, apparently."

Pilgrim blinked his eyes. He could feel the water building up. "And this Raymont Williams, this phony preacher, he walks away clean."

"I call it the Deadbeat Write-off. Meanwhile, for you, this could all get very expensive, particularly in addition to the other work you mentioned."

Pilgrim glowered, trying to shush her. He figured Corella had an ear pressed up to the door, trying to hear his business.

"Expensive is lying here doing nothing. I can't move. Don't mean I can't fight."

That night Pilgrim dreamed he had his body back. He and Lorene were in the throes, the way it used to be—give some, not too much, take a little away, then give it back till she's arching her spine and making that sound that made everything right. Damn near the only good he'd done his whole sorry life, pleasure that woman—that and turn himself into a quadriplegic piggy bank.

But no sooner did she make that gratified cry in his dream than the whole thing changed. He heard another sound, a low fierce hum, then the deafening broadside slam of the semi ramming his pickup, the fierce growl of the diesel inches from his bleeding face through the shattered glass of his window, the scream of air brakes and metal against metal, then the odd, hissing silence after. His head bobbing atop his twisted spine, body hanging limp in the shoulder harness. The smell of gas and smoldering rubber and that *tick-tick-tick* from the truck's radiator that he mistook for dripping blood.

Raymont Williams, dressed in pleated slacks and a cashmere V-neck, Italian loafers, and silk socks, heard the doorbell ring and glanced down from a second story window. A fluffy little white fella, baggy suit, small hat, stood on the porch. Something wrong with this picture, he thought. White people in the neighborhood didn't come to visit.

Raymont lifted the window: "Yeah?"

The man backed up, gripping his hat so it wouldn't fall off as he tilted his head back to see who was talking. "Reverend Raymont Williams?"

No collar, Raymont thought, touching his throat. "You're who?"

"Name's William Montgomery. I live down the block. I received some of your mail. By mistake. The names, I guess." He tugged on the brim of his puny hat. "Kind of similar in a backwards sort of way."

"Shove it through the slot."

The man winced. "There's a bit of a snafu." He looked at the wad of mail in his hand, like it might catch fire. "One of the letters is certified, I signed by mistake. I don't know, I didn't look carefully, I just . . ." He scrunched up his face. "I called the post office. I have to get your signature, too, next to mine, then take the receipt down to the main office on Evans. It's a hassle, I realize—"

"That don't make sense."

"They were very specific. I'm truly sorry, Reverend."

The hairs on Raymont's neck stood up. *You mocking me?* "Hold on." He closed the window, walked down the carpeted stairs to the entry. The crystal prisms on the chandelier refracted the sunshine streaming through the fanlight. In the dining room a bouquet of lilies and irises exploded from a crystal vase on the Hepplewhite side table. Lorene had this mania for Waterford lately, in addition to a number of other decorating obsessions. Out of control. They'd need to talk on that.

He flipped open the mail slot from inside. "Okay, slip it through."

The little man obliged. Raymont took the bundle of paper, at which point the voice through the mail slot said, "Reverend Raymont Williams, a.k.a. Raymont Williams, a.k.a. Raymond White, a.k.a. Montel Dickson—you've been served with a summons and a complaint in accordance with state law and local rules of the California Superior Court. You must appear on the specified date or a default judgment may be filed against you. If you have any questions, you can call the number that appears on the summons."

Why you schemey little bug, Raymont thought. He pulled himself up, booming through the door: "How dare you! Coming here, full of hostile intent and subterfuge. I am a man of the cloth. What's the difficulty, tell me—the difficulty in simply ringing the bell like a decent man with honest business?"

Beyond the door's beveled glass, the white man grinned, his eyes hard. He didn't look so fluffy now. "Yeah, right. Straight up, that's you." He turned and started down the steps, saying over his shoulder, "You're served."

Raymont threw the door open, came after him, one step, two. "You listen—"

The little man spun around. "Go ahead. Lay a hand on me, I'll sue you for every cent you're worth."

Raymont cocked his head, perplexed. "Will you now?" He reached out, lifted William Montgomery or whoever the hell he was off his little white feet, and tossed him down to the sidewalk. His head hit with a hollow, mean-sounding *thunk*. The man groaned, curled up, clutching his hat.

"Sue me for every cent I'm worth? Joke's on you."

The phone started ringing inside the house. Raymont slammed the door behind him, went to the hallway, and picked up. He could hear Lorene, sobbing.

"So. Lemme guess. They got you at work."

"We got ten days—to *get out*. That's *my house*—"

"What did you do? What did you say?"

"I tried, Raymont, I swear. But he is a stubborn, spiteful—"

"You best try again, woman. Try harder. Try till that horizontal nigger sees the motherfucking light of goddamn day."

"Mr. Baxter says I'm to stay in the room this time."

Robert opened the bedroom door so Lorene could go in. She put away the fifty dollars she'd planned to pass along, tidied her hair, gathered herself. "Fine then." She strode in like a shamed queen.

Pilgrim's voice stopped her cold. "You come here to try to weasel your way into my good graces, don't bother. You got ten days to quit. You and that hustling no-count you taken in. The two of you, not out by then, sheriff kicks you out."

Lorene gathered her pride. "From the very beginning, Pilgrim, you promised—"

"Promises don't always keep, Lorene. You crossed the line."

Lorene sat down and tried to collect her thoughts. *Crossed the line.* Yes. And what an interesting world it became, across that line. The things you never thought you could have, right there. But here and now she was running out of options. Still, she reminded herself: *I know this man.*

With the nurse there she couldn't be as bold as the moment called for. All she could do was lean forward, tip her cleavage into view, bite her lip. "What is it you want, Pilgrim?"

Marguerite sank back in the chair and tapped her foot. "I don't agree with this."

"Not your place to agree or disagree."

"That's not entirely true. I can withdraw."

"Just find me another lawyer, not so particular."

"Mr. Baxter, it may not be my place, but you might want to think of your estate plan as a way to take care of your loved ones, not settle scores."

"I want that kind of talk, I'll turn on Oprah."

"All right. Fine." Marguerite took the papers out of her briefcase. "I've drawn things up the way you asked. Both sets." She glanced up. "Are you all right?"

Pilgrim blinked. His face was wet. "Damn eyes is all."

Corella came that evening to visit and found her father sleeping. His breathing was faint, troubled. She put her hand to his forehead. Cool. Clammy.

Hurry up and die, she thought.

He'd always made no secret of his feelings. If her mother was in the room, Corella did not exist. Children are baggage.

How much time had she wasted, pounding her heart against his indifference—only to melt at the merest *Hey there, little girl.*

As fickle as the man could be, he still had it all over her mother. That woman was scandalous. Corella had tried to be gracious, turn a blind eye to the parade of men through that big old house—even this Raymont creature—but then the woman started spending money like a crack whore on holiday and Corella had to draw a line. Woman's gonna burn up my inheritance, she thought. That can't stand.

She pulled up a chair to wait until her father woke up. A manila envelope peeked out from under the bed covers. Carefully, she lifted it out. The lawyer's address label was on the front, with the notation: *"Pilgrim Baxter—Estate Plan— DRAFT."* About time he got to this, she thought.

Corella had earned her teacher's certificate just as the new governor was talking about taking pensions away and basing salaries on "merit"—meaning your career lay in the hands of bored kids cut loose by lazy parents. Schoolwork? Not even. Not when there's curb service for rock and herb on the street, Grand Theft Auto on the Game Boy, streaming porn on the web. The American dream. She was sorry for what had happened to her father but the money was luck and she'd need all she could muster. Otherwise the future just looked too grim.

She checked to be sure he was still dozing, then opened the envelope quietly, removed the papers inside. There was a living trust, a will, some other legal documents captioned *"Baxter v. Williams et al."* Not like I don't have a right to see, she thought. He'll need me to make the calls, transfer accounts, consult with the accountants and all.

She read every page, even the boiler plate. By the time she was done her whole body was shaking.

* * *

Raymont, wearing his preacher collar under a gray suit, stared out through the beveled glass of the Victorian's front door at Corella on the porch. Girl's nothing but a snitch for her father, he thought. He felt like telling her to just go away but Lorene hadn't come home the night before. He'd rattled around all night alone in their canopy bed, like a moth inside a lampshade, wondering if he shouldn't call the police. But, given his troubles, that could turn tricky. Besides, he figured she wasn't missing. She was hiding.

He cracked open the door. "Your mama's not around."

Corella had her hands folded before her, prim as a nun. "I didn't come to see her."

She might as well have thrown a rock. "Say that again?"

"Turns out you and I have something in common." She looked him square in the eye. "We need to talk."

They sat in the kitchen, Raymont sipping Hennessy with a splash of 7-Up, Corella content with tap water as she told him what she'd learned.

"The lawsuit and eviction remain in place—against you. Everything against my mother is dismissed in exchange for her cooperation and truthful testimony."

Girl sounds like a bad day on Court TV, he thought. "Your mama says I forced her into anything, that's a damn lie. I may have *suggested*—"

"She gets the house, too. He's quit-claiming it to her. But the debt comes with it."

Raymont shook his glass, the ice rattled. "There's his pound of flesh. Payments too steep. She can't keep up, they'll foreclose."

Corella shook her head. "She'll be able to hold them off for a while. And the insurance annuity that pays for my

father's care? It has a cash payout when he dies. Half a million dollars. He's giving half of that to my mother to pay
down the debt. That should make it manageable but still
steep enough it'll feel—if I know my mother and father—like
punishment."

Girl understands her blood, he thought, I'll grant her
that. "And the other half—who gets that?"

Corella shook her head, a little flinch of outrage. "It goes
to the nurse."

Raymont put down his drink. "The *bouncer?*"

"'For services rendered charitably, patiently, and gener-
ously.'" Corella seemed about to cry, but there was ice in her
voice, too. "I get nothing."

"You got a half-sister floating around somewhere, too, am
I right?"

He might as well have slapped her. "She doesn't deserve
anything! Where has she been? What has she done?"

"Easy. Easy. I just—"

"The nurse is bad enough. I'm the one in the family who's
been there. Every day."

"Fine. Agreed." Raymont juiced up his drink with a little
more Hennessy. The girl was getting on his nerves and he
needed to think. His mind boiled. "I'm gonna hire me a
lawyer," he said. "A real junkyard dog. You best find yourself
one, too, girl, before this all gets finalized."

Corella stood up from the table. "You're missing the
point."

Lorene left the hotel where she was hiding and arrived in
Hunter's Point shortly after dinner to visit with Pilgrim.
Robert let her in and said, "Mr. Baxter told me you and him
would be wanting some private time." She opened her purse,

figuring they were back on the old payment schedule, but Robert said, "No need for that, ma'am." He grabbed his hat, glanced at his watch, and added, "I'll come back in an hour."

She inferred from his cheerfulness that Pilgrim had informed him of his good fortune. Once Pilgrim executed his documents, the former wrestler and part-time bouncer would stand to inherit a princely sum. Pausing at the window, she watched him flounce out to his beat-up car. He'll buy himself a new one first thing, she thought, something everyone will stare at. New car, new clothes, flash and trash, waste it all. But who's the bigger fool for that—him or Pilgrim?

She went into the bedroom and stood beside the bed. Pilgrim gazed up at her. "You look tired," he said.

She smiled grimly, thinking: You have no idea. Tired of pretending I feel for you. Tired of keeping up that charade just so I can have the one thing I want, my home and the things in it, a safe place as I grow old. Tired of watching you hang on to your miserable life with all its petty jealousy and resentment and hate. Tired of trying to convince myself I can do what you want. You think you can control my life and who I love, now and forever, even from beyond the grave. So yes. I'm tired.

It's always the devil, she thought, who shows us who we really are. She knew Raymont was evil, but so? Love is not a choice and who would want it if it was? He'd taught her things. Fortune favors the bold. No risk, no reward. She did not intend to waste that lesson. And there were hatreds and resentments of her own to abide.

"Come here," Pilgrim whispered. "Visit with me."

She stepped out of her shoes, lowered the bed, climbed on, and straddled him, edging forward on her knees. Maybe you'll forgive me, she thought. Maybe not.

"Let me move this," she said, wrestling the pillow from beneath his head.

"Lorene, damn, careful—"

She clamped the pillow across his face and pressed down hard. The plump soft weight muffled his cries. Two minutes, she thought. That's how long they say it takes for old folks in nursing homes and Pilgrim lacked even that much strength. The killing would leave tiny red dots in his eyes but she would call her own doctor, not his, say he'd just stopped breathing. Her doctor would take her word, sign the death certificate before anyone was the wiser. And though Robert would be suspicious when he got back—he'd be out a quarter of a million dollars—he'd be in no position to make trouble. The police would see right through him. Besides, she made out no better than he did with Pilgrim dead and no documents signed—why would she kill him?

Her heart pounded and she was drenched with sweat by the time it was over. She couldn't bear to lift the pillow, see his face. She just leaned down, listened for sounds of breathing. Nothing.

From behind: "You just do what I think?"

Lorene spun around on the bed. Raymont stood in the doorway. Stranger still, Corella peeked out from behind him.

"We knew you'd be here," Raymont said. "We saw the nurse leave. Corella has a key."

Lorene held out her hand. "Help me down."

Raymont approached her like he thought she might turn into a bat but helped her as she climbed off Pilgrim's body. He caught her when she nearly fell. Her knees felt rubbery. She almost fainted.

"I couldn't go through with it," she said.

Puzzled, Raymont lifted the pillow. "You already did."

"No, I mean go through with what he wanted me to do. Turn against you." A shudder went through her and she began to weep softly. "I'm so sorry."

"It's all right, baby, stop." He stroked her face. "Don't fret. We got it all figured out."

"We?" She wiped her face.

"Corella and me. She's the one stands to inherit, she's the next of kin."

"But Cynthia—"

"To hell with Cynthia." It was Corella, holding herself so tight it looked like she might explode if she let go.

Raymont, more gently, said, "Anybody heard from this Cynthia? Anybody even know where she is?"

"St. Louis. Somewhere near—"

"No, Lorene." He grabbed her by the shoulders, shook her. "No. Listen to me. Corella and me, we've come to an understanding." He looked at Pilgrim's body, the face exposed now. Vacant. Still. "Corella's gonna file the probate. She'll say she heard some talk about another daughter, tried hard to find her, couldn't. We ransack this place, destroy any letters or anything else that might give us away, lead somebody to where she is. Hell, why can't we pretend she doesn't even exist?"

"What about the lawyer? The one he's been talking to. What if he's told her—"

"Why should she care? You pay her whatever she's owed, she'll go away, trust me. One thing I know, it's lawyers."

The next impulse took Lorene by surprise. She reached for Raymont's face, clamped her eyes shut, and pressed her mouth so hungrily against his she thought, again, she might faint. A cold pulse ran through her, it felt like laughter. He's dead, she thought. He's dead and I'm free and God help me but I have lived for this moment.

* * *

Watching her mother grab the bogus preacher within inches of her father's corpse, Corella suffered a moment of clarity so searing she nearly got sick. Nothing would change, she realized. She'd be used. These two revolting people would get what they wanted then toss her aside. She was a tool. She was, again, baggage.

Raymont had brought a gun in case Robert had to be dealt with. Corella crept up behind him, reached inside his coat pocket.

Raymont tried to catch her by the arm, missed. "What you playin' at?"

Corella gripped the weapon with both hands, waving it back and forth, at Raymont, at Lorene, at Raymont. She was crying.

Raymont held out his hand. "Put that down." Then: "This was your idea, girl."

Corella fired. Lorene screamed as the bullet hit Raymont in the shoulder. He howled in pain, cursed, reached for the wound, said, "I'll kill you," through clenched teeth, but then she fired again, this time aiming for his face. The round went through his eye. Lorene's screams grew piercing. Raymont tottered, reached for something that wasn't there, and slowly collapsed to the floor.

"My God, Corella, why, Lord, what—"

Corella raised the barrel till it pointed at her mother. "Quiet," she said, barely above a whisper, then fired. The bullet ripped through Lorene's throat. The second went straight through her heart.

Robert came back from the Philly cheese steak shop on Oakdale he liked, chewing gum to counter the smell of the greasy cheese and grilled onions on his breath. He found the door unlocked. Odd, he thought. Careless of me. Smokehounds could just waltz in.

He went straight for the bedroom, make sure all was well, and stopped in his tracks. A man he didn't recognize sat slumped against the wall, a bloody hole where one eye had been, another in his shoulder. Lorene lay in a heap beside the bed, ugly wounds on her chest and neck. And Mr. Baxter lay in his bed, motionless as a hunk of wood, eyes and mouth gaping.

Corella sat on the floor against the wall, clutching a pillow, staring at nothing. A pistol rested on the floor, not far from her feet.

"They killed him," she whispered. "I came in . . ." Her voice trailed away. She glanced up at Robert.

Robert's eyes bounced back and forth—the gun, Corella. "You?"

"They killed him," she said again. Practicing.

Robert studied her, then said, "It's all right. I understand."

He went to the bedside, checked to make sure Pilgrim was dead, then checked the other two as well. From a box beside the bed he withdrew a vinyl glove, slipped it on his hand.

"You hurt?" he asked Corella, walking over to the gun, picking it up.

She shook her head. Then, looking up into his face, she said, "He never signed those documents, you know. You get nothing."

Robert crouched down in front of her. "Sometimes it's not about the money." With one hand he forced her mouth open, with the other he worked the barrel in. "Sometimes it's just the right thing to do."

* * *

Two days after the funerals, Marguerite Johnstone sat in her office, meeting with Pilgrim's surviving daughter, Cynthia. She'd traveled from Hannibal, Missouri, for the services. Her mother had stayed behind.

"Your father had me draft two estate plans," Marguerite explained, "one he executed the last time I met with him, the other he was saving."

Cynthia tilted her head quizzically. "Saving?"

She was quite different from Corella, Marguerite thought. She had Midwestern manners, played the cello, wore Chanel. More to the point, she was Korean. Or half Korean, anyway.

"He wanted to see how his ex-wife followed through on certain promises. Obviously, that's all moot now."

Cynthia shuddered. "It sounds so terrible."

The night of the murders, the police received reports of gunfire in the neighborhood but that was like saying it was dark out at the time. No one could pinpoint where the shots came from till Robert called 911. The detectives working the case had their doubts about his story but he'd held up under questioning and passed his gunshot residue test. Besides, the new mayor was lighting bonfires up their buttholes—their phrase—because of their pitiful clear rate on the dozens of drive-bys and gang hits in that neighborhood. Last thing they wanted to do was waste time on a domestic. As it sat, the case had a family angle and a murder-suicide tidiness to it, and that permitted them to close it out with a clear conscience. If justice got served in the bargain, fabulous.

"The documents your father actually executed leave everything to you. The Excelsior house has so little equity and is so heavily leveraged, I'd consider just walking away.

Let the lenders fight over it. The Hunter's Point lot—forget the house—might bring fifty thousand. That's a guess, we'll have it appraised. That leaves the cash payout from the annuity."

Cynthia looked up. "And that would be?"

"In the ballpark of half a million."

The girl's eyes ballooned. "I had no idea. I mean, my father and I, we weren't in touch. My mother, she's become more and more . . . traditional. She felt ashamed. She and my father weren't married and they—" Her cheeks colored. She wrung her handkerchief in her lap. "I wrote from time to time but never visited. Not even after his accident. Corella was the one—"

"It wasn't Corella's decision to make. It was your father's property. That's the way it works."

"But—"

"From the way he talked about it, I gathered it was precisely the fact you didn't hang around, waiting for him to die, that made him feel benevolent toward you."

Cynthia pondered that, then shrugged. "It still feels a little like stealing, to be honest."

"You can't steal a gift, not under the law anyway." Marguerite glanced at the clock, reminding herself: billable hours. "Are there any questions you'd like to ask?"

Cynthia put her chin in her hand and tapped her cheek with her forefinger. Too cute, Marguerite thought. The innocence was beginning to grate.

"I hope this doesn't sound crass," Cynthia said finally, "but when will I get my check?"

Marguerite bit her lip to keep from grinning. Families, death, and money, she thought. Didn't matter your race or creed—or how far away you lived—the poison always bubbles up from somewhere, often long before the dear departed's body grows cold.

"That depends on the insurance company administering the annuity. Why?"

Cynthia shrugged. "Nothing. I was thinking about maybe traveling." She blushed again. "It's my boyfriend's idea, actually."

Interesting, Marguerite thought. "'Travel is a privilege of the young.' I read that somewhere. Why didn't your boyfriend come with you?"

"He lives here. We just met." The color in her cheeks deepened. "It's sudden, I realize, and he's really not my type, but I've felt lonely here and he's very kind. He introduced himself at the church service. You may know him, actually, he took care of my father."

DOUBLE ESPRESSO

BY SIN SORACCO

Russian River

There was a festival of tiny Virgin de Guadalupe statues casting nets into the water. They hopped along the edges of the flooded soccer field, whispering about uncles who used to fish there. Huge hairy homeless men huddled in the predawn drizzle: When will the sun come out again, Mothers? The men placed large eggs in front of the statues. Or not.

Gina trudged through the little park, her mouth opened in a big yawn, her heavy eyes unfocussed, her hair flattened in wet curls from the sputtering rain. Soccer field was flooded again—they built the thing on top of one of the Mission district's old springs. Whole place used to be one big marsh, birds and fish and everything. Maybe someone should put a couple ducks there or something. Remind folks. Except the birds would probably get eaten. Would that be a good thing or not? Gina wasn't sure. She'd figure it out over coffee.

She was trying to savor the last moments of night before a harsh winter's sun gave everything edges—

"Hey! Get outta my way!" An agitated man wearing burgundy plaid jogging shorts and blueberry running shoes continued pumping his legs as he glared at her.

She stared at his legs. Did he actually shave them? What was in his mind when he did that? Like leg hair would slow him down? "Shhhh," she said. "People sleepin here."

"Dickhead." A deep voice Gina recognized rumbled from the depths of a sleeping bag. She saw Lucas's head appear for a moment before he burrowed back beneath the gold-striped plastic tablecloth which covered the upper half of him. "Go home."

The jogger's knees lifted higher, *pop pop one-two one-two*, as he bounced in front of Gina. He huffed, in the direction of the tablecloth, "This is a public park! Not a hotel!"

A couple more sleeping bags twitched, someone groaned. "Every fuckin mornin."

Lucas turtled out, muttering, "Dickhead gets up befo the sun jus to spoil our mornin." He nodded to Gina. "Mornin, Gina."

"Sun's not comin up today. Go back to sleep."

The enraged jogger hissed, "You people are crap."

Gina put her hands on her hips. "What people? Who people? Just who izzit you callin crap?" Her hands clenched as he ran across the lawn and down the steps to his SUV parked at the curb. She hollered at his retreating butt, "You rich fuckin bastaaaard!" She turned to the park's no longer sleeping crew. "Oh. Sorry." She headed toward the little mall at Sixteenth and Bryant.

The people who opened Peet's in the morning didn't smile a lot—this was important to Gina: Just pour the damn espresso into the cup and give it to me.

Double espresso. Spoonfulla steam milk. She poured the sugar over the top, circling the cup three times—

"Got you a serious sugar jones, Gina?"

Bleary-eyed, Gina glared at her coffee, "Mornin, Lucas. Don't talk about jonesin before coffee." She lifted her head and motioned at the Safeway parking lot outside the window. "Gonna be a crappy day, Lucas. Another crappy day." She poured half her coffee into a paper cup, handed it to him.

"Yup. Yup." Lucas rubbed his stubbly chin, scratched his do-rag back over his graying curls, grinned his seven-tooth grin. "Up before the sun again. Haaaaah." He waved at the chaotic lot, the oily drizzle. "Yunno, the world is how ya make it." He shrugged deeper into his baseball jacket. "Got a extra cigarette you can spare?"

Gina smiled at her grubby pal. "Pfft. They don come with extra. Only twenty to a pack." Cocking her head toward the lot, she said, "Come on back out into the wilderness with me and we'll bring up the sun, smokin."

She lit two cigarettes. Not gonna share one with Lucas no matter how little he annoyed her in the morning, that man's mouth surely been some nasty places. She watched him cough on the exhale. "Sorry I woke yas this mornin."

Lucas blew the smoke into the sky over the lot. "Nahhh. Weren't you. That guy got somethin wrong with him. Yunno." He watched the crows and the cars bark and circle in the morning light. "Goin down Sixteenth this morning, Gina. Anythin you want?"

Gina snorted, an unladylike noise. "I want it all, Lucas. I want it all."

"All Sixteenth Street?" His laugh was a sustained growl. "C'n you *i-magine* what it'd be like just to keep it clean?"

"Pffft. What about the DPW?"

Lucas raised a grizzled eyebrow. "Yeah. What about em?"

"Right. Let it rot."

"No. If it's yers . . ." Solemn nod, years of living at the edges. "If you want it, you gotta care for it."

Grumpy, "Yeah. Sure. Okay." A creek used to run all the way from where they stood, started over on Seventh, emptied into the bay. Sewer line now. "You're right. I don't want it."

Last drag. "What you want, Lucas? What you willin to take care of?"

"Weeeeeee-ell. I cheer you, smokin the sun come up. That about good enough for my day."

"I'm not cheered up." Gina smiled up at him. "Not me. Not cheerful. Not in the mornin. Nope." She turned her head, her smile fading as she saw three cop cars slide into the parking lot, sharks circling closer to a shiny black car with three shiny brownskin teenagers inside it.

The boys were oblivious, windows down, coffee cups raised to each other, their laughter shading from ghetto falsetto to royal belly roars: "Didja see that man looooooook at us? OOoooooooh yeeeeeeah. He be one jealous mutha-fucka nowwwwww."

Six doors opened, six cops approached the car, three hung back, two at each side, one stepping forward. "Out. Out of the car. Now."

Gina saw the whole morning slide straight into the shit-ter, the tender motion of their wild night, their grand friendship—she watched their lives slip off their faces as the cops approached.

One of the cops pawed at his gun, his shoulders twitched with anticipation.

Wind it back. Way back. To the moment of celebration. Never moving forward.

Stolen car, beautiful car pounding through the night, windows down, rockin sound, good friends. Nothing on their minds, nowhere to be. Just cruisin. Maybe drivin across the bridge to Oakland howlin at the moon, back again headin west as the sun came up behind them, racin chasin and pullin into Safeway's big lot, grabbem some wake-up-the-day, no one even know the car be gonnnnne yet. Three coffees, lotsa cream, take the whole sugar jar. Oh lookit that fiiiine girl, just a fine young girl. Fine. Here's to all the fine young girls! Here's to a night under the moon at seventy eighty ninety a hunnert miles an hour! Here's to friends and Here's to Forever.

Gina's breath came slow and shallow, her eyes riveted on the three boys standing, leaning on the car, one foot behind the other, casual, doomed. The police talked then the kids talked, waving their hands in the air. Even though she stared and stared directly at them all, she couldn't stop the forward motion from falling into the gray nothing forever of jail.

She felt Lucas fade away to her left—a soft sound like a sucker punch—right at the edge of awareness. Her lips curled in a snarl, she flung her coffee cup at the closest police car. Failed to get a splash on the tires. Grand gesture. Didn't save a single soul.

Gina spun away, headed out Bryant Street, following some long buried waterway, work forgotten. The sound of her boots snapped the cement into grains of sand, the glare of her eyes destroyed every condom dropped in her path. She cut up to Seventh and Folsom, creek's mouth, digging in her pocket for bills to catch a bus ride out. North. Out of the city. Like her granma used to do when things got tight in the kitchen. Far away for a day of friendly trees. There'd be lots of green shit on the hills. Big ol winter river.

When she got to her seat she half-closed her eyes, peeking out from under her heavy lids as the city rolled by. She discovered a fondness for the city buried somewhere deep in her chest, most noticeable when she was leaving. Gina sat upright at the bridge, staring at the early-morning skyline: Dawnlight glowed on fairy tale city.

"What crap." Gina put her head back, went to sleep.

She had intended to call Karen from Santa Rosa: Get out the bong, the booze, the shrooms. I'm headin fer the high grass. The tall trees. Comin to break the monotony of yer sheltered rural ex-is-tence.

But the River Express bus was at the station when she arrived so she just kept moving, no breaks in the rhythm, not even to call work: Got stuck up the river, road's washed out, won't be in today. She kept moving toward the green, away from the city drizzle that hurt her eyes. Burned her heart.

Gina hopped off in Guerneville, fog swirling from the trees at the top of the ridge, Latinos waiting on the corners for day-wage dirt jobs, no traffic on the street, slow dogs pissing on the shrubbery. Nice one-street city. Tattoo shop, couple weird art shops. Coffee shop.

"Double espresso, please." Gina took a deep breath, felt her ribs expand in the country air. First big rib-stretcher in a long time. "Ahhhh. Please, where's the nearest phone?"

Karen answered, melodic with country cheer, "Alhambra here."

"Al Hambra? What? Like some Saudi cousin of Al Qaeda?"

"Giiina! How are you?" She laughed. "It's a palace in Spain."

"You moved to Spain? Or named yourself after a building?" Gina scowled: You let em move outta the city, they completely lose their little freakin minds.

"Hah. I just liked the sound of it. So, what's up, little grouch?"

"I'm in Guerneville. Filled with urban angst." For the first time Gina wondered if this had been a good idea. She decided not to mention bongs or shrooms—when people changed a perfectly good two-syllable name like Karen to something mouth-filling or edificial, you never knew what other changes might have taken place.

"Gotcha. I'll be there inna few. Don't go to the bridge."

"Okay." What the hell is that supposed to mean?

"Don't do anything weird there. The local citizen-watch has the place bugged and videotaped."

"You shittin me? What's up with that?" Gina turned around, slow, careful, looking left, looking right. The vigilantes were hunkered down somewhere out of sight.

"The lower river's tagged with being inna condition of urban blight. Garbage. And crime, Gina. Terrible crime. People smoke dope. Shoot the lights out. Make noise. The world will come to an end if the good citizens don't document everything."

"What should I do?" Gina asked.

"Oh hell, go to the bridge anyway. It's the easiest landmark. Besides, the river's huge, makes everything hum. Make ya feel alive. Meet you there."

"Eat my shorts."

The rain started pissing down again, it would never stop, the world was going to wash away or disappear in a poof of mold. Dozens of vultures lurked in the dripping trees by the bridge, shitting down their legs, watching Gina with lazy hungry eyes.

She walked out to the middle of the span and stared down at the wide coffee river rumbling along only a foot or two below her, the bridge itself thrumming with the crazy power of so much muddy water bombing past. Gina goggled down into deep river space then pulled her sweater off over her head, spread her arms wide open to the *sprizz* of the water. "Yeeeeah!"

"Hey! Get outta the way!"

Gina turned to see a skinny guy walking a purple and green painted wheelchair.

"Din't yo mommy teach you ta watch yer back?" He stopped next to her, crowding her against the metal screen railing. He peered at the delicate vines tattooed around her left arm, at the datura blossoms inked by the same Mission district master artist on her right. "Wow." Up and down, moving closer. "Nice ink, babe!"

Gina glared at the gimp, she slid away from him. His T-shirt exposed beef-jerky muscles covered with blackwork tattoos. Thick lines where the ink had bled through the skin made the ugly skeletal forms worse. Both lower legs were similarly covered. Badly executed fake-tribal. The whites of his eyes were dead yellow, no pupil, his face didn't move when he spoke. Not good. "Get the fuck away from me."

He grabbed her arm, turning it to examine it closely. "Looks like my work, here." He leaned forward. "This here jus like my design." He ran his tongue up her inner arm.

Relax arm, bend knees, step to the side, and twist sharp. "You simple-minded fuckhead—"

There was more she was going to say, but his fist slammed into her face, she felt her right eye crack like an egg, sudden yolk ran red down her neck. She took a deep breath, a low crooning subsonic kind of sound began in her belly, spun out of her mouth. Her toes curled back, she popped his dick with the ball of her foot, and while he crouched in the traditional male *oof* position, she jumped straight up in the air, clasped her hands together, and whacked his head into a steel girder. He made a satisfying *clang* sound.

She grabbed the wheelchair and heaved it over the railing into the river. A classic finishing move. *Hoo hoo hoo.*

Gina took fragile steps along the bridge, back the way she

had come, muttering to herself. She snapped her fingers at the spot where she figured the camera would be: *Kiss my ass.*

As she stepped off the bridge she saw Karen's lanky figure running toward her. Gina took her hand off her eye and waved, spattering drops of blood which disappeared in the drizzle before they hit the ground. Gina's one-eye vision wobbled. Karen? Long sweater, long skirt, cowboy hat? Two long black braids swung out behind the woman as she ran.

"What happened?"

"Uhhh," Gina said, waving at the staggering figure on the bridge. "Uhh. Tattoo pride. What can I say?"

"Put your hand over your eye, press down. Wait. No. Don't press on it, you might make it worse. Tilt your head back. Wait, no, don't tilt it back, you won't see where you're going—here, lean on me."

Gina grinned up at her friend. "Calm down, Allllhambrah. Just point me to your car. This ain't my first head wound, surely won't be the last. C'mon. Let's blow Guerneville."

Gina wrapped her sweater around her head before she got in the car so she wouldn't bloody-up the upholstery. Tires squealed, there was no traffic so Karen took it from zero to sixty in, well, it was an old wreck of a car so it made it to sixty in a couple, three, maybe four blocks. Held steady around the curves.

"Ahhh. That felt good. I mean, now it feels really bad— you do have dope at home, don't you? But outside of this ex-cruciatin pain here, I been needin to do that for months." Gina tipped her head into her hand. "I can see why they hava camera on that bridge. The Mission's a snooze in comparison. Izzit this excitin generally?"

Alhambra spoke through her teeth, "I have some

Percocet, and no, it's not usually like that. Generally people just hang out. Yunno. But that guy—well." A dozen turns, over a couple more bridges, onto a gravel and dirt road, some more curves, the old car still hanging tough around the corners, then *bounce bounce bounce*, Alhambra avoided the trees growing smack in the middle of the throughway, sharp right. "Home."

"Hardly a spot on your brocade." Gina's sweater was soaked through with great splotches of blood—head wounds always bled like some animal had been gutted—she dropped it on the porch.

Alhambra picked it up. "No need to advertise to the neighbors that you're a thug. I'll wash this." She looked at Gina's bloody clothes. "Gah. Take them all off. They'll get stiff and sticky if you don't."

Gina stripped on the porch, head tilted back, palm cupped over her eye. "This could be so romantic. But instead, how about you gimme some dope, like right now? Like even before I enter your Spanish palace?"

Alhambra wrapped Gina in a huge blanket, pushed her inside and onto the couch. "Here."

"Yum." Bright light, hydrogen peroxide, cotton balls, scissors, tape, gauze—"Thread and needle? Get away!"

"Shhh. That's just part of the kit, darlin, you aren't gettin the full treatment this time. Just gonna clean here and here."

"Ow. I would be stoic, but then you won't give me any more drugs. Ooooh owwww."

"Shit. Stop howlin. I need ta see if your eyeball is squished."

Gina tried to sit up, "My eyeball ain't just squished, I heard it crack like it was a egg!" She wondered how it would be to live one-eyed.

"It looks like his ring cut your eyelid. But your eyeball isn't scratched or cracked or anythin." Alhambra stepped back, smiling. "Gonna hava shinerrr."

"Crap. Come to the country. Be bucolic. Frolic. Man, this sucks."

Alhambra fixed a gauze patch over Gina's eye, handed her a package of frozen peas to put on her cheekbone, and set the kettle on the stove.

Gina lay back with her eyes closed. Half-dreaming, she heard the sound of chopping, then wood hitting the slate floor with a *clonk*, crunkle of paper, *skritch* of match, *whomp* of a fire starting—the smell of pitch pine and oak, the flicker on her eyelids of orange dancers, the whistle of the kettle. Peppermint ginger tea. Something gritty slid through her mind about rural livin bullshit and how it just ain't true, but she let it drift away. "I miss you sometimes in the city, yunno? I got a friend, he been on the streets now for I dunno how many years, but even with him, I don't see that reflection of who I am—like I see in your eyes." She muttered, "Lonely."

"You needa learn to be gentle with yourself."

"Gentle? No." Gina shifted, grunting. "Oh. Right. You can say that now cause you're the medicine woman of the woods. Livin clean. Chop wood, carry water." She took a gulp of tea. Gina thought she heard monsters roaring in the distance. "What the hell is that big noise?"

Alhambra laughed. "It's the river! Cool, huh?"

"Not cool. Wheelchair perverts anda howlin river. And you. I mean, you gotta cowboy hat now. A full medical kit. A rifle?"

"No rifle. Just an old Ruger with the numbers filed off. It was a gift, because it's a classic, like me."

"What?"

"That's what the guy said. I wasn't all that pleased with the man, but the gun is sweet."

Gina growled, "Convicts like us can't have guns, Karen. Can't have dope. Can't do medical stuff. We aren't allowed to protect ourselves. Not even if there's wolves at the door. Monsters in the woods. Once a convict, always a criminal."

Alhambra laughed, "There's no monsters in these woods."

"Ha. What you gotta gun for? What the hell you doin up here?"

"Safe haven, Gina. That's all. Sanctuary."

"Dayam. Sanctuary?"

Alhambra put her hand on Gina's shoulder. "If it makes you feel any better, that guy you clobbered isn't a gimp. He uses the wheelchair as a prop so people give him money. Dude's not even poor. His daddy's in grapes and development. Gonna shut the river down—says there isn't enough water to go around for the fish and all the people."

Gina listened to the growling of the river. "Seem to me there's plenty of water."

"Not for these greedy bastards. They're gonna make the river dry all up in the summer. Pretend it's good for the fish, then sell the water for development." Alhambra chewed on one of her braids. "Can't stand to let people just live, gotta always make money."

Gina looked up, her one eye huge and sad. "Used to be rivers in the city. In the Mission. All kindsa fish, too. My granma told me. She told me how she'd watch her uncles go off for a day of fishin insteada goin to school. They come home drunk. But sometimes they'd catch little trouts, then everybody would come over and . . . Well, it'd be great. All gone now."

Alhambra shivered. "Rivers are an endangered species. That guy's father maybe figures if the river dies, then his toad son come back home, become a wealthy lawyer."

"Same no matter where I go."

Gina took the package of not-really-frozen-anymore peas from her cheek, started to get up to put it back in the fridge.

"Siddown, you. I'm in charge here. Gimme that, it'll be pea soup innabout an hour." A frying pan sizzled as pancetta hit it, rattle of peas into a pot.

"Smells like hot dogs."

"Hah. Remember when we try to learn how to give a guy head?"

"Oh yeahhhhh. Stuck hot dogs down our throats till we gagged, so we gave up and cooked em. I never yet have had occasion to use whatever it was we learned. You?"

"Sure! I'm up for whatever comes along."

"Comes? Along? Oh yuck. Did you swallow?"

"Condoms are your friend, dimwit."

"Not my friend. I don't go that way." Gina leaned forward, staring into the flames. "How long has it been since I hadda fire inna fireplace? Forever? Never? You do this a lot?"

"Every night this time of year. Drops to freezin. Sometimes, if I don't bank it right, I need to start it up again in the mornin. But that's not hard cause the embers are still hot."

"You learn this up here or you knew it all already? Me . . . Well, I sort of figure if I don't know it, I'll fake it." Gina shifted her hips, trying to get comfortable. "Like, I suppose I could make a fire . . ." Her voice faded. "Just never expected to need to know."

Gina watched Alhambra cook. "We always at the mercy of rich fuckers. They want everythin to be their way—mean and narrow. Oh crap! I gotta call work! I just sort of up and left the city."

There was a huge boom. And another. Another. Gina bolted upright. The light on the table blinked, blinked, blinkblinked, then fizzed. The house was dark except for the firelight.

"But it's already dark, as you can see. They know you're not comin in, Gina. Besides, power's out. No regular phone." Alhambra placed the pot of soup on the wood stove. "Don't worry, if the phone lines didn't come down, you can still call out." Alhambra left the room, hollering over her shoulder, "Let me see if the land line is workin."

"Land line?" Gina felt around for her pack. "Jeez. What's a land line? A shortwave radio? I'm gonna call work on like a CB? Well, I gotta tellum I won't be in tomorrow neither." Her voice faded to tiny mutters, she peered out at the menacing tree shapes looming over the house. "Fuckin primitive out here. Hey, Karen? You realize I only have one workin eye and this is like purgatory? I can't see shit now." She didn't mention that the trees were reaching mean spiky fingers out at her. Smaller voice, "Shit. Can't find my cigarettes." Gina sat back on the couch clutching her backpack on her lap. "And my eye is startin to hurt. And . . ." She began to snicker. "And I can't get to work." The snickers turned into laughter. "And I can't call because they don't hava shortwave radio. Hah. Haaaaaah."

Gina grabbed the blanket loosely in her hands. "And I'm up here in total blackout boonie land with my best friend. Oh yeahhhhh."

Alhambra came up the hallway carrying a small lantern. She said, "Phone lines are down."

Gina leaped up, flailing the blanket in the air like a huge

bat. "We'll get the boogie man! You and me, Alhambra! We'll scare im right back into the hellhole he keep comin up out of! Every smartass self-righteous bastard that ever EVER tried to make us small. Every shitmouth rich bitch who plays the I'm-entitled card—we will smassssh her. We'll tear the prison walls DOWN, muthafucka, DOWN!"

Alhambra put the lantern on the floor, grabbing a corner of the blanket. She raced Gina out into the night, howling, "Down, muthafuckas! Get baaaaack! Mothafuckas!"

It wasn't until they got right to the edge of the swollen river that Gina noticed she had no clothes on. "Oh my god." She curled forward. "Karen! You let me go outside starkers."

Alhambra leaned against the huge belly of a redwood, laughter making it impossible for her to stand on her own.

Gina wrapped the blanket in tidy folds around herself. She lifted her head with a haughty twitch. "You bitch."

Too early in the morning, Alhambra put the kettle on a small butane gas ring, the *hoo* when it reached a boil woke Gina. "Coffee?" she said. "Still no power, so we'll go into town for the next cup. Phones probably work there."

The rain rattle-crashed on the windows, the evil trees slammed their devil branches on the roof of the little house, Gina pulled the covers over her head. "Oh ow oh ow oh ow."

"Shshshhh. You'll annoy the demons. Be brave, oh black-heart babe, be brave."

"Hey, I'm dyin here. One eye, purple cheek, held captive in a wilderness hellhole."

"What time they expect you at your place of gainful?"

"When I get there. I'm just the inventory monster trapped in the basement, any shipments get there before I do, they pile up. I suit up, show up, count em, log em, sort em, shelve em. Simple. I do it inna speed-stupor. Work one all-day-all-night shift and it's done. Commerce recommences. And I get paid. Do it again after I've slept some."

"You wanta callem, or what?"

"Yeah. I better. They aren't likely to call my PO, but they might start callin hospitals. Or morgues." Gina rolled off the futon onto the floor, crawled around for a while patting the slate. "Cigarette? Grrr. Cigarette? Ahhh." Inhale. "They think that highly of me. Right. Let's hava shot of coffee here—I'll take another Percoset, thank you—then make a break for civilization." She held out her coffee cup.

Alhambra poured. "Not civilization. I'm not happy with civilization. Yunno? It don't work for me."

Gina held her coffee cup in both hands, cigarette dangling from her lips, she couldn't figure out how to sip since the cigarette was in the way and she wasn't about to let go of the cup with either hand. Mornings were filled with dilemma. She growled, "Civilized is soothing drugs. You have soothing drugs. Ergo. Civilized." She sucked the cigarette down to the filter, put the cup in one hand, pinched the cigarette out of her mouth, and tossed it into the embers of last night's fire. She held her hand out for the pill. "Thank you."

Alhambra said, "Civilization treats pain with lectures. You know that."

"Right. I came all the way up here to get my face mashed in so I could get properly loaded. Got it." Gina pulled her shirt on. "Beats whatever else I had in mind."

They rattled into town, avoiding the fallen branches, hydroplaning through the rivulets streaming across the road. Monte Rio. Vacation Wonderland. Two bridges, one street. No beach in the winter, the river ate it. There was a movie theater in a Quonset hut with an immense mural on its side, runny with water. The metal ridges of the hut blurred the painted trees into menacing shapes. Gina muttered, "And my granma tol me this place was friendly. Ha."

A large red amanita mushroom graced the sign for the Wonderland Diner. Alhambra said, "You'll like it here, Gina."

Gina looked dubious, but as they entered she murmured, "Whoa. A real diner. Cool."

Knotty pine walls, sweet breakfast smells, a waitress with a sharp take-no-prisoners grin greeted them. "Good morning. Sit yourselves wherever you're most comfortable. Coffee?" Not even a small blink at Gina's broken face. Maybe smashed up faces were common. Maybe the waitress was just good.

Alhambra grinned back. "Mornin. Two double espressos, please, to start."

"Comes double. You want double double?"

"Yes, please." Alhambra whispered to Gina, "Great coffee. They tested every kind they could get their hands on—"

The waitress pulled the handles on the old espresso machine like an Italian barrista. Serious. No shortcuts like the machines at Peet's.

"Sounds like my kind of job."

"Pffft. You would be the worst waitress on the planet. It's an art."

Grumbling, "I wanta be the taster, not the server." Gina bit the lemon peel, sipped her double espresso. "Damn. Well. All right then."

"Country pleasures."

Gina didn't respond, she got up, bringing her coffee with her, walked to the side of the diner, called her job. They hadn't missed her, really, but they were aware that the work wasn't done. Not to worry. She'd deal with it when the roads opened up. Sometime in May. Monte Rio had a certain appeal.

"Okay, so tell me: What do people do up here?" Gina spoke through a mouthful of biscuit ten minutes from the oven with real Maple syrup poured over. She stabbed at her bacon and spun it around on her fork, pointing the whole arrangement at her friend.

Alhambra chewed her BLT on rye, considering an answer. "Same as anywhere. Folks try to get by, grab the energy of the earth and put it to work."

"Energy of the earth? Crap." Gina wasn't going to be mollified by an outstanding breakfast. "Diddlin. That's what happens when you don't have the energy of the city. Ya go soft in the head and spend all your time diddlin."

"Define."

Gina's mouth opened, closed. She scowled. "Eh. You know what I mean."

Alhambra looked up.

Gina felt a large ominous shadow on her right. She craned her neck, wincing for effect, focused her one functioning eye on the steel worker who stood by their table.

"I know you."

Gina's lips parted, starting to snarl then wiggling into a limp smile. "Yeah?"

The six-foot steel worker with the blond buzz cut spoke in a melodic soprano, she stood sort of shy, one foot on top of the other. "Uh-huh." She shifted to another self-effacing position. Her eyebrows lifted, her head tipped to the side, one shoulder raised up—a sort of traditional body language for you-know-where-we've-been.

"Jail?" As soon as Gina spoke she would have eaten her own head if only she could've fit it in her mouth. In for a nickel. "Which one?" In for a dime.

"Bryant Street. You were on your way somewheres else,

probably don't remember me. Name's Joey. They called me *Big Rig*."

It would be impolite to admit she didn't remember anyone quite so large, impossible to say she had no memory at all of someone who tried so hard to be small. And failed so utterly. "Ah." Perhaps the woman was smaller then?

Joey pointed, a small movement, at Gina's arm. "That my design, that one there."

Gina took a long breath, blew it out. This person was too sizable to insult, but truth is truth. "No. It ain't. It ain't yers. It's from the hand and mind and soul of a monster great master in the Mission. I watched it bein born in his psyche, I watched it get drawn here on my arm, and I watched him, in total tattoo trance, ink this sucker by hand with needles he tied together right there in front of me with secret knots, and with ink he ground up hisself from pine sap. So don't give me no shit about it's yours." Her lower jaw stuck out: Nobody fucked with Mission history.

Joey shrunk back, her lilting voice floating as if it was a whisper of wind. "Oh. I see."

"No. You don't see." Gina made a small grunt as Alhambra kicked her under the table. "Yesterday a complete toad haulin around a Day-Glo wheelchair told me the same thing." She moved her chair back in order to speak directly up at Joey. "I apologize for bein harsh to you, but the skinny fucker popped me in the eye when I told him to go fuck himself."

"That asshole! He been stealing my designs, calling them his own." The color rose in Joey-Big Rig's face, her eyes went glinty gray, her arms swelled up like pumpkins as she clenched her fists. "That gnarly bastard couldn't put a tattoo on a fucking grapefruit."

Gina thought better of pointing out that the design on her arm wasn't Joey's. Instead she nodded, glad to have support in her appraisal of the man. "Dead eyes? Mummy face? Crap ink?"

Joey nodded, her color shading to something less volcanic. "He kills people. He uses the same needles on everyone. Steals other folks' work and twists it into something ugly."

"Carryin bad tattoo art is death in itself." Alhambra spoke, cool waters to soothe a restless soul.

"You know what I'm talking about, then." Joey became their comrade again. "You staying clean and sober? Yes?"

"Yes. Well, no. I mean . . ."

Joey laughed, a hearty trill—it would have been a trill except it came from a mountain, so it was, well, hearty. "Been seventeen months for me. Clean. And. Sober." The laugh stopped and her eyes went flinty. "I ain't never going back." She paused, looked at each of them in turn, her huge hands opening and closing in spasm. "Never. Never going back."

The air had gone out of the diner with a psychic *whoosh*.

"Never. You got that?"

Alhambra sighed, softly refilling the place with air. "We got it, Joey. Good for you."

"Good for you." Gina's voice clicked in her throat, stuck on something she hadn't known was in there.

The big woman's face shifted into a smile, she leaned forward and knocked on the table, "Good talking with yas. Hope to see yas around, then." She straightened up, "Don't forget what I told yas. None of us ever going back. No way. None of us."

The door closed behind her with a small *plock*.

"We done here, I think?"

"Dayam. We be done and done again." Gina stared at her hands clenched tight as two poodles fucking. "Holy crap."

"Let's walk down to the river and catch a breath of massive water power?"

"Wash away all our sins?"

"Take more than a river in full mud raging flood to do that."

They passed a sign: *Welcome to Monte Rio! HATE STOPS HERE.*

"You guys hava different definition of *hate* up here than we do down in the Mission where folks aren't all completely bonkers?"

Alhambra, lost in her own thoughts, nodded *uh-huh*.

They crossed the parking lot, started down a scrubby slope to the curve of the rumbling river. "Jeezuz! She's goin in the water!"

Joey-Big Rig, hip deep where the water curled against a set of rocks, was wrestling something out of the scrub.

"Holy Christ, it's that wheelchair I tossed." Gina didn't know whether to jump right in, in some goofy heroic attempt to help, or back away in shame at the calamity she had set in motion: Joey was going to be slushed away to drown.

Alhambra's hand touched Gina's shoulder. "She'll be fine long as she doesn't go past the rocks. Water boils around in there but there's no big current, that's more to the center. See the logs out there?"

"That's not a log—"

One of the logs flipped upright at Joey's side, eye-blink fast he grabbed for the chair, hissing.

"Crap. That's the guy."

"Too right." Alhambra's full lips curled up. "This is gonna be good."

"Uh, Alhambra? Karen? Those two people can drown in there. What happened to Miss Sunshine No Sorrow?"

Alhambra stepped to the edge of the icy water, a short leap away from the spectacle. "The snake and the elephant."

"Should we interfere? Or scream?"

The wheelchair, flung by one of the combatants, skidded on the gravel to their left. Someone screamed.

"Ah. Screaming is what we do." But Gina didn't scream. It wasn't in her nature to scream. She shouted, "Tha's right, Joey! Pound that slimy fucker! Tha's right, Joey! Take im out!" The chant swelled, backed by the river's grumble, "Take im out! Take im out! Take im out!"

Joey had the fake gimp's arms twisted up behind his back, held easy in one of her huge hands, with the other she had hold of his hair, dunking him face first into the river. The muscles of her arms pumped up and down, relentless pistons pushing him under the water, out again, snap back into the river. Her eyes had gone flat and gray, her mouth twisted.

Alhambra said, matter-of-fact, "Let him get a breath now, Joey."

Joey shrugged, lifted his head, peered at the fake gimp's face with scientific detachment.

He gagged, green-brown river water puked from his mouth. He took a stuttering gulp of air, his eyes fluttering.

Joey shook him, wrinkled her nose, straight-armed his head back under.

Gina stepped toward the river. "That fucker isn't never comin up."

Bubbles.

"He ain't worth it, Joey," Alhambra said. Simple statement.

Gina's voice rose up over the river's howl, "Hey! Never goin back? Joey—you ain't never goin back. Remember?"

Bubbles. An eternity of bubbles rising *pock pock pock* to the surface.

Joey looked up, took a breath. Nodded. She thrust the man from her, into the current, staggered up to the shore. "Thank you." She popped her knuckles, tipped her head left and right to get the tension out of her neck. "Thank you."

They watched the limp form spin in the current, catch on the next curve, and lie there for a moment before the man began to pull himself up the gravel.

Gina muttered, "Fuckers like that never die."

Joey sighed, "I'm keeping the wheelchair though. Damn." She folded the thing up, hoisted it over one shoulder, waved to Alhambra and Gina. "Have yerselves a jolly day. Clean and sober. Oh yeahhhh."

The rain had let up, Gina and Alhambra were walking down the same path they'd rocketed down the night before. The only sound was the steady noise of hundreds of thousands of gallons of water rushing to the sea. Billions of gallons?

"Tell me, Alhambra. What you find up here you never got in the city?"

"Look up at the damn trees, Gina. Listen to the goddam river. Pay attention to what's right here."

"I want answers to questions this here river and tree world doesn't care about—lookin at trees ain't gonna make the hurt stop."

"Sometimes it's the only thing make the hurt stop. Come here and look over there across the river."

Gina saw a power pole on the far shore with a wooden box on top. Snaggly sticks poked out in all directions.

"Young osprey built a nest up there. First year she was ready to mate, she built her nest on the only tall thing didn't already have someone else's nest on it. Her babies died when they hit the electric wires. One of the locals climbed up there, built her a platform."

Gina stared at the ungainly nest in a box. She whispered, "Maybe next year the babies will live?" She looked at Alhambra. "You think?"

Alhambra lifted her shoulders, "There's a chance. Yeah."

Gina tipped back on her heels, hands in her pockets. "So. What you're sayin is—what you're sayin is?"

"Somethin like that. Yeah."

Gina got off the bus at Sixteenth and Bryant, stretched her back, lit a cigarette, looked at the city. Not too shabby. It was home. She understood it, knew pretty much when to shift aside, when to stand firm. She headed up the steps to the park. She had a whole pack of American Spirits for Lucas, they'd smoke her welcome home, talk about rivers underfoot that were, and one that still is. For another winter season at least.

"Hey. You seen Lucas?"

"Nah. He not been here, day, two days, mebbe."

"Hey. You seen Lucas?"

"Family trouble. He gone."

Gina set off for the freeway underpass, right where another spring used to bubble. "Anybody seen Lucas?"

"Nope." The man in front of the tents glared at her, made her uncomfortable until she realized the glare was permanent, one eye blind. She touched her own bruised face, said, "Mine's only a day or two. Gettin used to bein a pirate with one eye. How long yours?" She shook out a few cigarettes from Lucas's pack.

He smiled. "Hah. Ten years ago." He allowed Gina to

light his cigarette. "Funny you ask about Lucas. He was there. When it happen to me. Was his son's eighth birthday. We got drunk and—" Still smiling, "Was a helluva lotta fun."

"Where his son now?"

The man's mouth curled down. "Where else? He in jail." He wandered away shaking his head. "Least ways tha's what Lucas said."

Three boys whoopin in the parking lot. Here's to a night under the moon, a hunnert miles an hour. Here's to the girls that smiled at us.

Here's to the father that loved us.

"You see Lucas, you please tellim I gotta story fer him. Yunno? So tellim I'm goin for coffee in the morning at the other place, down the street t'other way. Ain't goin back to that Peet's. Okay? Tellim I got to start the day off with him. Otherwise the mornin ain't right. Yunno?"

The old man didn't stop his slow amble away through the puddles, but Gina saw his hand raise up, as if to say, "Sure thing, girl. Sure thing."

Under the dim freeway buttresses, several statues of La Virgin de Guadalupe dipped their bowls into the clear head-waters of the creek and, chuckling like pigeons, poured it over their heads.

AFTER HOURS AT LA CHINITA

BY BARRY GIFFORD

The Bayview

Spooky backside of town, Third Street, San Francisco, late at night, in a motel office. The furnishings were shabby. La Chinita, once an elegant, Spanish-style motel built in the 1930s, was now, in 1963, run-down; paint was peeling off the walls and the wooden registration desk was chipped and gouged. A decrepit, moth-eaten easy chair and a few other rickety wickers with ripped seats and backs were placed against the walls. Hanging blinds, with several slats missing or broken, covered the glass-paned door. The office was clean, however, and presided over by a bespectacled woman who looked to be in her mid-sixties. She was seated in a lounge chair in front of the desk, knitting and humming softly to herself. Her name was Vermillion Chaney. The tune she was humming was "Just a Closer Walk with Thee." It was two weeks before Christmas.

The telephone behind the motel desk rang. Vermillion did not move. The telephone continued to ring. It was as if Vermillion did not hear it. The telephone rang eight times before it finally stopped. After the ringing stopped, Vermillion put down her knitting, stood up and walked behind the registration desk, picked up the telephone receiver, and dialed a number.

"Was that you just called?" Vermillion asked into the phone. "Um, okay. Don't matter. What you doin', anyway?

Sure I know it's 3 o'clock in the mornin', I'm at work!"

Vermillion hung up the phone. She came back around the desk, sat back down in her chair, and resumed knitting. She started singing again, only this time it was "What a Friend We Have in Jesus."

The office door began to shake. Somebody was trying to open it but the door was locked. This was followed by a loud knocking. The knocking was hard, insistent.

From behind the door came a woman's scream. "Open up! Open the door!"

Vermillion stopped singing and stared at the door. The knocking continued. The woman's voice became hysterical.

"You got to help me! Open up!"

Vermillion put down her knitting, got up, and went to the door. She looked out through one of the missing slats as the woman outside continued to yell.

"Miz Chaney, it's me! Revancha!"

Vermillion unlocked the door and a woman in her early twenties burst into the office, forcing the older woman back as she brushed past her.

"Shut it!" said Revancha. "Lock the door before he gets here!"

Vermillion stared at the young woman, who was half-dressed, wearing only a bra and panties. Clutched to her chest were other garments. Vermillion closed the door. Revancha ran back to it and fastened the chain lock.

"What's goin' on, Revancha? You look like a chicken in a bag full of snakes."

Revancha retreated from the door and stopped with her back against the desk.

"He beatin' on me, Miz Chaney! Chokin' me! Usin' a strap!"

"Man get what he pay for."

"He gone too far, cat flip his wig. Call for security!"

Vermillion walked back behind the desk, reached down, and came up with a revolver in her right hand.

"This the onliest security I got tonight, baby."

"Where's Myron?" asked Revancha.

Vermillion shook her head. "He out the loop. Fool got hisself arrested yestiday for receivin' stolen property. Fake beaver coats. Can you beat that? I'm alone here this evenin'."

The office door started to shake.

A man shouted, "Vermillion! Let me in!" He rattled the door.

"Don't do it, Miz Chaney!" said Revancha.

"Bitch stole my pants!"

"You'd best go on, Ray," said Vermillion.

"Not without my pants!"

Vermillion looked at Revancha.

"You got Ray's pants?"

"I scooped it all up, what was piled on the floor. Thought maybe he wouldn't follow me."

"Man ain't gonna go away without you give up his trousers."

Ray forced himself against the door, breaking the lock on the handle. Only the chain now prevented him from opening it. He stuck his hand through and attempted to undo the chain.

"Don't do it, Ray," said Vermillion. "I got a piece."

Ray pushed against the door, breaking the chain. The door flew open and Ray entered. He was a handsome man in his mid-thirties, wearing only a half-unbuttoned white dress shirt, under-shorts, socks, and shoes. He moved toward Revancha.

"Give me my wallet," he said.

Vermillion pointed the gun at him.

"Stop right there, Ray," she said. "I'll get it for you."

Ray stopped.

"I ain't got your wallet!" shrieked Revancha.

Ray brushed past Vermillion and grabbed the garments out of Revancha's hands. He felt around in them.

"It ain't here."

He dropped the garments on the floor and grabbed hold of Revancha.

"Where is it?!"

"Let go the girl, Ray!" said Vermillion.

Ray put his hands around Revancha's throat and began choking her. Revancha screamed; she kept screaming.

"Turn her loose, Ray, or I got to shoot!"

Ray turned his head and looked at Vermillion but continued strangling the girl.

"You old whore," Ray said to Vermillion, "you prob'ly in on the game."

Vermillion trained the barrel of her revolver on Ray and pulled the trigger, shooting him in the side. Ray, stunned, looked down at himself and watched as blood began to stain his shirt. Revancha continued to scream. Ray looked back at the girl and tightened his grip around her throat. Vermillion fired again, this time hitting Ray square in the back. His hands came away from Revancha's throat. He turned slowly and faced the old lady. She fired a third bullet, which entered his body in the middle of his chest. Ray dropped to his knees, holding his hands up, as if in prayer. He remained motionless in that position for several moments before toppling over onto his face.

Revancha stopped screaming. She looked down at Ray. Blood was everywhere.

From behind them came a man's voice. "Mother of God."

Vermillion turned and saw a short, middle-aged, long-bearded man, dressed like a tramp, standing in the doorway. He took a closer look at Ray's corpse, crossed himself, and said, "If God knew what He was doing, He wouldn't be doing this."

The stage was dark. A single spotlight lit up, shining on an empty stool set in the middle of the stage. A microphone lay on the stool.

The voice of the club announcer boomed out at the audience: "And now, ladies and gentlemen, the moment you have all been waiting for. The Blackhawk, San Francisco's premier nightclub, is proud to welcome America's favorite recording artist, Mr. Smooth himself, Ray Sparks!"

As the audience applauded, Ray Sparks, the man who had been gunned down in the motel office, skipped on stage. He was nattily dressed in a sharp suit and tie. Lights came up behind him, revealing an orchestra, which began to play. Ray smiled and bowed to the audience, who continued to applaud. He then turned and picked up the microphone, sat down on the stool, and began to sing.

Twenty years later. In the corridor of a decrepit nursing home, elderly people in wheelchairs, mostly black, were either sitting in or being pushed along by attendants. One of the former, a woman in her eighties, sat in a wheelchair placed flush against a wall, ignored by the overworked staff. The woman, now blind, wearing dark glasses, was Vermillion Chaney.

"I don't recall that night too good," said Vermillion. "I'm old enough now I don't recall most too good, though sometimes I surprise myself, rememberin' the tiniest detail from way back in the day. I know Revancha was a workin' girl, sure I did. Used to be she hung out at the Toro Club down Bayshore. Almost always she'd bring her man to the Chinita. Never had no trouble about her till that night.

"Ray Sparks? Everybody knowed Ray Sparks. Famous singer like him? Nobody miss that face. I heard he sometimes hung at the Toro, sat in with the band, after hours, like that. Maybe he just run into Revancha for the first time. Can't say one way or another. About the shootin', it's like I told the police when it happen, I was just defendin' the girl and myself."

Revancha Lopez, now in her mid-forties, was seated on a bed in a crummy hotel room. The evidence of a hard life showed in her face.

"My name is Esquerita Revancha Lopez y Arrieta. I ain't been usin' for six years, since before my last holiday at Tehachapi, and I won't start again, the Good Lord willin'. The street broke me. If you can believe this, I got me a straight job now, cleanin' rooms at the Chinita. Ain't that a twist? 'Bout that night, I heard so many stories, 'bout the man bein' set up and all, 'bout Miz Chaney be in on a hustle, even that she and I was hired by the FBI or a black militant group to put him out the way. People make up shit like that don't need no TV. They got enough goin' on inside they own mind entertain' theyself.

"I knew Ray Sparks for a while before that. He had this image, you know, clean-livin' man, good family, still singin' gospel some Sundays. Cat was a player! Not only that but I heard his wife was runnin' the streets, too. I had just got back to the Toro Club after doin' a piece of business when in walk Ray with his cousin, Anthony. Was Anthony come over to me, buy me a drink. We shootin' the shit for a few moments, then here come Ray. Puts his arm around me, says somethin' like, *Señorita Lopez, I figure it's about time you treat me right.* I said, *You got what it takes, Ray.* We was playin', straight up. He'd had a few drinks already, he didn't want no more, and he was all over me, tellin' me how beautiful I look, he don't know why we ain't got together before, makin' me feel good. Back then, it don't take but fifty dollars to make me feel good, but Ray, he liked to have some style, you know what I mean. He know it's gonna cost him, but he liked to play like it's on the house. One thing, with this girl was nothin' doin' on the house.

"Now I'd been with Anthony before, so Ray, he know the deal. The three of us was havin' a good time. Ray be rubbin' against me, I knew he was ready to do some business. Inside an hour, we get in his red Corvette, tool over to the Chinita. I ask him, *Don't you want to do better than this?* He say, *Baby, I'm in a hurry to get at you.* Okay by me. I didn't figure him to be a freak. I ask for a hundred dollars. Star like him can't think under that. He pay for the privilege of bein' a star. He took off his pants. I got to my underwear and next thing I know, he starts beatin' on me. I mean, *serious*, usin' a belt. I tell him to quit, he don't need to be doin' that. He say, *Don't tell me what I need!* He throw me down on the bed, push my face into the pillow so I can't scream, hittin' me. Then he sticks his dick in from behind, finish in a hurry. Then he get up, go into the bathroom.

"When I hear him relievin' himself, I jump up, scoop up all the clothes off the floor, and run out the room. I run to the office. Miz Chaney let me in, she by herself, lock the door. A few seconds later, Ray bust it down. Miz Chaney be afraid for her life, that's the truth. He come at me, shoutin' I stolen his wallet. Chokin' me. Miz Chaney come up with a hand cannon, tell Ray to turn me loose. Next thing I know, there's Ray on the floor, everywhere is red. It weren't the worst time in my life, but it was sure the beginin' of a downhill. I keep thinkin', slide gotta stop sometime. I keep thinkin', but it don't really stop."

Ray Sparks was half-seated on a nightclub stool.

"Who you looking at ain't Ray Sparks, it's the ghost of Ray Sparks. Here it is twenty years later, and I look the same, not like Revancha Lopez and Vermillion Chaney. You'll have to decide for yourself if it's a comfort to look like you did when you died on into eternity. They don't look so good as me but they got to live a lot longer. What people do with their lives is mostly fuck 'em up. Almost no way they could do anything else. I always liked that saying, *Give a man enough rope and he'll hang himself.* Just some folks got themselves a longer rope to hang with.

"People like to blame other people for their own troubles. Even me. One thing I picked up on recently—in eternity, all thoughts and things are recent—is how there is no particular way to avoid what you do or how you do it. It's like waking up in the middle of the night, hung over, and snoring in the bed next to you is an ugly whore. And you think to yourself, this can't be me, shacked up with some nasty skank. Me is little Ray, running with my dog down along the river. Seven years old, me and my dog running next to the river and it's about to rain. Nobody bothering us. But no mistake, it's you in that bed, feeling like a bomb gone off in your head, and it ain't no cute puppy lying there. You got to ask yourself why, and then if you got a lick of sense, do something to change your situation. If you never ask yourself the question *Why?* then you ain't got a chance. You got to be brave."

"Don't you be listenin' to that man!" said Vermillion Chaney, who rolled herself up to Ray in her wheelchair. "Talk like he sang, smooth as silk. Didn't shoot you on purpose," she said.

"What do you mean, didn't do it on purpose?" said Ray. "That was on purpose as possible to be. You shot me three times. Once in the back."

"Pistol felt light as a feather in my hand."

"You got to like pulling that trigger."

"Light as a feather," said Vermillion.

Revancha walked up to Ray and said, "I didn't mean to steal your clothes."

"Only my wallet."

"Your wallet was up in those clothes somewhere. I would have left it, after I took what was owed me."

"There is no such thing as an honest whore," said Ray.

"Man gets violent, what's a woman to do?" said Vermillion. "God put that gun in my hand, told me to use it."

"Better leave God out of this," said Ray.

"When I was a little girl, eight years old," said Revancha, "Mamacita took me down on Mission Street to La Iglesia Espiritu Santu to pray for my father, who was in the prison hospital. He had got stabbed in the stomach in a fight. We didn't know it then, but at the same moment we was in the church, he died. I liked lightin' the candles.

"We was about to leave when a man comes in off the street, wearin' nothin' but dirty rags. Had a long beard. I said, *Mama, look it's Jesus Cristo!* The man started blowin' out all the candles, then picked 'em up and stuffed as many as he could inside his shirt. He looked up at the cross and shook his fist at it. He shouted, *There's no hiding place for the damned!* Then he ran out of the church, droppin' candles as he went.

"When Mama and I got home, we found out my father was dead. I asked Mamacita, *Is Papa damned? No se,* she said, *I don't know.*"

"I heard that after I died," said Ray, "there was a church created in my name. The Church of Ray Sparks."

"You coulda been a saint, Ray," said Vermillion, "but instead you was a fool."

"I'd like to've gone to the Church of Ray Sparks, shown up with nobody knowing I was coming. Got up in front of the choir and sung, 'He's My Friend Until the End.'"

"There ain't no such church," said Revancha.

"Heard there was."

"The devil got your ear, son," said Vermillion, "way he go about flatterin' folks. He do that. Vain man fallin' for the devil's malarkey, all that is."

"What you had to go smackin' me around like that for, anyway?" asked Revancha. "Use me so bad."

"Standin' in satan's shoes," said Vermillion, "even back then."

"Man spoke the truth," said Ray.

"What man?" asked Revancha.

"One you saw in church, stole all the candles. No place to hide."

"John the Baptis'," said Vermillion.

"I know him, I know that man."

"How could you?" asked Revancha.

"Look at him, sugar, a child of darkness. All the devil's children the same. Ask him can he sing, Revancha. Go on."

"Can you sing, Ray?"

"'Course I can sing."

"Tell him go ahead and try," said Vermillion.

"Sing, Ray, sing 'He's My Friend Until the End.'"

Ray opened his mouth to sing but no sound came out. He tried again with the same result.

"I can't."

"The Lord giveth and the Lord taketh away," said Vermillion. "You ain't got no gift left, Mr. Church of Ray Sparks."

Ray got up and walked away.

"Damn, Miz Chaney," said Revancha, "that's hard."

"He ask for it."

Revancha began to cry.

"Only time I ever have an orgasm," she said, "is when I imagine the man doin' me's the one dressed in rags come in the church the day my father died."

"God bless you, girl," said Vermillion.

"God bless you, too, Miz Chaney."

PART II

IN MEMORIAM TO IDENTITY

THE NEUTRAL ZONE

BY KATE BRAVERMAN

Fisherman's Wharf

Zoë and Clarissa meet at irregular intervals at Fisherman's Wharf. This is the neutral zone. The landscape of perpetual unmolested childhood. The carousel spins in predictable orbits and the original primitive neon alphabet does not deviate. These hieroglyphics are permanent and intelligible in all hemispheres and dialects. No translation is necessary. The carousel does not require calculus, rehab, or absolution. No complications with immigration or the IRS. Just buy a token.

"I'm here," Zoë says from her cell phone.

"At the wharf?" Clarissa must clarify the conditions.

"Little anemic waves at my feet. Corn dogs that give you cancer. Old men catching perch with so much mercury they explode as they reel them in," Zoë reports.

"What color is the water?" Clarissa asks.

"Last-ditch leukemia IV drip blue," Zoë decides.

"Half an hour," Clarissa assures her. "I'm coming."

Zoë has no interest in who Clarissa will abandon or strand at a conference table, restaurant, or health club. No callbacks, a medical emergency, cancel everything, Clarissa will inform her staff. It's a day for experimental time travel.

They meet episodically. Conventional friendship, with its narrative of consensual commitments and behaviors, has proved too intimate and demanding. Between them are houses never seen, husbands dead or divorced, known only by anecdote or photograph. Entire strata of their lives are less than footnotes. Years passed when they did not know one another's addresses or current last names. Decades when they could have been driftwood to one another, vessels lost at sea. A drowned stranger, perhaps, why bother?

"This litany of blame is becoming tedious," Zoë once recognized.

"Human perimeters are collective background razor wire. We're too hip for that shit," Clarissa responded. "It's residual static from a Baptist radio broadcast in Mississippi. It's irrelevant and obsolete."

"We'll bite it off with our teeth," Zoë offered. "Napalm it. Grenade launchers and M-16s. Tec-9s. We'll have our own Cultural Revolution. We'll go post-modern, but fully armed."

"We'll invent rituals appropriate for our circumstances. We'll whisper endearments while strolling the killing fields," Clarissa was enthusiastic. "We'll crawl our Ho Chi Minh trail, hand-in-hand, trusting each other with our lives."

"But we'll abide by the Geneva Convention," Zoë prompted. "Despite our emotional residue."

"Directed psychological evolution. It'll be more brutal than weight training," Clarissa agreed. "But we'll become better human beings."

"We'll redefine and transcend ourselves," Zoë said.

It was an earlier autumn on Fisherman's Wharf. It was bluer than Maui, bay studded with cobalt that looked charged, technologically modified. Zoë had lived two years without electricity in a shack on a nameless river of red orchids in the jungle near Hana. She wasn't in contact with Clarissa then. Clarissa probably didn't know there were seasons in Maui, too. A faint reddening, a moistening, and the mosquitoes went in temporary remission.

"I like it conceptually. But let's go further," Clarissa suggested. "We'll be molecular. Just strands of light from one radiance to another."

"Should we reject linearity entirely?" Zoë asked. "Sporadic moments of illumination in extreme altitudes requiring oxygen masks?"

"Discreet and unpredictable meetings with spectacular voltage. We'll communicate by blowtorch," Clarissa replied. "We'll wear asbestos jackets."

A process of accommodation and evolution was plausible, they agreed. True, they had failed the traditional strategies of giving and receiving. But the standard methods by which one registers recognition and regret do not apply to them. They would have a pact, an armistice, like aggressive radical improvisational surgery. Their psychiatrists were cautiously optimistic. The possibility of malignant complications was an acceptable risk. Then they had shaken hands.

Now Zoë sees Clarissa. She is exiting a black Lincoln town car, wearing her standard business outfit—aerobics pants and jacket, Gucci sunglasses and Giants baseball cap. It's the camouflaged movie star look designed to create the impression that you're attempting to be incognito. Clarissa is carrying not a gym bag, which would be appropriate and predictable, but a Chanel purse with leather quilting and gold braid handles. It's the uniform the narcissistic personality disorder dictates.

They kiss on each cheek. "You forgot my birthday," Clarissa begins. She dismisses the car and driver with a hand gesture.

"I didn't sign on as a soccer mom. I don't decorate for

holidays. I don't bake or send thank-you cards. I don't answer the phone. I throw away personal mail. You know this," Zoë reminds her.

"Don't you go to bed before Thanksgiving and not get up until after Valentine's Day?" Clarissa's voice is light.

"That was my mother," Zoë says. "I simply leave the country at appropriate junctures."

Actually, Zoë is fond of Christmas in Southeast Asia. Ornately decorated pine trees in the air-conditioned hotel lobbies like vestiges from another planet. Bamboo balconies draped in green velvets, antique brocades, and holly wreaths. More fetishes. And Christmas carols rendered in versions so mangled by distance and erroneous translation they're almost tolerable. Rivers smell of rotting vegetables, petrol, wood cooking fires, and hunger. Air is layers of decaying prayers that remind her of a satellite losing orbit, falling down not as metal but as streams of origami. In Bangkok, in December, it is 103 degrees.

"Let's just be here now," Clarissa says. "We know the rules. It's play time." Her mouth glistens with a red lipstick that seems to have small stars encrusted within it. There are implications in the sheen Zoë doesn't want to consider.

The wharf is almost deserted. It's mid-day, mid-week, in an undifferentiated season. It's another windswept early November. They walk hand-in-hand down the pier past occasional immigrant men fishing and stray teenagers who appear eager for corruption. Zoë and Clarissa know where they live. They, too, grew up in tenements designed for transience, already shabby decades ago, festering like sun sores. They were an integral part of the blueprint for the millennial slums in the sun. They were the penciled-in stick figures on the diagrams.

"Don't look," Clarissa cautions. "They're contagious. We'll get a contact psychotic flashback."

The Last Edge Saloon perches on the furthest border of the pier. Their reunions begin here. They choose a booth facing the bay on three sides. They might drink coffee, perhaps with Dexedrine. Or get drunk on something festive, like White Russians or champagne. Since Zoë is technically in AA, she decides to let Clarissa set the tenor. Clarissa orders Bloody Marys. From a caloric standpoint, it's the obvious choice.

"You still look like a hippy," Clarissa observes. She regards her with a smile that is speciously conciliatory, perhaps even condescending. Zoë interprets this as disturbing. Anxiety is inseparable from the air. It's in the oxygen molecules and how their biochemistry fails to correctly process them. It's a perpetual uneasy truce.

"It's my signature classic bohemian style," Zoë replies. "And I want to formalize our alliance."

"Do you want to get married?" Clarissa asks.

"I want a document with terms, precise specifications," Zoë realizes. "And I want a weapons check."

"Contracts are worthless," Clarissa points out. "They're a wish list for Santa." She's a lawyer, after all. She knows.

"We could become cousins," Zoë suggests. This appeals to her.

Survivors of cataclysmic childhoods defined by poverty and isolation compulsively seek validation. They know they lack proper emotional documentation. Cousins evokes a blood connection that would both substantiate and obviate certain complexities, the ebbs and flows, droughts and monsoons of their relationship. Such a device would highlight and justify their erratic and pathologically intense conjunction. In regions of bamboo and sun-rotted petals, wind propels sand like tiny bullets, and there are always too few artifacts. Cousins is an inspiration.

"I could draw up the papers," Clarissa is expansive. "But adoption is superior."

Zoë came to San Francisco when she was seven. Her father, Marvin, had terminal cancer. Her mother was mentally ill. They were bankrupt. She used to think heaven was a foster home. If Marvin would just finally die, perhaps she could even get adopted.

"I've missed you like a first love," Zoë says.

"I *was* your first love," Clarissa reminds her. "And you mine."

They lean across the faux-wood table etched with knife-gouged gang insignias and logos of metal bands and kiss again. They are both manic this autumn day. Zoë and Clarissa share numerous personality disorders. They are both bipolar 2 with borderline features. Substance abuse is a persistent irritant. Recently, they have both been diagnosed with post-traumatic stress syndrome.

Today, sun turns San Francisco Bay the purple of noon irises in country gardens in July. To articulate such facets, to know and chart them, is a spasm of thunder inside, a tiny birth the size of a violet's mouth. If she extracted this entity from her body, she could give it to Clarissa like an infant.

Zoë examines her almost cousin's eyes. Even through dark sunglasses, they are inordinately bright. Zoë senses that she, too, is also glowing. Yes, her eyes are brass corridors reflecting fluorescent light. They are both candles today, unusually in sync, radiant with clarity and energy. Clarissa wears a silk scarf, a vivid purple implying motion. It might contain vertical waves.

"Do you like it?" Clarissa asks. "Hérmes. Take it. I just stole it on Maiden Lane."

"You still shoplift?" Zoë holds the scarf. It feels moist and sanctified, an embrace around her neck.

"It's an attitude like guerrilla warfare," Clarissa explains. They've finished their second round of drinks. "A thrill kill requires mental discipline. Put it on and keep walking. I know, I've had it for years. I bought it on the Champs-Élysées. It was raining. I was at the George V. I remember the details absolutely. No one could dare question me. And no one does. Let's ride the carousel."

They carry their drinks across the stained wooden planks of the pier. The carousel is closed. Clarissa makes a cell phone call and a man appears. She produces three hundred-dollar bills. They wait for the right seats, choosing recently painted twin horses, white and intricately decorated like certain porcelain, and ride for half an hour. Clarissa vomits twice.

Zoë searches her theoretical arsenal. Is it time for a hand grenade? Should she call for a chopper with medics? Then she remembers her mission. "Are you okay?" she manages.

"I understand how children discover bulimia," Clarissa reports, excited. "It's an accidental miracle."

"Maybe you'll get retroactive psychiatric insight points," Zoë says.

Despite the gym-suit camouflage, it's obvious Clarissa has gained weight. But even they have taboos. Eating disorders are a forbidden topic. They meet on neutral ground, but there are still no-fly zones, areas of fragmentation bombs and landmines. Shrapnel is a constant.

Clarissa borrows the purple scarf to wipe her mouth. She has contaminated the silk, but Zoë still wants it back. She thinks, suddenly, of flower bouquets and their inadequacy.

The floral arrangements of her life have been too much and not enough. The petals stained. They were debris.

"If a contract is insufficient, what can we do?" Zoë wonders.

They are standing on the pier where the carousel is no longer operating. Gone are the circles they inscribed in the loitering too-thin aqua air. Her body carved the afternoon as they whirled and spun, engraving trails of midnight-blue ink like marks made by fins. Somewhere these etchings floated into a river winding down to a bay, more invisible origami.

"We could get a tattoo," Clarissa proposes. "Our names together in a heart."

"A tattoo?" Zoë repeats, delighted. "Won't it be painful and dangerous? The possibility of AIDS and infection?"

"But you love needles." Clarissa is annoyed. "You're a professional junky."

"I'm in remission," Zoë replies quickly, unexpectedly defensive.

In truth, during one particularly virulent carousel rotation, she began to think about a drug dealer she knew in North Beach. It's walking distance, over a steep sequence of stone steps and hills, through a sudden unexpected gate. There is a combination lock. Within, a creek is dammed and trapped, the water a stalled green with slime and duck excrement. She knows this Victorian house, the grain in every wooden floorboard and the way sunset displays itself through each glass pane in every room. There is geometry to how sun impales and dissects the Golden Gate Bridge. If you comprehend this mathematics, you can construct spaceships and time machines with common household appliances. You listen to the radio and talk to any god. This is encrypted information she will be buried with.

"You always relapse," Clarissa observes, as if stating an historical date or chemical formula. "And don't you already have AIDS?"

Zoë is shocked. She stares at Clarissa. Even with Gucci sunglasses, there's a distinct softening around the chin, a loss of definition in her cheeks. "No, dear potential cousin. I have hepatitis C. And you need to get your face done."

"What part?" Clarissa is concerned.

They are walking from the pier toward a tattoo parlor on Columbus Avenue. Shops offer stacks of cheap plaster statues, saints and children, dwarves and frogs. Someone will purchase and paint these objects, display them, give them as gifts. And plastic replicas of Alcatraz and T-shirts that say *Prisoner* and *Psycho Ward*.

"What part?" Zoë repeats. "It isn't a fucking contract. It's a composition. Just give the guy a blank check. And don't use a Pacific Heights or Marin surgeon. You'll end up looking like everybody else. I found an Italian in Pittsburgh."

"I noticed you finally got your father off your face," Clarissa slowly admits.

"Well, the police wouldn't do it," Zoë says. "And Mommy was so busy."

Slow swells are below the wharf now. The bay is a liquid representation of fall. It's in continual transition. It's a form of treachery. All fluid bodies are autumnal and promise betrayal. That's what leaves changing mean, the reds and ochre, the yellows like lanterns. It's about packing and disappearing. It's a season for divestiture. That's the fundamental imperative winds hint at. Time of the severing. That's the obvious subtext. And it occurs to Zoë that her elation could dissipate. Emotions have their own seasons, inexplicable currents and random lightning storms.

Zoë follows Clarissa into the tattoo parlor. "Let's rock," Clarissa says. "Lock and load."

The Eagles are playing. It's "Hotel California," of course. A tanned man with a blond ponytail who looks like a yoga instructor opens a book of designs. Dragons. Butterflies. Demons. Flowers. Guitars. Spiders. Zoë vaguely remembers negotiations including the procurement of a fifth of vodka, tomato juice, and a complicated argument about the aesthetic implications of script choices. Eventually they selected a gothic font. Then she may have passed out.

Zoë realizes they are in an arcade on Pier 39. It's three hours and six Bloody Marys later. They have gauze and adhesive tape on their shoulders where their names are carved into their left upper arms in identical navy-blue. They decided to leave the encircling heart in red ink for their next reunion. Banks of garish video games surround them; hip-hop music blasts from speakers in the ceilings and floors. Boys who all look part Asian or Mexican are armed with laser levers and plastic machine guns. They keep the real Glocks in their pockets.

"This is not the global village I envisioned," Zoë says.

"That's politically incorrect enough to get me disbarred," Clarissa whispers. She places two fingers against her red lacquered lips in a gesture of mock fright.

The automatic photographic booth is on the far side of the arcade. Four shots. They have been taking pictures here since they rode buses and walked from Daly City in seventh grade. Zoë remembers when it cost a quarter. Now it takes dollars. This photographic session is a ritual element in each of their meetings. It's their sacrament. When they leave the booth, they cut the strip in half. Zoë saves her photographs in a shoebox where she keeps her passport and birth certificate.

She assumes Clarissa saves hers in her jewelry vault. Or perhaps she just throws them away.

The photographs are a necessary component of their liturgy. Zoë knows they can only see one another by laminated representations. It would be too disturbing and intrusive if they could actually perceive one another without artificial mediation. They communicate by email, fax, and newspaper clippings. The telephone is unbearable. They only use it to arrange an imminent unplanned meeting.

"Marvin's jowls are definitely gone." Clarissa studies the thin strip of four facial shots. "You have cheekbones. Are those implants? Jesus. You're gorgeous. You never looked this good, not at sixteen, even. Cosmetic surgery already."

"We're breathing on forty," Zoë says, bewildered. Certainly Clarissa comprehends the necessity of proactive facial procedures. This is San Francisco and Clarissa is an entertainment business attorney with a penthouse office above a Chinese bank. Is Clarissa in denial? Are her medications interfering with her functioning on so obvious and rudimentary a level?

"I thought you had to wait as long as possible." Clarissa's words are slurred.

"After you psychologically remove the slap across the face, and its more damaging verbal resonances—" Zoë begins.

"And that takes decades and costs what? A quarter of a million?" Clarissa is still staring at the strip of photographs.

"Then the next step is actual surgical removal. It's a natural progression. It's how to treat emotional cancer. Keep them," Zoë says. "Get some reference points."

They sit on a bench on the south side of the pier, sun tamed and restrained. The water is becoming agitated. White caps like mouths opening, baring teeth. The bay reminds Zoe of women in autumn in a medical imaging office. First the locker, the paper bathrobe, the chatty blonde with the clipboard who walks you into the room containing the mammogram machines. Then the stasis before the X-rays are read. Yes, the bay is waiting for its results. Poppies encrusted with resins or blood float like prayer offerings in the dangerous toxic waters.

"We used to walk here. What were we? Eleven, twelve?" Clarissa asks. Her mood is also shifting. They're both still drunk.

Zoë and Clarissa, gauze and bandages on their shoulders, hold hands. Zoë's childhood is sequences of yellows composed of trailer park kitchen cabinets and the invisible poisons leaking from the pores of fathers undergoing chemotherapy. Take a breath of rancid lemon. You've seen the Pacific, reached the end of the trail and don't linger at the edges of death too long. They had a final punctuation for that. It was called the iron lung.

"They hadn't invented a vocabulary for us yet," Clarissa says to the waves. "Dysfunctional families. Latchkey children. Remember when I lost my key? What my father did? Jerry tied me up in the carport in pajamas for a week."

"I brought you a canteen with orange juice. A bottle of vitamins," Zoë recalls. "And a few joints. I cut up a cantaloupe in tiny pieces. You were handcuffed. I fed you like a sick bird."

"How did you get a canteen?" Clarissa asks.

"I took it from the hospital outpatient closet," Zoë says. Her head is throbbing.

She stares at sea swells that are the process by which autumn becomes water. If you understand the bay, it smells of slow-burning cedar. Midnight currents are actually leaves brushing the ocean with russet and amber. Only adepts recognize this. Waves answer to the moon and immutable laws of spin and fall. They don't get dinner on the table at the appointed hour. They don't carpool or pick up the suits on time, have the cuff links and invitations ready.

"Only you know," Clarissa says. She looks like she may vomit again.

Zoë nods. Yes, only I was at ground zero when it happened. This is why we tattooed ourselves. Who else could comprehend adolescence in the margins of a hardscrabble town in the conceptual latitudes? The late '50s and their village was subdivided wood frame houses and stucco bungalows nailed in rows like the fruit trees above gashes of alley, oranges and lemons so bitter they burned your mouth.

"We sat next to each other in homeroom," Zoë says.

It was seventh grade and they were learning about cities. Their names were Sherry and Judy then but they do not ever mention this.

"We rode buses, trying to find the city," Clarissa remembers. "We had library cards."

True, Zoë thinks, but they could not find their geography or circumstances in literature. Nature was oaks and maples, not a riot of magenta bougainvillea, not a blaze of red and yellow canna bursting through bamboo fences sticky with pink oleander. Families had two parents and pastel houses behind lawns with white picket fences where characters experienced angst rather than hunger and rage. Such children did not sift through trashcans in dusk alleys searching for glass soda bottles redeemable for two cents apiece. Gather enough glass and you had bus fare. On a fortunate hunt, you could trap enough coins for lunch.

"Remember digging for bottles for food money?" Zoë asks.

"I remember what you said," Clarissa smiles. "You said Holden Caulfield would have taken a taxi."

Zoë laughs. "Remember our black berets? We were trying to meet Ginsberg and Kerouac. We wore those berets every day. We got lice."

Clarissa shrugs. "We looked for beatniks right here, on this pier. Boys with sketchbooks and guitars. We said we were French. We practiced our accents at recess."

Recess in the region of broken families, of divorcées and single mothers, of stigma and words that could not be spoken out loud. Alcoholism. Cancer. Child abuse. Illegitimacy. Domestic violence. The special yellow smell of Sunday evenings when the mothers who worked as secretaries poured peroxide on their hair. The tiny implications of illumination from the one lamp you were allowed to turn on. Electricity was an extravagance. Their San Francisco was a medieval oasis, ocean at your face, desert at your back. There were warlords at the utility companies with incomprehensible capabilities and powers. Phones were instruments of terror. It cost money every time you touched them. Long distance calls were rationed, like chocolate during a war. The world as it was, before hotlines that could put your father in prison.

"I still have nightmares about the apartment in Daly City," Clarissa reveals. "At every St. Regis and Ritz, from Beijing to Buenos Aires, I wake up shaking. At the Bora Bora Lagoon Resort Hotel. At the Palazzo Sasso in Ravello, for Christ's sake. The plot complications vary but somehow I'm back there."

"Remember the neighbors?" Zoë asks. They lived next door, with a cement hall between them. She is dizzy. Her arm burns.

"The wetbacks and hillbillies? The identical blondes with

drawls?" Clarissa is unusually bright. "It was still the Depression. I had a friend once. Another friend, not like you, Zoë. A hillbilly. Jerry found us listening to the radio. It was Elvis. Jerry started yelling, *You're playing colored music? You're putting colored music in my house?* He threw the radio at my face. Took out my front tooth. That's how I discovered caps."

"That was me," Zoë corrects. "It was Marvin, not Jerry. And he used the 'n' word."

"We had the same father, metamorphically. A barbarian with bad grammar who thought a *yarmulke* was a ticket to prison. A guy who could plaster and drywall. They were house painters. When they were employed. House painters." Clarissa stares at the bay.

"Like Hitler," Zoë points out. Then, "Had your mother run away yet?"

"Rachel? She was on the verge. She was becoming River or Rainbow or something in secret. Preparing for her first commune. After Jerry, a sleeping bag and a candle was a good time."

Zoë remembers Clarissa's mother. A woman sheathed in dark fabrics who sank into shadows, kept her back to the wall, found her own periphery, rarely spoke. Jerry had pushed her out of a moving car. He kicked in her ribs and put her in a cast. Clarissa's mother, a bruised woman in the process of metamorphosis. Yes, molting like the hibiscus and night-blooming jasmine beside the alleys, sheathed in long skirts, shawls, and kimonos. She was younger than they are now.

Then Clarissa had a family of subtraction. Zoë envied her. All the neighbors had incomplete families. The brothers in juvenile detention. The sisters who disappeared. Soon, if Marvin stopped lingering, if he would just die, she could have a similar reduction. Perhaps she could escape the anomalous caste consigned to stucco tenements with torn mesh screen doors and vacant lots behind wires and no white picket fences. And the mothers and aunts who rode buses and worked as file clerks between nervous breakdowns. Even secondhand cars were an aberration. If she got placed in foster care, adoption might follow. She had straight As and then won the poetry and science competition. Maybe she could be given a new name with syllables that formed church steeples on your lips, like the women in books. A stay-at-home mother with a ruffled apron who baked cookies could call her Elizabeth or Margaret or Christine.

"Did you realize we were Jewish?" Zoë wonders.

"I was instructed to never to reveal this. The hillbillies thought we were Christ killers and owned all the banks," Clarissa answers. "And Jerry said they'd deport us. Send us back to Poland."

"I wanted a bat mitzvah," Zoë suddenly remembers. "I don't know how I even knew the word. Marvin said, *You mean a Jew thing? It costs a fortune to get into that club. They inspect you first. You have to shave your head and show them your penis.*"

"Speaking of Marvin's penis, remember the Polanski scandal? When he sodomized a thirteen-year-old?" Clarissa asks.

It happened in California. It was front-page news in an era when newspapers were read and discussed. The details were graphic and comprehensive, indelible like a personal mutilation.

"Jerry said, *I knew that guy in Warsaw. He's 5'2". He's got a three-inch dick.* He mimed the organ dimensions with his fingers." Clarissa repeats the demonstration for her. "Then he said, *Why is this a headline? What kind of damage can you do with a dick that small?*" Clarissa turns back to the bay.

"Is that when it happened? When you moved away? You disappeared. The phone was disconnected. I couldn't find you for a year." Zoë tries to form a chronology.

"Brillstein says it wasn't rape. It was an inevitable appropriation. Jerry thought a ditch with a turnip in it was a party. I was chattel. Rachel left and he just moved me into their bedroom. I came home from school and my clothes were hanging in their closet. My pajamas were folded on their bed. Then he found us an apartment in Oakland. He let me pick out curtains," Clarissa explains. "Hey, I was the first trophy wife on the block. It's my mother I hate. She knew what would happen. I was expendable."

"But she came back for you," Zoë says. "She took you to a commune. You went to college. You got out."

"You don't get out, for Christ's sake." Clarissa is angry. "You chance to survive."

Zoë examines the bay. There is less agitation, swells softer; a haze grazes what was amethyst. The diagnosis has come. The bay had its biopsy. This stretch of ocean is terminal.

"Didn't Marvin break your wrist?" Clarissa suddenly asks. "You had bandages all summer. You had to stay on the pier, reading."

"Mommy did it, actually. She was between mental hospitals that month. Maybe a weekend pass. Her contemptuous glare. It cut right through the chemo and antipsychotics. She ratted me out. She said, *Marvin, look, that kid's talking with her fingers again. Don't you know only Jews and Gypsies talk with their hands?* I remember precisely. She said, *You think you're a neurosurgeon? You think you're a symphony conductor? You're not even human.* Then she seized my hand. I had three fractured fingers and they took her in the ambulance."

They are quiet. The bay, too, is still. Through haze, the sun is lemon-yellow on the heavy waters. There are floating orchards rooted in sand. Wave break and dog bark are a language. Accuracy is a necessary requirement of civilization. Daddy knocked out your tooth. Mommy broke your fingers. There's an elegant mathematics to this, to these coordinates and their relationship to one another. The accumulation of slights. The weight of insults. The random resurrection of coherence. The way you are no longer blind, cold, bereft. Then the indelible vulgarity you finally have the vocabulary to name.

Zoë and Clarissa's fingers entwine. Clarissa wears a platinum set Tiffany diamond of at least four carats. And a gold Rolex with the oyster diamond setting. She withdraws her hand.

"You know how it is," Clarissa dismisses the implication. "When other women evaluate their black velvets and red silk jackets, I consider a cool set of razor blades."

"So you transcend the genre?" Zoë is enraged.

"What genre would that be? Survivors of squalid adolescences? Best aberration in the most abhorred class?" Clarissa stares at her, hard. Her red lipstick with the embedded stars that are like tiny metallic studs or hooks—they help you shred flesh.

Zoë considers their shared childhood in the already faltering city without seasons. Their parents were Jews who had been disenfranchised for generations; pre-urban and unprepared in a remote town perched at the edge of the implausible Pacific. Plumbing and appliances amazed them. The garbage disposal must never be touched. What if it broke? The refrigerator must be strategically opened and immediately closed. What if it burned out? Then their offspring, who became mute with shock, there in the dirty secret city, deep within a colossus of yellow hibiscus and magenta bougainvillea, behind banks of startled red geraniums and brittle canna.

"We are what coalesced at the end of the trail. After the bandits, cactus, and coyotes. We are the indigenous spawn of this saint. His bastards," Zoë realizes.

"We were spillage," Clarissa replies. "Don't romanticize." They stand and everything is suspended. The bay is barely breathing. Perhaps it's just been wheeled back from a fifth round of chemo. Maybe it's hung over. Or in a coma. It needs a respirator. Come on. Code blue. It needs CPR.

"But we have instincts." Zoë is exhausted. Her arm with the gauze-bandaged shoulder extends. She can talk with her limbs now. Marvin and her mother are dead. She gestures with her fingers, a motion that includes the bay, an outcropping that is Marin and Sonoma, and a suggestion of something beyond.

"We understand ambushes and unconventional warfare. We're expert with camouflage," Clarissa agrees, offering encouragement.

"They'll never take us by surprise," Zoë laughs. She feels a complete lack of conviction and a sudden intense longing to get a manicure.

Silence. Palms sway, windswept and brazen. Sudden vertical shadows from fronds appear without warning, random spears. They are beyond known choreography. One must relentlessly improvise. Holden Caulfield would get knifed in the gut.

"I have to go now," Clarissa abruptly announces. "But you look stunning. I'm impressed. Have you considered a wardrobe update? Do schmattes prove you're an artist? Listen, I brought some Prada that don't fit right. They were sized wrong. I'd sue if I had time. They're in my car."

"That's okay," Zoë manages. This is emotional aerobics for the crippled, she thinks. Then, "I appreciate the gesture."

"I don't have a generous impulse in my repertoire." Clarissa seems tired. "This is a search-and-destroy in the triple-tier. But we must keep trying. And we must end our reunion with a celebratory benediction."

This is their ritual of conclusion. They exchange tokens of mutual acceptance. It's how they prove their capacity to transcend themselves. It's the equivalent of boot camp five-mile runs in mud and climbing obstacle course ropes in rainstorms.

"I brought you a postcard you sent me from Fiji sixteen years ago." Zoë produces it from her backpack. She reads it out loud. "*On the beach under green cliffs, I feel God's nude breath. I make my daughter smile. She laughs like an orchestra of bells and sea birds fed on fresh fruits. Her hair is moss against my lips. How pink the infant fingernails are. I wish you such sea pearls.*" Zoë offers the postcard to Clarissa.

"I forgot that completely." Clarissa doesn't sound surprised. "That was Anna. We don't speak anymore. I don't know where she lives. A guy with the name of a reptile, Snake or Scorpion, took her away on a Harley to Arizona."

Zoë takes the postcard back. She is convinced their reunions are conceptually well-intentioned. But leaches and bloodletting were considered purifying and curative. Also barbequing women at the stake. And garlic for vampire protection.

There is a long pause during which she considers radium poisoning, Madame Curie, and the extent of her fatigue. Then Zoë says, "You still doing the venture capital thing? Private jets? Yachts to beaches too chic to be on a map? Everybody loses but you?"

"When the Israeli money dried up, I thought I was through. Then the Persians. No sensibility and billions, all liquid. An entire race with an innate passion for schlock. Payday." Clarissa is more alert. "Then détente. Russian mafia money poured in. Cossacks with unlimited cash. Who would have thought?" Clarissa places the strip of photographs in her Chanel purse. And as an afterthought, asks, "What about you?"

"I'm getting married," Zoë says. "I'm moving to Pennsylvania."

"Jesus. The grand finale. OD in a barn with a woodstove? Twenty below without the wind chill? Your halfway-house skirts in a broom closet? What now? Another alcoholic painter fighting his way back to the Whitney? Or a seething genius with a great novel and a small narcotics problem?" Clarissa extracts her cell phone.

"Fuck you." Zoë is incensed.

"I apologize. That was completely inappropriate," Clarissa says immediately. "Forgive me, please. It's separation anxiety. We have extreme difficulty individuating. Partings are turbulent. The overlay and resonances. It's unspeakable. But Brillstein says we're improving."

"You're still with Brillstein? Jerry's psychiatrist? The Freudian with the high colonics and weekend mud baths?" Zoë stares at her, so startled she's almost sober.

"He's eclectic, I know. But it's like a family plan. I'm grandfathered in at the original price," Clarissa says.

The stylish phone opens, the keyboard glows like the panels on an airplane. It's the millennium and we have cockpits on our wrists and in our pockets. Clarissa's phone is voice-activated. She says, "Driver." Then, "Pier 39. Now."

"Does your arm hurt?" Zoë wonders. Her shoulder feels like it's on fire.

"No pain, no gain. My dear cousin," Clarissa smiles, "keep your finger on the trigger. We must soldier on. The cause is just."

Zoë realizes Clarissa has already moved on. The conference is over. The documents will be studied. Further discussions to be scheduled. My people will calendar with yours. We'll synchronize by palm pilot.

Suddenly Zoë feels she is on a borderless layover. It's last Christmas in India again. She began in a broken taxi five hours from Goa. Then the six-hour delay in the airport and the run across the tarmac for the last and totally unscheduled miraculous flight to Bombay. A day room for seven hours. The flight to Frankfurt and another day room and delay. Finally the fourteen-hour flight to New York. Seventy hours of continual travel and she was just finding her rhythm. She could continue for weeks or months, in a perpetual montage of stalled entrances and exits, corridors and steps, tunnels and lobbies of vertigo in free fall where no time zones apply.

Clarissa and Zoë no longer hold hands. A distance of texture and intention forms between them. The geometry is calculated. Not even their shadows collide.

"Another bittersweet reunion barely survived," Clarissa says. "My beloved cousin."

"And you, my first and greatest love," Zoë says. "Another high-risk foray we deserve purple hearts for."

"We'll get red hearts around our names next time. Our next tattoo," Clarissa smiles.

They kiss on both cheeks. The glitter has departed from their eyes. They have slid into an interminable foreign film neither of them has interest or affection for. She knows the name of Clarissa's lipstick now. It's called Khmer Rouge.

There is a certain pause just before sunset, when the bay is veiled in azure.

It's the moment of redemption or drowning. Inland, cyclone-fenced freeways carve cement scars beside bungalows with miniature balconies where parched geraniums decay in air soiled from the fumes of manufacturing and human wounds. The bay is a muted defeated blue, subjugated and contained. At night, they pump the antidepressants in. Or maybe there's enough Prozac and beer already in the sewage. Pollution turns the setting sun into strata of brandy and lurid claret, smears of curry and iodine. It looks like a massacre.

"My car can take you where you're going," Clarissa offers.

Clarissa's driver has short hair, a thick neck, sunglasses with an ear attachment she imagines CIA field operatives employ. Clarissa indicates the car door. It is open like a dark mouth with the teeth knocked out. And she's waving the purple scarf like a banner. Zoë refuses to admit that she doesn't know where she's going. She turns away and starts walking. If those are words issuing from Clarissa's mouth, which needs immediate surgical attention, Zoë can't hear them. There are shadows along the boardwalk now, in the alleys and sides of residential streets with ridiculous, insipid seaside names. Bay Street. Marine Drive. North Point View. Who do they think they're kidding?

Keep walking and shadows find you. They are the distilled essence of all harbors and bays. Such shadows taste like a wounded sherry you can drink or pour on your cuts. Use them for bath oil and become immune to infection. Shadows are graceful and do not require explanations. They know you are more dangerous than they imagine. They cannot fill in your blanks. Simply surrender and they do everything.

There are no neutral zones. They're an illusion, a delusionary construct, like movie and real-estate contracts. Satellites map each zip code and tap every telephone. Cities are enclaves between combat arenas. We are born with weapons of mass destruction. They're in our genes, passed down the generations, like poisonous heirlooms. It's ground zero now and forever. Zoë senses the car moving behind and away from her, and she is grateful. She never wants to see Clarissa again.

LE ROUGE ET LE NOIR

BY ALVIN LU

Chinatown

For K & T

Face à face avec la profondeur, l'homme, front penché, se recueille.
Que voit-il au fond du trou caverneux? La nuit sous la terre,
l'Empire d'ombre.

—Victor Segalen

The young people in Chinatown are afraid and confused. We don't know what to do with our lives," Michael Munroe read in the February 1970 issue of *Getting Together*, a mimeographed newsletter published by I Wor Kuen, a Chinatown-based anti-imperialist group somewhat ludicrously named after the late-nineteenth-century Chinese secret society whose members believed mystic rituals and spirit possession would make them invulnerable.

Three years out of Princeton, Michael had thrown in with the revolution. He had turned his back on a life of privilege, by any standard, and left his home in Illinois for the West Coast.

He worked as a postman in the East Bay, inside a stretch of black neighborhoods, and organized there. Recently he had been coming across the bridge to discuss tactics with another postal organizer, Francis Chao. Organization was effective in the post office. The P.O. had a high percentage of black workers, who in those days were highly politicized.

Meeting Francis in Chinatown, coming from the East Bay, was an abrupt transition. Walking routes in West Oakland, Michael felt he had miraculously made the great leap from one world to another; his role as deliverer of welfare checks afforded him access to ordinary black lives few white men experienced. But Chinatown was different. There were a few of the cadre there, both American- and foreign-born, who could move, not always with ease, through that underground world, an entirely other country only two blocks wide extending from Bush to Broadway, and they offered Michael glimpses of how it worked. Francis was one of them.

The struggle for Chinatown's soul between Kuomintang and CPC (Communist Party of China) sympathizers was then at its peak. IWK and Wei Min She (literally, the "Serve the People" Association) opened storefronts in the basement of the International Hotel, located in Manilatown on the corner of Jackson and Kearny Streets, and plotted to overthrow the power structure. Radical activists, propelled by Third World strikes at San Francisco State and Berkeley, descended on the bewildered community, some of them calling themselves Red Guards, talking about Yellow Soul. Politics in turn exacerbated already existing petty rivalries between American-born and foreign-born gangs. A pool hall–soda fountain run by a group of reformed American-born at 615 Jackson was adorned with posters of Huey P. Newton and Mao Tse-tung, while a large gang known as the Jo-Boys amounted to strongarms for the tongs, who continued to assert their fading influence.

What all these groups, including the ruling Six

Companies oligarchy, fought to represent could be narrowed down to one square block, Portsmouth Square, in the heart of the community, which had been recently defaced by stenciled graffiti bearing the image of Chiang Ching. It was the site of innocuous fairs, well-meaning rallies, and, increasingly, conflicts. One could imagine, in the years of the Barbary Coast, when it was the makeshift center of San Francisco's gambling traffic, a gallows being erected there. But most of the time now, it was just the immortal old men, playing Chinese chess or a variation on bridge. Some nights, the fog would stroll down the hills of Washington and Clay Streets, you could hear the foghorns, and the Stockton bus would roll up. No one knew the future.

Michael and Francis regularly met at the Hunan Cafe, across the street from the I-Hotel, but the atmosphere there had grown too thick with intrigue, and Francis suggested a little-known restaurant elsewhere, frequented entirely by locals who spoke only in Toisan dialect. The two of them were to meet an acquaintance of Francis's there, who was researching a documentary film on the nascent Asian-American "movement" and wanted to interview Francis incognito.

Francis wore a blue Mao tunic, jeans, and black kung-fu shoes. He was clean-shaven, and a helmet of straight hair covered his ears. Though smallish, he projected confidence and power—rumor had it that he was a black belt, and even Michael, who was a big man and a star college lacrosse player before he blew out his knee, felt tough walking beside him. The two of them, as members of the rather rigidly Maoist Revolutionary Union, worked closely with WMS, their Chinatown affiliate, and tended to regard IWK, who after all were from New York and were behind the curve that way, as suspiciously reformist. Nevertheless, at this optimistic time, there was still hope a united front could be built in Chinatown.

"I hear you're going to be sent somewhere," Francis said.

"Where?"

Francis leaned his head to one side, then made a kind of quarter-turn with it, his abbreviation for shaking his head. He took a gulp of very attenuated jasmine tea from a porcelain cup with the faded image of a red, green, and yellow dragon printed on it.

"Why?"

"To retrieve something."

That could mean anything. To San Leandro? For burritos? But Michael had an idea of what Francis was talking about. Both of them had joined RU around the same time, coming from very different directions, and they'd risen quickly through the ranks. In the spirit of competition, Francis liked to keep Michael off balance with hints that made it sound as if he were closer to directives being made in the inner circle, but Michael knew it was just smoke. Michael had personal ties to the upper echelons of the leadership that Francis didn't have. On the other hand, one never knew what one faction might be planning without another's knowledge. And there were plenty of factions.

"So tell me about these Red Guard guys," Michael said.

"They have a lot less to do with the Red Guard in China than with talking black and acting like the Panthers, but without half the political commitment. Most are ex-Leway and are in it strictly for the image."

Francis had a way of sizing up, dissecting, and dismissing someone in a sentence or two that matched RU's reputation for sectarianism. Michael, who was prone to see both sides of an issue, thought there was truth to the accusation that they didn't get along with anybody, because they didn't cut anybody any slack. He also knew it was worse cutting everybody slack all the time, over anything. One needed parameters. But even in their own group, Francis was thought to have a very refined palate.

"Look at their position on militancy." He pointed to a line printed in the newsletter. "*Our Constitution says we have the right to bear arms.* Our? This is about bringing the whole system down. As far as their politics go, it's strictly 'black cat, white cat.'"

He was making reference to rifts that had grown within the ranks of the CPC itself, demonstrating a fairly high-level awareness of issues that Michael only understood in a blurry way. Groups like IWK and elements within RU's own national ranks reflected the rightist thought of the Liu Hsiao-chi/Teng Hsiao-ping revisionist party clique that the radicals, including the student Red Guard and Mao himself, were resisting. Somehow that internecine struggle had radiated out from the capital of worldwide revolution to this remote outpost.

Michael had only heard of the Red Guard less than two years ago, before he joined RU. He didn't know much about China then, much less the Cultural Revolution. But there had been a great deal of hoopla around an American, a white man, who had returned to the Bay Area from China and had participated in the Great Proletarian Cultural Revolution as a Red Guard himself. By chance, Michael had gone to his presentation and was mesmerized, particularly by the photos that were passed around, clipped from *Life* magazine. One showed a group of Red Guards in surgical masks hammering apart a Peking opera house. Michael didn't understand exactly why they were destroying the building, but he thought it was probably because opera was something for rich people.

In later, grimmer years Francis would go to jail for infiltrating a U.N. Security Council meeting and throwing plastic bags filled with pig's blood at the U.S. and Soviet councilmembers.

Francis's acquaintance, the filmmaker Cletus Dong, arrived at the same time as the twice-cooked pork and honey walnut prawns. As he approached their table, conspicuous in cowboy boots and big silver belt buckle, Francis muttered under his breath, "Cultural nationalist," which to Michael was a codeword for "reverse racist."

Cletus introduced himself as "the Chinese-American Jean-Luc Godard," which struck Michael as an odd thing to aspire to be, considering Cletus was the only Chinese-American filmmaker he'd ever heard of. Couldn't you pretty much call yourself the Chinese-American anything? But with a name like Cletus Dong he wasn't going to be the Jean-Luc Godard of anybody.

Michael's attention was immediately taken away from Cletus anyway, because he'd brought a girl. At first Michael had taken her to be his girlfriend, but it later came out she was his sister, in the literal sense. Unlike the girls Asian "movement" guys tended to hang out with, the ones who wore granny glasses over humorless expressions, she had all the qualities of a classical Chinese beauty: green eyebrows, reedy silhouette, straight ass-length hair. There might be something too brittle about her, as in one of those lamenting maidens in a poem by Li Po, but on closer look one saw this was not the case, especially in the eyes, which were steely and unsentimental. Thick, bold strokes made up her face. She had dark eyes and a full mouth. Her name was Candy. She chewed gum.

Michael immediately fell in love with her.

She stuck her gum to a napkin and smoked a cigarette with heartwrenching elegance, while Cletus and Francis went over the details of the party platform. If it wasn't for the entertainment Candy provided, Michael would have quickly grown bored. He respected Francis, because he knew he was dedicated, but even then, he always thought the worst thing about being a Communist were the endless meetings, speeches, and discussions over total abstractions. Despite his own class background, which he was still trying to live down, he tended to connect more with ordinary working-class people, the good citizens who lived on his delivery route.

"Your idea of revolution, like most people's, is romantic," Francis concluded. "In fact, our work is like 'washing one's face,' as Chairman Mao put it; that is, it takes place on a daily basis. Chinatown is capital-scarce, deteriorated, urban terrain. We have to be frugal and diligent and, as Mao says again, 'do more with less money.'"

"What's so different about that from your run-of-the-mill penny-pinching Chinaman?"

"Well, there are comrades, even when talking about revolution, who only see it in terms of economics and benefits. Of course, we should try to do more with less—as guerrillas we have no choice about that—but not at the expense of political awareness. Getting results is one thing, but isn't it as important to understand how all the pieces fit together? The correct path is to see economic pragmatism and political consciousness as a dialectic. My point was, we can't achieve our goals with sweeping gestures. That's what the capitalists did when they wiped out Japantown and the Fillmore."

"Speaking of less money," Candy suddenly broke in, "I have to get to work."

Francis acknowledged her existence for the first time by nodding his head.

"I was giving her a ride to the Richmond," Cletus mumbled apologetically.

"Who do you think's supporting this kid?" she went on.

"And what do you do?" Francis asked.

"I'm a bartender."

"What kind?"

"What do you mean, *what kind*? What kind of question is that?"

"I meant, are you happy with your work? Is it a good job?"

"What do you mean? It's the kind of job that makes money. What do you do?"

"We're postal workers."

"You mean mailmen?"

"Okay, so you make a lot of money. And what are you going to do with all of that money when, if, you get enough of it?"

"Get outta this place! A girlfriend of mine just moved to Vancouver." She pronounced it *Van-koo-fah*. "She says it's real nice. Plenty of jobs. Big houses. No Chinese. Once I save up some money, I'm moving there." She gestured theatrically to that promised land, like one of those actors in the opera house wrecked by Red Guards. "This time next year, I'll be there, I promise. I hate this place. It stinks."

Michael was impressed. He was always moved by hope. He introduced himself and held his hand out. She didn't take it. He took a deep breath. He didn't normally give in to impulses, he was one of those people who tended to mull things over and act only when it was too late, but it was as if a spirit had taken over him. He wrote something down on the back of a chopstick wrapper and handed it to her.

"Here's my number. Call me when you get to Canada."

"What for?"

"I just want to know if you get there, like you said."

"Who are you?"

He looked around. "The only white person in this restaurant, it looks like."

She laughed at that. She wrote something on the wrapper and handed it back to him. "This is the number of the restaurant my girlfriend works at. Call a year from now and ask her if I got there. Okay? Bye bye."

With that, she dragged Cletus off into the cool San Francisco night. Only after they were out the door did Michael realize everyone in the restaurant was staring at him. Francis just went about opening his fortune cookie. Michael couldn't help grinning. He was aglow. Here, in a hole-in-the-wall restaurant he in all likelihood would never be able to find his way back to again, in Chinatown, where it seemed, for someone like himself, it was all but impossible to make a human connection, he'd had one. Not just any connection, either, but with her. The people in the restaurant eventually went back to their business. Michael couldn't understand a word above the din they were making. They could have been talking about anything within the confines of those four walls, and without.

The following summer, Michael traveled back to the Midwest to see some old friends and to have his draft physical. He wore a T-shirt with Mao Tse-tung's face silk-screened on the front and the phrase, "*All political power grows from the barrel of a gun*," on the back. He flunked the physical.

Before he flew back to the Bay Area, he took a detour to see a fellow RU member of high standing.

Ariel Rabenstein was a former CPUSA member, who now lent RU a certain legitimacy. Like Michael and Francis, he was employed by the post office. Unlike most of the young cadre, he had actual experience with mass organizing mayhem on a grand scale. The rest of RU were in comparison children, working in a vacuum, sealed off from history by McCarthy and the fact that the Soviet Union had stopped being revolutionary. Ariel was hiding in Chicago after having been out of the country for a number of years. He had run afoul of the police in San Francisco when a reporter for the *Examiner*, acting as an FBI informant, had exposed him, and he had to leave the country. He took a freighter to China and somehow made it into circles that reached as high as Chou En-lai. There had been a handful of Americans in China then, a collection of outright defectors, Korean War deserters, double agents, and old CPUSA and Soviet sympathizers who'd run into bad police situations, all of whom knew each other and did similar things like teach English. The Chinese premier's group became Ariel's main contact, and they arranged for Ariel to bring $600,000 back to the States, where he was "to start organizing a new revolutionary group." This was in 1968. It wasn't clear what the significance of the six-hundred-thousand figure was, but when Michael first heard the story, he assumed it must have been a round or lucky number in Chinese.

Ariel's apartment was located in a weathered brick tenement on the South Side. It was around eight million degrees that day and seemed hotter inside the tortuous hallways. Michael had been told Ariel had something for him, nothing more. It could have been materials or it could have been information. After winding his way through the building's infernal interior, he was prepared for just about anything, except what greeted him there.

A beautiful, young black woman with a natural, wearing a wine-colored Chinese silk robe, answered the door. She escorted him in without a word. The apartment looked like the interior of a souvenir store on Grant Avenue, full of things Ariel had brought back with him—lanterns, screens, embroidery, bronzes, scrolls. Ariel, in a black robe, waited for Michael in the inner room, seated with one knee upright on a kang, smoking from a copper water pipe, writing in a notebook. Michael didn't know how old Ariel was, but he looked a hundred, and not a good hundred. He'd lived a hard, uncompromised life, and he smoked from that water pipe nonstop.

Ariel and the woman exchanged some words in what must have been Mandarin. She left and then returned with a freshly brewed pot of tea and performed what seemed like a brief ritual involving pouring the tea from the pot into variously sized cups and then repouring them into other cups. When she was done, she left the room.

"We met in China," his host explained, going into no further detail. "Drink up. This pot and these cups are made of yi-hsing clay. It's said to enhance the flavor of the tea. Let me know if you taste anything. My taste buds are shot." He stuck his tongue out.

Michael declined because he was dying in the heat, but his host insisted, saying the Chinese believed drinking hot tea actually cooled the body, which sounded like utter madness.

"You're to be sent somewhere," Ariel declared. "You'll be traveling with me to pick up some money. I can't say when or where, for now. Everything will be conducted on a 'need to know' basis. We don't want you to lose your job at the post office, where you're doing good work. So as we get closer to the date, we'll tell you how long you'll be gone."

"It won't be that long then?"

"About a week."

"Will it be just you and me?"

"There will be checkpoints and handoffs. But yes, most of the time it will be just you and me. That's all I can tell you for now."

Michael nodded. Ariel stopped talking. It was very odd, regardless of the bizarre trappings of the apartment, to see this rough-hewn man taking such delicate sips from a teacup the size of a thimble. Ariel didn't have any materials for him to bring back. Probably the purpose of this visit was just to check Michael out. Michael took a sip of the offered tea, now lukewarm, before he left. It was green and stronger than it looked.

On his way back, he felt an uneasy sense of elation. When Ariel mentioned money, he immediately thought of the $600,000 the old man had delivered from China. Michael could only assume they were going there for more. That he was being sent to the command center of world revolution at this juncture in his young career, for such a sensitive task, was quite unbelievable. Very little in his life, besides a few trips to Chinatown to discuss tactics with Francis, had prepared him. "China" had always been to him more a revolutionary ideal than an actual place, existing only in cloudy rumors he and the other local cadre, like courtiers stationed in a distant colony, attempted to decode, or else otherwise in those abstract, stiffly translated tracts they were sent, their lifeline to interpretation. Very few of them had access to cleaner information—Francis, who could understand some

Chinese, and Ariel, with his contacts there, among them—
and even their throughlines were questionable, though
enough to lend them a certain priestlike authority. But the
more Michael thought about it, the more he was convinced
his life, so far, had been a preparation for such a trip. What,
for instance, had led him that night to the lecture by the former Red Guard, which sent him off on his own trajectory into
the revolution? As an advocate of science, Michael didn't
believe in fate, but he trusted the unconscious. His life so far
had been defined by great, blind leaps. He had gone from the
Midwest to the Ivy League to San Francisco. He had never
left the country before. Now he was going to China.

When he thought of why he had been selected to go,
though, the picture grew darker. It was clear he was going, on
the one hand, to take care of the money and keep it from
capitalists and opportunists, in case Ariel, who was old as
shit, had a heart attack or otherwise dropped dead. On the
other, and this was the part of his job he was uncomfortable
with, he was probably there to keep an eye on his companion.
Or rather, they were to keep an eye on each other, in case
either person, and the people who backed them, tried to
muscle out the other. This was not something he liked to
think about. Ariel had built factions within the organization,
probably based in the Midwest. Things were lining up,
Michael understood though only very vaguely, along the
same faults that were fracturing the CPC. Everyone knew
Ariel was a Chou En-lai guy, but which way did Chou go?
With Liu Hsiao-chi? Lin Piao and the PLA? Or the radicals?
Michael had been selected, he believed, because he was
trusted on all sides. That had always been his best trait: he
got along with everybody. And he could also take care of
himself, if he had to. Certainly he could against an old man.

But he did not want to think he couldn't trust Ariel, or the organization. He was sure of his own commitment. He believed the group was sure too and would take the necessary precautions for his safety. One good sign was his receiving only the information he needed to know, which, he understood, was for his own protection.

On returning to the Bay Area, he ran into Francis. Michael was on his way to the People's Bookstore on Brenham Street, off Portsmouth Square. Francis was coming out with some books tucked under his arm. On that gray day, he looked uncharacteristically like an ineffably old Chinese scholar, strolling through Tien An Men on his way to the Forbidden City.

The two of them talked among the pigeons. The square was unusually empty. Droplets of mist condensed in the air. Playing their game of one-upmanship, Michael mentioned the job he was being assigned and that he was traveling with Ariel. His disclosure was strategic as well. He wanted to gauge how much Francis knew.

"Well, you know the score," Francis replied, unperturbed. "Don't let Ariel out of your sight once the two of you pick up the money."

Michael nodded. He couldn't tell if Francis was playing the same game, talking as if he knew more than he did. All of them did that to some degree, Michael supposed. But maybe Francis did know things about Ariel that Michael didn't.

Without having mentioned that China was the place he was being sent, he asked Francis where he might buy a decent Chinese phrasebook and maps. "I came here for that, but I was thinking there are other places in Chinatown I could look."

"There are places you could buy maps," Francis replied,

without missing a beat, "but because most of them are printed in Hong Kong or Taiwan, they're inaccurate." They depicted nonexistent rail lines and provincial boundaries, he explained, and some still drew the national borders as if it were the height of the Ching Dynasty. "The capital is Nanking, while Peking doesn't exist at all. It's called 'Peiping,' *the Pacified North.* You're better off sticking to our own bookstore."

"All right then."

Michael went ahead and bought all the maps he could find anyway. When he went home and compared them all, including the one in the World Atlas in his local library, he wasn't surprised to find the discrepancies Francis had mentioned. He was no stranger to political fictions. In practice, he lived to fight against them, but he had to admit, he was dismayed to encounter such a black-and-white instance of contested reality. On the one hand, there was the version promulgated by the United States, which pretended a government representing one billion people practically did not exist. On the other, there were remote areas in the southwest of China the size of California that he knew could not be considered under Communist control, no matter how cleanly delineated. The maps, far from providing a composite picture of something resembling the truth, only made the place he assumed he was traveling to seem all the more unreal.

When they arrived in Seattle, having driven up, just the two of them, they stored Michael's car at the local organization headquarters. He and Ariel moved into the backseat of another car. Two local cadre sat up front to drive them past the border.

In Vancouver, they made a brief stop. Michael stayed in

the car. Ariel entered an apartment building. A few minutes later, he reemerged with two passports with their photographs and new identities. Michael felt a chill. He hadn't handed a photograph of himself to anybody, and this particular photo he'd had taken in a photo booth at Ocean Beach, with the only prints he knew somewhere in his desk at home. Ariel told him, none too reassuringly, everything was being taken care of "on the other end." He also had another item with him: a suitcase full of something, clothes presumably.

"You're going to check this piece of luggage in under your own name," one of the Seattle operatives told Michael. "You'll get a ticket for it, but you won't need to replace the contents with anything. In fact, once you check it in, you won't see it again until you get back to Canada."

On the long flight across the Pacific Ocean, the two of them didn't speak much, sleeping most of the way, but for the few hours both of them were awake, Ariel turned surprisingly chatty. He broke into his life's story, how he once ran off to join a puppet troupe, decided to become a Communist before he turned forty, even going a bit into China. Michael appreciated how friendly he'd become, after the long, tense drive from San Francisco, but grew unsettled the more it went on. Somehow, every time Michael tried to steer the topic of conversation toward actual information, such as going into greater detail over the handoff protocol, Ariel batted it away. It was very subtle, Michael couldn't say at what precise moment he'd been deflected, but it happened repeatedly. Despite the fact that Ariel's stories sounded too nutty to be made up, Michael eventually realized that what seemed like casual candor was boldly executed diversion. The more Ariel talked, the less Michael knew.

Ariel was in a grand mood, though, and, once he got

going, went into his theory on why Vietnam was just a prelude to a global war between the U.S. and China.

"Either the two superpowers are going to enter into an
alliance against China or, more likely, the U.S. is going to simply beat the Soviets into reneging on their commitments to
international socialist solidarity, to the point, if you ask me,
where we'll see the collapse of the U.S.S.R. as a political
entity. At that point, we enter a new phase of the Cold War,
where the balance of power isn't between the U.S. and
Soviets, but between the U.S. and China. This will all happen within the next twenty years, by the way. Moreover,
everyone knows this already, which is why the real target of
U.S. strategy right now the world over isn't the U.S.S.R., but
China. By the time the crucial battleground will have shifted
to the Pacific Rim, the Eastern Bloc will be just a memory."

Michael couldn't help feeling excited. Or maybe it was
just the straight drive, without stopping, and to finally have
got up in the air. Either way, he thought there was a grain of
respectability to the scenario Ariel had just painted. The collapse of the U.S.S.R. in twenty years? China as the world's
second superpower? A shift in the global balance of power to
the Pacific nations? It seemed unbelievable, and yet here they
were, suspended in the stratosphere, somewhere between
San Francisco and Tokyo, on a mission to change the world.

Japan was no different than, say, La Guardia, but once they
boarded a Russian passenger jet bound for Shanghai,
Michael felt he had entered another world. The cabin
looked like the interior of a kids' clubhouse. There was no
crew to speak of. Or passengers, for that matter. Just a few
black-haired heads scattered about the narrow cabin, none
of them in a seat next to another. He and Ariel sat in the

first row, with their interpreter/guide/watchdog, a thin woman in a blue pantsuit with a bob haircut.

A minor hubbub went up when their guide remarked in fluid Queen's English that they had entered Chinese airspace. Out the window, Michael could see the coastline of the continent, marked by a few small fires here and there. It was happening. It was one thing to take cues from translated texts that wore the dry air of the exotic and esoteric, another to be confronted with a glimpse of a world of real lives and a landmass that, reaching across impassable stretches of time and space, had bore the near totality of human civilization. The idea of that history, rolling back from the shoreline he was now tracing through the dark, was incomprehensible. All that made such a thought tolerable was the counterforce of the equally impossible fact that the most radical social revolution the world had ever known was taking place here too. Michael had spent a lifetime in exile from everything. For the first time, he felt as if he had come home.

They touched down at Hung Chiao International Airport in the dead of night. Michael picked up the luggage he'd packed for himself, but not the suitcase he was given in Vancouver. The streets of Shanghai, one of the world's most populous cities, former Whore of the Orient, Paris of the East, as seen from the backseat of a Chinese government sedan, were pitch dark.

They were put up in a hotel room. The next day Ariel went out for a few hours, but Michael was forced to stay the whole time in the sparse, narrow room. Most of those hours were spent catching up with his jet lag. A rotation of chainsmoking young men in the same kind of blue jackets Francis wore stood watch outside the door. They didn't speak English. Every time Michael opened it and asked if he could go out, the response was the same sheepish smile and bout of mute head shaking and hand waving.

Around 3 in the afternoon, he was staring out the window when he saw, miraculously, three white people walk by. He tried to get their attention by banging on the window and yelling, but they didn't hear him, or acted as if they didn't. He tried to see where they were headed, but they quickly disappeared from view.

That evening they were put on the train and spent the night in an isolated car. They arrived in Peking by morning. They were put in another hotel room.

They spent most of day two cooped up in the hotel room together, with Ariel being called out for a few hours in mid-morning.

When Ariel came back, he was not any more forthcoming about whatever he was doing, or what was going on, than he was about anything else. But like almost everyone else they had met on this trip so far, he had a case of nerves.

It was apparent they were being handled very carefully. So far, every time they had been met by someone, picked up, or taken around, the atmosphere was tense. No one looked directly at anyone or anything. The passing off of the Americans from one handler to another was an especially serious affair. Their sponsors tended to be young men, and occasionally women, dressed in identical blue suits, although there were a few seniors here and there. So far everyone they encountered either spoke fluent English or none at all. They all smoked constantly. People were only grudgingly friendly. They ground their teeth when they smiled and were otherwise businesslike. Too businesslike for Michael's taste. There was something flinty in their behavior; with any misstep in the complex operation going on, Michael felt he (and Ariel?)

would be sacrificed. Michael recognized some of the m.o.: They tended to travel in pairs in which the partners clearly did not like each other. As with Ariel and himself, they were there to keep an eye on each other as much as on their charges.

Admittedly he hadn't seen much of China so far besides the interior of cars, trains, and hotel rooms, but the whole country seemed on edge. In September, the Minister of Defense, Lin Piao, had died in a plane crash in Mongolia, while trying to flee the country. Michael didn't know Lin had failed to execute the "571 Plot," an attempt on the life of Mao Tse-tung while aboard his special train. Nor could Michael have known—it would have peeved him if he had—that his journey to China was preceded by that of Henry Kissinger, who had made a secret trip in July to prepare the way for Nixon's planned visit the following year.

While Michael and Ariel told each other that their sponsors were being overcautious—after all, they weren't here to cause any trouble—Michael understood the danger was real. The secrecy was for their own protection. What if one of them got out and fell into the hands of one faction or the other, and something happened? Somebody could make a big deal over it. And what if something were made to happen?

What if they had already fallen into the hands of the Chou group, Ariel's group?

Thoughts like this occupied him while he waited for Ariel to return from a second, afternoon summoning. It wasn't pleasant, wondering whether Ariel was plotting against him, while he was kept in a hotel room, a sitting duck.

He went over again in his mind what would happen when they returned to Vancouver. It was his understanding that the money was to come to both of them at the same time. Everything had been prepared, he had been told between Seattle and Vancouver, to ensure that no one had a particular advantage in seizing it. A clear chain of pickups and handoffs would occur after they received it. Who would be in a certain place at a certain time. Who would hand the money to whom. If the right people weren't in the right place at the right time, they were not to hand off the money. Instead, there was a backup handoff plan they were to go to.

Michael understood his role once the money landed in their hands. No one was to pry Ariel away from him for any length of time, and he was to keep anyone from stealing it. There were people within the organization who might try to steal it from Michael, and both Ariel and he knew that. To avoid anyone trying to engineer a setup, each team only knew who they were getting from and giving to. No one knew the entire chain, where the money would eventually wind up. Michael supposed that the people on Ariel's side might try to kill the people on his side when the money was given over. A balance in the number of men on each team was meant to ensure that wouldn't happen. Michael supposed one or more people might switch teams, or that Ariel's people might have killed his people by the time he arrived at the handoff point. If that happened, if it was only him against the others and he was outnumbered, then, Michael decided, he wasn't going to fight. Then they would kill him, or maybe something would happen right there on the spot. Michael had traveled for four days with Ariel. Despite some testy moments, they had gotten along. He didn't like to think Ariel might kill him or that he might have to kill Ariel. They didn't teach you this stuff at Princeton. This was what it was like getting into the movement. Trouble was real trouble, and it came real quick.

It was all very strange. He was in China.

To take his mind off its current depressing trajectory, he tried focusing on the environment around him. The room they were given couldn't be considered a cell, but it wasn't exactly luxurious either. It was like much of what he'd seen of the entire country itself. There did not seem to be one item that was anything other than absolutely essential. Two beds, with two layers of sheets, one slightly heavier than the other. Each of them had been issued a thin hand towel, about one foot wide by two feet long, that was to be used for the duration of their stay. There was a light. No phone. No pen or paper. No ashtray, but cigarette burns in the carpet. Toilet paper, of sorts, was brought in once a day. Somehow their hosts were able to calculate exactly what amount was just enough.

There was no mirror. In those days, Michael kept up a thin Fu Manchu. Both his hair and mustache he wore much longer in his hippie days, but these days he tried to keep up a neat appearance. It was a proletarian thing; his attire consisted of T-shirts, a single sweatshirt, jeans, boots. He'd meant to trim his mustache before he left, but he'd been in a rush to get out. Now he didn't want his hosts to get the wrong idea about him, so with the free time fate had granted him, he learned how to shave without a mirror.

That night, under curfew, the old man started to lose it.

"I want to go out, see the sights, get laid. This sitting around here all night, man, is driving me nuts."

"Hey, at least you're out during the day. Think about me. I burned through the two books I brought with me by the time we left Vancouver."

That seemed to elicit some sympathy at least. Ariel told Michael he would talk to someone tomorrow about letting him out, even just for a few hours with a chaperone.

"You haven't told me a thing about what goes on when you go out there with them."

"I haven't told you anything because I don't know what the fuck is going on."

"There's some shit going down, isn't there? Who are we dealing with?"

"I have no idea. I don't know these people." Ariel lit a cigarette, one of the Chinese ones a youth stationed outside the door had given him. It smelled awful and quickly suffocated the entire room. Michael thought his roommate was using this method to kill him. Having not gotten over his jet lag yet, Ariel chain-smoked for most of the night, but by morning Michael was still alive.

"Hey, Ariel," Michael asked as the dawn was breaking. Neither one of them had said a word for hours. "Are we in trouble?"

The old man detected the note of fear in the younger man's voice and his stony expression softened.

"You'll be all right," he said.

Michael didn't know what to make of that. Did it mean that Ariel wasn't? Or was he just reassuring Michael? Either way, Michael felt ashamed.

On day three, there was considerably more traffic going back and forth from the room, and Ariel spent more time out than in. His pleas on Michael's behalf worked to the degree that Michael was handed a stack of English-language *Peking Reviews*.

Michael felt better in the morning. At least he got the sense that the old man was as confused and frustrated as he was. Of course, all of that may have been a put-on, but he preferred not to think so. He seized the day, trying to make the best of the hospitality that was offered. He sat down to read the *Peking Review*. In the first issue he read, he found an article, in the "Arts" section, with the headline, "*Music with No Words Is Reactionary*":

> *Beethoven's music is inherently reactionary. Because there are no words, you can't know what it means.*

The prose style and reasoning reminded him of something Camus had written about Saint-Just's writing style: "*It is the style of the guillotine.*" This, then, was the style of the dull butcher knife.

In the afternoon, he poked his head out the door and saw a girl sitting in the hallway. He assumed she was "guarding" him, though this was the first time he saw someone sitting instead of standing. Maybe they were getting the idea he wasn't going to challenge them.

When she looked up, he was startled. He thought he recognized her, but that would have been impossible: He didn't know anyone in China. Then it occurred to him that she resembled Cletus Dong's sister, Candy. It took a bit of imagination to make the transfer: imagine Candy without makeup, her long, straight hair chopped off just above the chin, wearing a sexless blue suit. When she stood up, he could tell they were about the same height, too.

"I'm sorry. I fell asleep for a little while," she said, in only slightly labored English. That was a major plus. Every single person that had been posted outside his door until now hadn't said a word to him.

"Uh, that's okay. If I'd known earlier, I would have made a run for it."

"Do you enjoy your visit to China?"

"Sure. It's been great."

"Good. Please let me know if I can do anything for you."
Michael pondered that when she followed up with a question: "Where are you from?"

"Me? America."

"What city?"

"San Francisco. Well, not exactly the city itself. I live in the East Bay."

"Is that near New York?"

"No, it's on the opposite side of the country."

"Really? I thought it was next to New York."

"No. You're thinking of New Jersey."

"Would you like a cigarette?"

"Do you smoke?"

"No. I am offering you."

"That's okay."

"Yes, or no?"

"'That's okay' means 'no'."

"Strange. You don't like Chinese cigarette, eh?"

"I don't smoke . . . tobacco."

"American cigarette taste better, right? That's what I hear."

"My friend," he gestured inside, meaning Ariel, "says that Chinese cigarettes are better. More tar."

She shook her head. "How much does one cost in America?"

"One cigarette? Or a pack?"

"Pack."

"I dunno. I never bought one."

"That's very strange. Is it true Americans eat raw vegetables?"

He blinked at that one. It took him a moment to realize what she was talking about. "Yes. We eat salad. You don't eat salad in China?"

She shook her head. "We cook. Only barbarians eat raw food. Like Japanese."

He nodded. It made sense.

Their conversation went on in this manner, with her peppering him with questions that sounded genuinely curious. It was the most fun he'd had in days, though he couldn't help noticing that every time he tried to come back with a question about China, she would clam up and ask another question about America. He got the message after a few tries: Talk about America, don't talk about China.

"You're very curious about America."

"I would like to travel there someday. I know it's difficult right now, but I think the relationship between our two countries will improve in the future."

"I hope so. There are a lot of Chinese people in America, especially in San Francisco."

"I would like to see them. There are a lot of things I would like to see in the world."

"Light out for the territory, huh?"

"Excuse me?"

"'I reckon I got to light out for the territory ahead of the rest, because Aunt Sally she's going to adopt me and sivilize me, and I can't stand it. I been there before.' That's from *The Adventures of Huckleberry Finn* by Mark Twain."

"Marx . . . ?"

"Not Karl Marx. Mark Twain. American author."

"I don't know him. Have you read any Chinese authors?"

"Just Mao."

She took him down to the basement, where he met the hotel kitchen staff. Nobody could speak English, but they all waved at him, smiling. A crowd began to grow around him. He was, he supposed, something of an attraction. The enthusiastic reception he received seemed to go beyond mere obligation. The spontaneity was a welcome relief from the uptightness of the bureaucrats and flunkies he'd encountered so far. His guide asked the staff to show him what they were making, and they took him around the kitchen. In one spot, a group of women were wrapping what looked like won tons. The people there had the friendly, unpretentious appeal of blue-collar workers who, while they weren't exactly happy, weren't as miserable as they once were. It reminded him very much of the post office.

The next day, he and Ariel were taken out for a drive to a village on the outskirts of Peking. He got a good look at the countryside surrounding that gray city. It was a brisk autumn day, and the trees were in full color.

Their hosts were going to treat them to a banquet and took them to a restaurant that resembled a union hall. Michael and Ariel and a group of men in blue suits sat around a table and ate and drank. One of those in attendance, Michael believed, was Wang Hung-wen, the former Shanghai cotton mill worker who had been promoted by Mao to the number-three position in the party hierarchy, and who later joined Chiang Ching in promoting the "Criticize Lin Piao, Criticize Confucius" campaign.

Their hosts ordered a number of "delicacies." There was an ugly thing that felt like eating a dead rat. Then they ordered a round of sea slugs, which didn't have any taste at all. It was like sucking down snot. What fucking culture considered this sort of thing a delicacy? Michael thought their gracious hosts were bringing out these dishes out of sheer perversity—they weren't delicacies at all. By the end of the night, their hosts had drunk them under table with *moutai*, a clear liquor that tasted like turpentine. They repeatedly toasted the Americans in Chinese and laughed, and the whole time Michael thought they were saying, *"Don't hold your breath waiting for the revolution in the U.S.A. This is the best we got! Ah ha ha ha!"*

That was their last day in China.

Michael picked up his luggage at the carousel. There was the suitcase he'd originally packed, and following, the suitcase he'd received in Vancouver, which he hadn't seen since he'd checked it in for the Pan Am flight to Tokyo. It felt heavier than he remembered, but that was hard to say. He looked at Ariel once he had it, expecting some kind of response, a raised eyebrow, smirk, or nod, but Ariel had his poker face on. They went through customs. The officer checked his luggage ticket and waved him through.

They entered the arrivals lobby. There was no one to pick them up.

In the seconds that he scanned the crowd again, looking for the people who should have been there but weren't, a flood of thoughts went through Michael's mind. He was sure the exact same thoughts were now going through Ariel's mind. Michael was carrying the suitcase. It wouldn't be hard for him to outrun the old man. Pushing him down or hitting him would only cause a disturbance that would draw attention to him. If he just ran, it would take the sparse crowd around them awhile, whatever Ariel's response, to realize what was going on, and even then, if that, security was light. Ariel didn't have a chance.

He could lie low in Canada. There would be a lot of people out to kill him. It was a lot of money. He could steal the money and become a capitalist.

The two men from the Seattle group came running up.

"Sorry we're late. Traffic."

They followed them to their car.

In Seattle, the four met another two, and the money was handed over. The two with the money left in a separate car. Michael and Ariel were driven back to Seattle HQ.

Michael thought he was driving to San Francisco with Ariel, but Ariel told him he would be staying on.

At the curb, Ariel stopped him. "You weren't thinking about running off with the money back there, were you?"

Michael just smiled. They didn't say goodbye or shake hands. It was the last they saw of each other.

In 1983, long after he'd stopped being a Communist, Michael came across an obit in the *Chronicle*. Ariel Rabenstein, a patient who had suffered from Alzheimer's, passed away in a Jewish old folk's home in East Oakland.

Some time after that, on a trip very unlike his first one there, Michael stepped into a bar in Vancouver and saw behind the counter a woman he believed to be Candy Dong. Her youthful beauty had long since withered away, but the vitality she had displayed that night in Chinatown was still in force.

He reintroduced himself, and she remembered him. He told her this story and mentioned how he had passed up a chance to run off with the money.

"I was going to take it and find you. I still kept the chopstick wrapper with your friend's phone number on it."

She looked at him with an unreadable expression. Then she mentioned she had left for Vancouver shortly after they'd met and hadn't been back to San Francisco since. Was the restaurant still there?

He had tried looking for it, but couldn't find it.

Chinatown hadn't changed much, though. In that way it seemed to exist in cyclical as opposed to linear time, life went on there much as it had before. Of course, politically, everything had changed. All the old battle lines that had been drawn up and which they'd all fought over so heatedly had been irrevocably erased. Things that used to matter, like the Kuomintang, now mattered little. The old I-Hotel, he didn't know if she'd heard, had been torn down after a great struggle. All that was left on the corner of Jackson and Kearny was a hole in the ground that had remained for almost twenty-five years.

"And your friend Francis? How's he doing?" she asked.

"He went to jail and kind of disappeared from view after that. What about your brother, the filmmaker?"

"He went into real estate," she said. "He bought up properties all over the avenues, and now he's immensely rich."

LARRY'S PLACE

BY MICHELLE TEA

Bernal Heights

I t was the beginning of October and it felt like the height of summer, even way the fuck up on the rotting hillside that was my Bernal Hill neighborhood. Not that the weather would dry my moldering basement apartment; we'd need a year of San Francisco Octobers for my home to become livable, to staunch the flow of moisture that dappled my crumbling walls—my own little waterfall, I liked to think of it. This was when I wasn't depressed, when I had some levity to spare. My own little waterfall, like I'm living in the tropics.

And it's true that my back door opened up to a lush back-yard, it's true that though it was horribly overgrown and almost entirely weeds, it was green. On the days when my depression had receded like a landlord's hairline, I could appreciate it all—the chest-high weeds tossing in the perpetual wind, the sheen of dew pimpling the walls of my subterranean apartment, my overall fungal existence. I was some sort of elf, a smallish person dwelling in a mushroom, which bloomed on the gloomy backside of Bernal Hill.

Two things happened that first week of October, and they both involved breaking and entering. First, I was the victim, later, the perpetrator. I'd come home from a call and I was feeling cranky. It was an early-morning client, unusual, a business guy from Seattle in town for a conference. I should pay more attention to what my tricks do. Some of them are almost certainly controlling the world—balding white businessmen, past middle age, with a lot of cash to blow on hookers. Their suits are expensive and their briefcases look like they come from the leather of a superior cow. I visit them at the Fairmont, at the Mandarin, at every single downtown hotel; a blur of elevator buttons and soft-carpeted hallways that muffle the clack of my heels. These guys are involved in dirty business, they're profiting from the war, are Republican, are getting rich on the backs of girls like me, I know. Sometimes, I think I should be a spy, fuck them better, make them like me, seduce them into telling me the secrets of their occupations so that I could do—something. So close to these rulers, in plush locked rooms, with their curdled white bodies. Surely I could do something; a certain sabotage seems close, so close, but no. I zone out when they speak to me, leave my body when they climb onto me, give them the dullest fuck, and they don't bat an eye. They've been having lousy sex since they were fourteen, they've been getting it on with women who want nothing to do with them since puberty, they can't tell the difference. They roll off me and I'm gone. Down the elevator, I've got my hand jammed into my purse, wrapped around the money, counting the bills from touch, discretely. I've already forgotten what he looked like.

Usually I'm nice to the cabbies. I have them drop me off at the tip of the sharply angled, dead-end block my ramshackle house sits, melting, at the end of. I walk myself careful down the steeply sloping sidewalk, gashes cut into the concrete sidewalk for traction. Getting to my front door is like rappelling down the side of a cliff. If you ask me, houses shouldn't have been built down here. These little block-long streets cease abruptly at the open space that remains on the side of the hill, and the hill is angry that development has crept so close. It whips these pathetic homes with a battering, constant wind. It sends soggy clouds to sit damply atop the roofs, trickling stagnant moisture, birthing deep green molds. It sends its monsters, the horrifying Jerusalem crickets, up from the soil to invade basement apartments, looking like greasy, translucent alien insects. They drive me crying into the bathroom to strategize their eviction from my home.

The hill hates the houses, and my dead-end street is a study in bad feng-shui—the sinister vibes rising on the wind. It's my plan to move someday, when I've saved enough money to afford it. It's my hope that the rents will go down in this town. I'm biding my time here on the side of the hill, a growing stack of cash in a box on my bookshelf. I worry about it there, the soft paper of it. I check in on it daily, to make sure the damp hasn't dissolved it into a mushy lump of pulp.

Anyway. My street is difficult to drive down, harder to get out of. You can back up but it's sort of scary. You can turn around in the driveway across the street, but that's a bitch. Plus, the scrappy little dog that lives there will bark at you the whole time, making the task even more hellish. Usually I tell the cabbies to let me off at the corner and I hike down to my door.

That morning I felt surly and bossy, like a tired old whore, even though I was only twenty-five. I'd been up till 4 a.m. fielding late-night alcoholic phone calls from my recent ex, Jenny. They'd started around last call, from the pay phone mounted on the wall at the bar. I could hear the rumble of voices behind her, smacked with sharp laughs and the sound of glasses, music low from the jukebox at the other end of the room. Jenny was louder than all of it. She must have thought

I couldn't hear her, but I heard her fine, she was screaming. I heard her fine and I bet half the bar did, too; heard all my business and Jenny's drunk opinion of it. The call would last until her money ran out and then I'd have a break as she hit the bar for more change or bummed some off her friends. I'd lay on my futon in the silence, listening to the subtle *ping* of water falling somewhere in my apartment. Waited for the phone to ring and it did. Heard the bartender holler last call; later heard her say, Hey, Jen, Don't You Got A Phone At Home, Come On. We're Closed. Mentally tracked the eight-minute walk down Mission, to Jen's place upstairs from the produce and piñata store. Counted minutes for the huffing climb of the stairs, the drunken fiddle with the locks. Imagined her pause at the narrow closet that held her toilet, to piss out a bunch of what she'd just drank; figured in some time for her trip into the kitchen to check the empty fridge for beer; then another sixty seconds for her to stomp into her room, fling herself onto her bed, and start calling me again. I picked up the phone; I didn't have anything else going on. I laid the phone on my ear and stayed rolled on my side upon the futon.

She sounded crazy because she was crazy. This was good for me to remember. These phone calls were the best break-up present Jenny could have given me. I listened to her psycho-ramble, and sometimes, when it was appropriate, I'd say, Yeah, I'm Sorry For That. Sometimes, the sharp reality of her pain really got me and I'd feel it, too; a haunting glimpse of what it must be like to be trapped on the inside of Jenny's brain. As shitty as our tortured relationship was for me—this shitty, dramatic ending was worse for Jenny. I was getting away, but she was going to be stuck there inside her head for the rest of her life.

The morning of my call with the guy from Seattle, my face was puffy and I was almost hallucinating with sleep deprivation. I smeared some Preparation H under my eyes, which had submitted to a bit of crying during some of Jenny's more expressive calls. I learned the Preparation H thing from a girl I worked with at a house in Oakland. It shrinks the little red saddlebags under my eyeballs right down. I wobbled into an outfit, packed my purse with the minimum; no toys, too early, just the condoms and the lube, my wallet, key, and that smear-proof lipstick. I swear, a million whores rejoiced when they finally came out with this stuff. Blowjobs require enough of a sacrifice of dignity without having to worry about looking like a clown, red smears all over the place, when you're done.

The call was easy; the guy was still sleepy himself. I left him fumbling with the hotel coffee pot and hailed a cab outside. *Down there?* the cabbie asked as he crested my street. Yup. He sighed. I could feel him asking if he could just dump me out at the corner. Not that morning, not in those shoes, not in the condition I was in. I was ready to plunge back into my damp bed and sleep the day away. Barely 10 a.m. and I'd already made my money. The cab turned down my block, crawling carefully.

That little fucking dog started its yapping. The poor thing never saw the inside of a house; it was just roped there to the chain-link fence that separated our paltry civilization from the wild roll of hillside. Its hair was long and its body was small. It looked like a bad wig someone had tossed onto the street, sort of matted and dingy. I bet it'd look like a real fancy pooch if someone ever cared to clean it up, but for now it looked like a piece of trash come to life. I tipped the driver well. If he were a good driver he'd be off my precarious street

in about two minutes; if he were a hack he'd be out there forever, the dog ruining the day with its noise.

I knew something was wrong right away, because my door
was open. The latch that held it shut had been busted off. It
hung there on its hinge, the door. Thankfully, we were expe-
riencing this summery weather up here, or else the wind
would have been flapping it open and closed, open and
closed, like that damn dog's mouth, advertising to the shady
neighborhood that my apartment was accepting explorers.

My neighborhood consists of: a gang of young boys who
try to be intimidating and usually succeed; a shiftless family
who occasionally steal my mail; the dude across the street
who owns the dog, an Archie Bunker–type who looks like
he's stockpiling weapons and has American flags hung in his
window in lieu of curtains; the little boy who lives downstairs
from him whose efforts to befriend the ragamuffin canine
result in bellows from the patriot and a scolding from the
boy's squat grandmother; a lesbian couple who bought the
nicest house on the block—a dubious compliment—and
who've allowed fear of their new surroundings to turn them
into hostile bitches. Oh, and there's Larry, lord of the mold,
the man I pay rent to, who lives in the apartment above
mine. It's not exactly Mister Roger's Neighborhood here. It's
like everyone has Seasonal Affective Disorder and we spend
a good ten months of the year ensconced in clouds. The sero-
tonin has all gone away, we're unhappy people here on Porter
Street.

I kicked off my heels and grabbed one in my fist, stiletto
out, as a weapon. My front door gaped open behind me. I
descended into the cave that was my home. Hello? I yelled.
Hello, Motherfucker? Show Yourself, Fucker! I paused. Larry?
I called. He has been known to come into my apartment on

landlordy business, unannounced, totally illegal, I know, but what am I really going to do? Like I said, I'm biding my time here.

In my kitchen there's a note. It's on the back of a take-out menu, scrawled in a dried-up Sharpie. It's faint and hard to read. I could decipher the word *"you"* and the word *"fucking"* and there was an arrow that went in the general direction of my back door, which was also wide open. Kicked open, busted. I felt a swell of anger. Whoever did this had to break my front door in order to get in. Okay, I get that. But the back door was easily unlocked from inside my house. Whoever did this broke my door just for the fuck of it, just to be a dickface.

I grabbed the menu and walked toward the door. I tried to study the text in the sunlight that shot down from the sky and pooled in the slight clearing of weeds outside my door. The phrase *"nice fucking life"* was visible at the bottom of the page.

Out in my yard, there was a clear path where the weeds had been trampled. I followed it, barefoot, my feet getting all gunked up. In the middle of the yard, I looked up at Larry's apartment. What a jackass. What a totally useless landlord. He makes no repairs; he lets the yard turn into a jungle and my apartment into a mold-ridden health hazard. The only thing he was good for was simple presence; he was reliable like that. He rarely left his upstairs apartment, save for beer runs. He sat up there and drank and watched cable. He was a bulky guy with a lousy attitude, and I figured I could at least rely on him to ward off burglars, a simple crime deterrent. But he wasn't even good for that. The sun reflected off his windows, making it impossible for me to see into his place. He could have been standing at the window looking out at me. I flipped him off just in case.

I followed the skinny trail of crushed weeds to the back of the yard. There was a depression there, a cement clearing that maybe an optimistic former tenant had once tried to garden in. It was filled with dirt that had turned muddy with trash and pooled rainwater. Who knows what else was in there. Today my life savings was. I could see the tips of bills sticking out from the sludge, like they'd been packed into the wet dirt and then stomped deeply into the skank of it. Yeah. There were footprints mashed into it, overlapping footprints going in all directions, like someone had just freaked out and moshed my money into the ground. The box it had all been stored in was off to the side, lying in the weeds, open and empty to the sky above us.

At first I felt nothing; and then quickly, swiftly, I wanted to die. As I stood there wanting to die, I could feel the sensation morph. I could feel it become energized and then it became the more dynamic feeling of wanting to kill. Then it lessened, became heavy, and I was filled with the desire to just kill myself.

I looked down at the mud. Maybe it was salvageable. I gently tugged the protruding corner of a hundred-dollar bill and it came off in my fingers. The mud was sopping, it was like coffee with a lot of grounds in it. It was, as I probed it with my fingers, more of a puddle than anything. I scooped up a liquidy pile of cash. I draped the paper across some bent stalks of weeds and it tore there, slunk into the ground like slurry.

My life was dissolving. I plunged my hands back into the puddle and brought out some more palmfuls of dark, indistinguishable nothing.

I started to cry. I started to hyperventilate. I thought of all the guys I'd fucked. I thought of all the mouths, gummy and slick, that had suctioned themselves to my breasts. I thought of my sweet, chafed pussy, and all it had been through. The gropes. The sweat—that beaded chests like the condensation on my bedroom walls—how it had splattered upon me. Oh, the noxious grunts, the gross sounds they made, the plain and hideous sight of their nudity. It was as if I had fucked them all for free. All I had were the bills in my purse, and rent was due today.

Fucking Jenny. Fucking sick Jenny. She didn't even steal it. She was as broke as me, broker even, with a bigger drinking problem, more of a need for cash, and she didn't even steal it. Her need to hurt me had blotted out even basic self-preservation. Under all my despair was a new fear now; fear of Jenny. She might as well have killed me, I thought, or at least sent someone to kick my ass.

I thought again about the men. The simple destruction of the money, the basis of those consensual trysts, now made every call an act of violence survived. I was shaking. I went back into my room and laid down on my futon. With both doors open to the beautiful day, I passed out.

When I awoke it was evening. The wind had stirred up on the hill and was blowing through my apartment like a little hurricane. My broken doors whined on their hinges. I padded into my kitchen, still in my whore clothes: a shimmery skirt—cheap from Ross—and a blousey lady-shirt, sheer, the ghost of my push-up bra a hazy vision beneath the fabric. Jenny had loved me in my whore outfits, months back when we had first hooked up. She had thought the getup hilarious, and it was. I remember her sitting squat on the dank wooden floor of my bedroom, her tiny hand spidering out around the fat bottle she was drinking from. Red-cheeked and giggling, she watched my transformation. I strung the lingerie around my body, pulling back my fried hair, removing my heavy horn-rimmed eyeglasses, and dusting my lids with shimmery powder. We'd fucked that first time, there on the floor, the splintery wood scraping my ass, scuffing my Payless pumps, and I didn't even care; her mouth cold from the beer and tasting of bubbles.

Three months is not a long time for a relationship unless you're a dyke. After the first few days, we were together all the time; I knew her story and she knew mine. We had one real good month together, and then things started to slip. She'd get moody and I'd turn bitchy in reply. We stopped fucking at home and instead did it in bar bathrooms, when the first flush of alcohol-induced good mood washed over her. By the time we got back to one of our places she'd be in a different state, sour, and we'd fight. I always regretted it. I know better than to argue with a drunk person—both my folks were drunks and it's like trying to have a logical conversation with some loony on the street. My points may have been good, may have been right, but in the morning Jenny wouldn't remember anything I said. It took a full month of things being real lousy between us for me to call it off, and I was ashamed that I'd stuck around that long. But she never stopped looking good to me; and she had charm, a glow that the beer both fed and ruined.

In my kitchen, I startled a small, feral cat; a black thing mottled with bits of orange. So tiny, it hissed ferociously and darted out my back door into the weeds. I tried to jam the door shut but it was useless. Same with the one upstairs. I made coffee and emptied the dregs of a box of cereal into a bowl, dousing it with soy milk. I tried to get a plan together. Even though I always had my rent ready on the first of the

month, I made a point not to pay Larry until the fifth. I liked
to put off spending my money until the last possible moment.
The first was four days ago; at the time I had had all my rent
and more. Today was the fifth and I had one hundred and
fifty dollars. Rent for this damp but spacious basement apartment was seven hundred dollars. People liked to tell me I had
a good deal. They would gasp when I told them. Seven
Hundred Dollars? And You Live All By Yourself? They would
moon dreamily. I suppose it was a good deal, and that said a
lot about this town. I would have to tell Larry that I didn't
have the money. I decided against telling him about the
break-in. I didn't want him knowing I kept my cash in a box
rather than a bank; didn't want him to know about my
romantic drama, or anything about me whatsoever. It was
none of his business. I'd tell him that I'd have it for him as
soon as possible, and leave it at that. Let the fucker evict me,
what did I care. I seemed to have awoken at a certain bottom. All I could figure to do was call my service and have
them put me on call twenty-four hours a day for the indefi-
nite future, and then try not to think too hard about what
that would really entail.

Out on the street, I banged on Larry's front door. I'd
given it about a half-dozen whacks before I remembered the
man had a doorbell. I guess I just wanted to hit something.
The rag of a dog across the street responded to my violence
with a series of futile yaps. The sky above was perfect and blue,
but a bank of clouds were in the distance, blowing my way.

Larry! I hollered. I banged and rang.

The dog was barking itself a sore throat. Then I looked
down. Coming out from under Larry's door was a bit of hair,
brown hair, sort of oily. Just a little greasy tuft, sliding out
from inside the house.

Larry? I asked, in a normal voice.

I crouched down and touched it. It felt like real hair. A wig? Why would Larry have a wig? I had a flash of him, drunk and outfitted in attire common to the opposite gender, and then a flash of sympathy for him and his poor attitude. We all have our secrets, don't we? I gave the wig a tug, but it didn't shift. It felt attached to something heavy, like a body. I cracked open Larry's mail slot and peered into the darkness. The crumpled mass lumped on the other side of the door looked like my landlord.

You lookin for something?

The voice made me jump; I sprung up in my stocking feet and spun around to greet my neighbor, the militia man. His belly preceded him, jutting out of his undershirt like a round, hard melon. He looked like he was sneering but it was simply the set of his face. A rifle would not have looked out of place in his arms.

I Live Here, I reminded him.

Every so often, this would happen. The guy would accost me as I fumbled for my keys, or as I lingered outside my door awaiting a taxi. I'd notice him peering out from behind his tattered flag, and then he'd be galumphing down his front stairs and confronting me in the street like I was set to burgle the neighborhood. I rapped my fingers on the door again, and moved a fish-netted foot to cover the lock of Larry's hair, which protruded onto the sidewalk.

You live here? he asked suspiciously. *How come I ain't seen ya?*

You Have, I said. We Do This All The Time. You See Me Out Here, Ask Me What I'm Doing, And I Tell You I Live Here. I sighed patiently.

That other girl lives here, he informed me. *The redheaded one?*

Forgot her keys this morning and busted her own damn door in.
He chuckled with affection for who I could only imagine was
Jenny, breaking into my house.

Oh, Yeah, I nodded. She Lives Here, Too.

Uh-huh, he nodded, looking me up and down. Stalling
briefly on the gauzy outline of my bra and moving on up to
my face. *You all keep leaving your keys behind and breaking your
doors down, that man up there's gonna get rid of ya.* He gave his
chin a chuck in the general direction of Larry's apartment.
He your dad? You two sisters?

Six months I've lived on Porter Street and this guy has
never spoken to me beyond clarifying that I'm not a criminal.
He picks this moment, this bizarre and creepy moment on
this strange and terrible day, to inquire about my life.

No, I tell him. Larry's The Landlord. Me And That Girl,
We're Just—Roommates.

Norma, he nods.

Right, I'm Norma. I'm losing patience. He frowns.

No, that other girl, she said her name was Norma. Now he's
suspicious again.

Well, She's Fucking With You. She Likes To Do That.
And Actually, She Didn't Lose Her Keys. She Broke The
Door Down Cause She's Crazy, And If You See Her Around
Here Again Breaking Things, I'd Appreciate It If You Could
Call The Cops.

The man took a step back, as if the breath my speech had
been carried out on was laced with something noxious.

*No need to use language like that. I don't believe in calling
police. I don't think our tax dollars should be going to a gang of
government thugs. I don't believe in a police state. You'll have to
handle your differences with Norma yourself, she seemed like a
nice person to me. We had a nice little talk about the government*

*out here this morning, all about the unconstitutionality of the pre-
sent tax system.* He swallowed and nodded. *That's right. You
girls just settle your grievances without bringing the government
into it, why don't you. Can't go crying to the government every
time life throws a problem your way.*

All Right, I agreed. All Right Then. Thanks A Lot.

Down the street the lesbians who bought the house on
the corner paused at their SUV, watching us.

Then there's all that, the guy said, gesturing toward them.

Yeah, I said.

You okay over there? the butchier one yelled over in an
uncharacteristic display of neighborliness. Where were all
these concerned citizens when my house was being robbed? I
ask you. Well, we know where the guy was. He was chatting
up and befriending Jenny, perhaps even helping her out with
a weighty hip-chuck to my front door.

Fine, Thanks! I gave a wave. They paused a moment and
turned to look at one another, perhaps communicating via a
special telepathy lesbian couples acquire when they manage
to stay together past three months. Then they climbed into
their mammoth automobile, lumbered over the crest of our
street, and were gone.

SUVs, the man said. He flung a meaty hand at the wake
of dust and trash their car had stirred. *Don't get me started.*

This Has Been Nice, I said. It's Nice To Be Neighborly.
But I've Got To Run.

Maybe you girls want to leave a spare set of keys with me, he
suggested. *If you're always locking yourself out.*

I Don't Think It'll Happen Again, I told him.

Better safe 'n sorry, he said.

I turned my back on him and descended into my subterranean apartment. I stood at the bottom of the stairs and

watched the crack of light in my busted door, expecting him to follow. I waited there for a few minutes and when he didn't come, ran through my house and out the back door, climbing the shabby back stairs to Larry's. The stairs shook with the slam of my feet, a snowfall of dried paint sifted down onto the weeds.

Larry! I banged on his back door. My voice carried out into the quiet.

Larry was an unconscious heap at his front door. I don't know why I was attracting all this attention to myself when I knew I was going to have to break into his place. I pulled and pushed and otherwise strained at his back door. I wasn't good at this. I'd never broken into a place before; my particular illegal inclinations hadn't ever brought me to such a situation. I've picked a pocket, shoplifted, and been guilty of an occasional drunken assault on equally drunken men behaving rudely in bars or on street corners. But I'd never broken into a home. I rattled the dully gleaming doorknob. It figures that Larry's doors have adequate locks. Doesn't that just sum up the whole thing?

Larry had a few ceramic pots on his back stairs. The plants inside them were long dead, all dried up. Cigarette butts were stubbed out in the dirt. I grabbed one and hurled it against his kitchen window, where it shattered in a rain of terra cotta and dirt that plunged to the yard below. I threw a second pot at the window and experienced a similar explosion. Jesus, I whined. The dirt was in my hair, smudged over my blouse. I grabbed a shard of pottery and used it to gouge a hole in the screen, tore it away. Now it was just the glass and me. The third pot bust through, sending a whole mess onto Larry's linoleum floor. Huh. Linoleum. Must be nice.

As I climbed in through the shattered window, ruining

my fishnet stockings on a jutting piece of glass, I realized I had never been inside Larry's apartment. I stepped gingerly onto a recycling box piled high with beer cans.

Larry? I called.

I walked into a small pile of dirt and plant roots. Broken glass glittered. I skipped quickly to the fridge and leaned onto it for balance.

Larry? I cried out again, my voice little more than a croak.

Oh fuck. I pulled open the fridge and spied a lone Budweiser, its plastic loop of rings still noosed around its aluminum neck. I yanked it out, set it free, cracked it.

I moved through Larry's place. It *was* nice, much nicer than my watery grave below. Good stove in the kitchen, ample cabinets. The floor was linoleum, and where it wasn't, carpet provided a soft relief on my feet. The living room was in disarray. The rest of the six-pack rolled empty on the floor alongside a glass bottle of something stronger. The television was set to ESPN. Some electronic device whirred in the corner. I studied it and discovered it was a dehumidifier. Fucking genius. I made a note to buy one when I had money again. Then I remembered that Larry was almost certainly dead and I could probably just take it.

I crept to the edge of the hall stairs, took a deep breath, a gulp from the can, and then switched on the light. There was Larry. His head was smooshed against the front door at an awful angle. His neck looked incorrect. His eyes were disturbingly open, as was his mouth. He was not alive.

Larry? I asked, just in case.

Nothing. Outside, the dog barked and barked. In the living room a sports team won something and the crowds in the stands cheered in unison. I finished my beer.

* * *

That was all about a month ago, perhaps a little longer. San Francisco's autumn summertime is all but gone, and the winds have brought their cold damp; they lash the house with it like a locker room of jocks snapping soggy towels. The wind is so forceful that it actually shakes the house. Before I became used to it, I would wake in the night thinking an earthquake had struck. I would stare at the ceiling in terror and wait for the upstairs apartment to cave in onto my bed in the basement. Then I would remember that I was upstairs, and it was only the wind. I would turn up the heat that hummed gently out from the vent in Larry's bedroom and fall back asleep.

I haven't seen Larry since I drug him into the bathroom and heaved him into his claw-footed bathtub. I shut the door with a click and I do not open it. I pee in an empty pickle jar and, when I must, slip out into the backyard and shit in the weeds like that tiny black-and-orange cat who lives out there, too. I shower in the hotels and private homes of the men that I trick with. One shower before and a longer one after. I can't bring myself to return to my basement, not even to use the toilet. I poked my head in only once, and it was as if the mold had accelerated in my absence. The moisture seemed heavier, wetter; the decay, palpable. It scented the very air of the place. There was an animal turd in plain view on the wooden kitchen floor, and a scurrying sound in the corner I did not investigate.

Upstairs, in Larry's place, I can hear my broken doors squeak like a strange wind chime in the gusting air. Upstairs, in Larry's place, I watch cable TV and eat the last of his food; bring home six-packs for the fridge. I drive his car to my calls. I've taken up smoking. When I cannot sleep, which is more and more frequent, I stand out on the back porch amidst the dirt and smashed pottery, and I smoke. The kitchen window is secured with cardboard and shiny gray duct tape; the light from inside does not shine on me there.

I stand in the dark night and the powerful wind steals the smoke as it streams from my mouth. I know that this will all end soon, and the understanding makes me jumpy. Last night, as I stood smoking, I saw beams of light in the wild hill below; the wide swath of land between my home and the housing projects at the bottom. It was a cop or two, prowling with flashlights, searching in the unruly grass. It seemed an omen. I'm not sure what I've done or what sort of punishment I need to outrun.

Late at night, as I smoke cigarettes, I can hear my telephone ringing through the open door downstairs. It's just past last call and I know the ringing won't stop for hours. I stand and smoke in the chill until it's quiet. The man across the street tries to speak to me when I let myself into Larry's with the key I took from his pocket. I ignore him. It makes him mad and he yells, and his yells inspire the dog, and I close my door on the decaying block and all of its angry inhabitants.

In the night, it is the hardest to be here; when I come back from a call and the television greets me. I have thousands of dollars in my box. I've been working so hard, so very hard.

Lately, I imagine I can smell him—the scent of Larry's collapsing body coming out from under the bathroom door on a terrible breeze. Certainly it is time to leave. I think I would like to live in Russian Hill; in a glinting apartment with a chandelier in the lobby and a man who holds the door open as I come and go.

I stand on the back stairs in the afternoon light; and

when my cigarette is half-done, I look down and see that man—the one who lives in his undershirt—standing in the weeds beneath me, looking up. And I know before I see her that Jenny is behind him.

THE OTHER BARRIO

BY ALEJANDRO MURGUÍA

The Mission

I t stood on the corner of Sixteenth and Valencia—the Apache Hotel, a once elegant residence for out of town visitors, more recently a rundown joint for several dozen single men and some desperate families. Every time I go by the spot I still hear the screams, the cries for help of those who were caught in the fire the night the Apache Hotel burned down.

The newspapers screamed the headlines the next day: SEVEN DEAD IN FIRE. It didn't state the cause, but I knew I would be dragged into it. And I didn't want to be dragged into it. I had cited the place three times, but not for fire hazards, just the common stuff—garbage and rodent infestations. Had there been a fire hazard, God himself could not have stopped me from making sure the owner took care of it that very day. Now it was going to come down on me. That's why Choy had taken me off the case. He was my shithead boss at the Department of Building Inspections, and my job was on the line if my report had failed to mention a fire hazard, which it did not. Seven people had died and I wasn't going to carry those dead. They weren't my dead. Let whoever killed them carry them.

It was Friday evening, and Choy's order to report for a Monday morning meeting had appeared on my desk as I was leaving work. I decided to take my file on the Apache Hotel with me; I had the weekend to find the cause of the fire. Sometime after my Wednesday inspection, maybe thirty-six hours afterwards, the place had burned down in a raging fire. It's not easy for a building that size to burn that fast. No one downtown was talking, to the papers anyway. This wasn't going to be easy or fun to be involved with. But it wasn't just my skin on the line—there was my own outrage at what had happened. There was no reason for those people to have died. No reason at all.

The fire had likely started early Friday, about 3:00 in the morning. The newspapers mentioned witnesses and I had to track them down and get their story firsthand. In particular, the person who'd called 911. They'd been identified as workers leaving a nightclub. I'd have to hang around the 'hood till 2 a.m. to interview them. In the meantime, I was nursing a beer in a little dive on Twenty-fourth Street; mindlessly staring at the yellow spot on the brown bottle neck, trying to make sense of this case and my own life.

I was living in a former can factory on Alabama Street, now converted into a den of unwashed but creative folks, who'd taken the iron-age dinosaur and made it somewhat habitable. Now the dot-comers were popping up like mushrooms in cow shit. Or you'd see them cruising in their beemers, calculating how much it would take to run everybody out of here. And in all irony, I was working for the city as a building inspector. I wasn't interested in being a cop, I just made sure that rental units were habitable for human beings. My girlfriend Amanda had left me. Going to our formerly happy loft usually put me in a funk of depression, so I stayed away as much as I could. Usually in places like this, bars without names outside, a couple of Mexicanos shooting an easy game of pool, and Miss Mary from San

Pedro Sula, with her smile wide as her hips, pouring a beer.

Don't get me wrong, the city is beautiful, but I live in another barrio. The dirty, low-down, underbelly side of town. Places that practically make the hovels of Calcutta look like the Taj Mahal. The garages turned into in-laws where three families live packed tight and desperate as boat people. Closets redone into bedroom suites. Such is life. And death. I was going to go visit death at 9 o'clock in General Hospital. In the morgue where the dead are kept. She wasn't dressed liked you expect but there is no mistaking her when you meet her.

At 9 o'clock I met La Pelona face-to-face in the basement morgue of General Hospital. A Samoan in scrubs and flip-flops led me into a walk-in cooler the size of a taquería. Inside were row upon row of gurneys, each with their own stiff. He pointed out a corner where seven of them were stretched out on the floor. "We ran out of tables," he laughed. I took no offense.

When I lifted the sheet on the first one, I was surprised to see the face was contorted like those mummies of Guanajuato, but unburned. "What happened?" I asked.

"They died of smoke inhalation," the Samoan said.

Nobody even knew these poor bastards' names. I could see the process that would now start: immigration tracking clues, an envelope with a name, or perhaps a phone number in one of their pockets. Find their hometown, relatives most likely, and tell them. Arrange for transportation. These guys were human sacrifices—but to what god? Why did I go see them? I wanted the rage to keep me going.

Valencia Street on a Friday night is an hormiguero. Suburbanites afraid of their own shadow crawling around in groups of ten. Sometimes more. One of them was standing on the corner, speaking into his little cell phone, asking for directions, looking like a character in that TV show *Lost*. It's for them the ruins are being created, the families forced out, the murals destroyed. The other night I overheard one of them ask, "What's this neighborhood called?" And her blond friend replied, "I don't know, but it used to be called the Mission."

I slid behind the counter at the Havana Social Club, the walls covered with the photos of poetas, famous and obscure, many of them dead. I ordered the specialty of the house, *ropa vieja*. Don Victor had the box booming "Chan Chan" by Compay Segundo. I'd just heard that Compay had checked out after ninety-three years of smoking cigars and that his real name was Francisco Repilado. This year my poet-friend-brother Pedro Pietri had moved to the other barrio, too. And today was the anniversary of my *comadre's* death, whom I'd known thirty years. Now there were seven more checked into the other barrio.

The dead were all around me, urging me to keep on living, to keep their memory alive.

I paid up about midnight and still had two hours to kill.

I stepped outside and there was a white SUV with its engine running at the curb. Two creeps with necks like wrestlers sat inside. The uglier one rolled out.

"You Morales?"

"Who wants to know?"

"Mike Callahan wants to speak with you."

"I'll have to check my social calendar."

The creep said nothing but opened the back door for me. He was maybe six-feet-four, three hundred pounds with his suit on.

"I was going that way myself," I said.

I named the muscle-head driving *Huey*, and the ugly one *Dewey*. I knew Callahan, Irish Mafioso, head of a renegade builder's association; he moved around City Hall like a man with a lot of muscle behind him, which he had. Muscle, but not the brains. The thugs he'd sent to pick me up were quiet the whole time they drove. Except when Dewey farted and Huey said to him in all seriousness, "God bless you."

We drove to another part of the city. We were in that industrial area near the freeway. A long time ago, we used to play in these empty lots as kids; riding our bikes down Pot Hill, as we called it. Now, giant commercial buildings, all chrome and steel, were in the throes of birth. We went under the freeway, took a side road behind a construction site, and parked. We were in Mission Creek. I knew this place well, another childhood hangout where we'd gone swimming. Now, fancy houseboats were docked with an occasional massive catamaran or sailboat. The pier creaked like backpacks on Guatemalan Indians. Nearby, the freeway roared with traffic headed downtown, and I could see the skyline of the city like a giant neon dollar sign flashing billions.

Huey indicated I should go to dock number 10. It was a fancy houseboat, but without any class; in fact, it was painted whorehouse-red. Callahan was alone in the back room, the air thick with scotch I could smell from where I was standing, ten feet away. He indicated I should sit down.

"You smoke cigars, Morales?" He was about to light a big stogie with a gold-plated lighter.

"I hate cigars and Republicans."

"Don't be so uptight. We're relaxing . . . follow me?"

"Okay. So we're relaxing . . ."

"You know what these are?" He handled the stogie like a

pool stick in his big hamlike hands. "*Cohibas*. The finest of all Cuban cigars." He let that sink in for a moment. "And—illegal in this country."

"What's it to do with me?"

"Hey—I'm trying to show you that we all have our imperfections. But you're not listening. So what you pissed off about? Go on, spit it out."

"I cited the Apache Hotel."

"The one that burned?"

"But never for a fire hazard. Because none existed."

"I don't follow you."

"It burned on my watch. I'm the fall guy, and I don't want to be the fall guy."

"If that's what you're worried about . . ."

"You don't get it. Seven people died. I don't think it was an accident."

"It was a fleabag hotel. Everything changes."

"It's against city ordinance to tear down low-income housing."

He shrugged. "Someone was careless . . . that's the way to look at it. It won't be an inconvenience to you."

The way they looked at people as an inconvenience made me sick.

"Why don't you explain it to the seven stiffs in the morgue?"

He rose from his chair, cigar swinging in his mouth. "Take a look outside. There, out the window." He gestured to the lit-up skyline, the buildings glowing, sucking up whole dinosaur herds of energy, perched like toxic towers spewing radiation. "That there, let me tell you, is the highway to the future. You can ride it or you can, well . . . be run over by it." He laughed at his own joke, his jowls trembling with fat.

To me it seemed like a nightmare. "I intend to find the source of the Apache Hotel fire . . . in case you're wondering."

His eyes turned gray like those of a great white shark. "You have a loft that's not warranted. It's, ah, how shall I say? . . . a safety hazard."

"I have the permits."

"That's a matter of opinion. One of your neighbors might file a complaint. Claim it was illegal."

"We're all illegal here. Except the Rammaytush. And we killed them all."

"So you're a do-gooder, is that it? Look, Morales, nobody appreciates a smart-ass like you stirring up trouble for other people. Let me remind you—with your illegal loft, your shit smells just as bad. So think about it."

He went back to his cigar and I knew the interview was over.

Huey was waiting for me.

"That's all right," I said. "I'll walk."

At 2:00 in the morning, Sixteenth and Valencia is a current of human electricity, AC-DC all the way. I'd caught the last show at Esta Noche, the tranny club on Sixteenth. I wanted to see "La Jessica," advertised as one of the most beautiful illusionists in the world. The soft spotlight in the smoky club made her indeed seem beautiful, at least the illusion of beauty, draped in sequins and sheer glittering gowns that gave the impression she had a body like Angelina Jolie.

But at 3 a.m., when La Jessica was out of costume, she looked like any other vato hanging around waiting to pick up a drunk to bounce or bed for money.

She smoked a filtered cigarette and the apple in her throat bobbed with each phrase.

"Mira, I was standing right here, *mismito*. And the flames just shot up at once, dios mio, it was like a *woosh*, licking up the side of the building."

"The flames didn't come from inside of the hotel?"

"No, chulo, from the outside."

"What else you see?"

"Two men running away."

"You sure of that?"

"I'm sure they were men. As sure as I'm La Jessica."

That was proof enough for me. That and the burned-out hulk of the building across the street, standing like some pre-Hispanic ruins in the jungles of the city.

"These men, could you identify them?"

"Maybe."

"Maybe? Did you get a good look at them!"

"Well, they had big muscles, they were you know, muy fuerte."

I thanked La Jessica and went home to Alabama Street. I would have to return the next day, sift around for evidence. I walked into my loft without turning on the lights, without checking for messages, just letting the glow from the street fill up the emptiness inside me.

I had nightmares, screams and bodies burning, people leaping from buildings to their deaths. I woke up early and reached for my file. There wasn't much there—kinda like Oakland. The notes on my three visits, including the one Wednesday, three days ago, described the minor stuff I'd cited. The listed owner was F. *Delgado, et al*. The address was on South Van Ness, one of those old Victorian mansions in the heart of the barrio. It was on my way to the ruins of the Apache Hotel, so I dropped by on the off chance F. Delgado might be around. I didn't know what I was going to say, but I can look someone in the eye and right away tell you if they're up to something evil.

In another century, the nineteenth to be exact, South Van Ness was millionaire's row. Victorian mansions lined the blocks, ornate ladies in wood lace and wrought-iron curlicues. Even old man Spreckles, the sugar baron, had his digs here, on the corner of Twenty-first and South Van Ness. Later, after the earthquake, most of these notable scoundrels parked their hats on Snob Hill, leaving the best weather to us poor folks in the flats.

At the door of one of these mansions from that era, all restored and pretty, I knocked once, twice, nothing happened. After I leaned on the doorbell, a maid finally cracked the door, but kept the security chain latched.

"Look lady," I said, "I carry no stinking badges."

She blinked once but didn't budge. So I repeated: "No soy policía. Busco a un tal F. Delgado."

"No Delgado here . . . this Señora Lopez house."

Then a voice came from behind the door: "What's the matter, Carmen?"

A woman I had not seen in years and thought I would never see again stepped out. Sofia Nido was beautiful as ever. And seeing her brought back that summer in Puerto Escondido, so long ago it seemed like another lifetime. Ten years ago we had spent a torrid summer together, dancing on tables, making love on the beach, living like the apocalypse was here. But to her it had been a fling; she had come back to her fiancé, and we had gone our separate ways. I had never gotten over her and had drunk many a beer in her memory.

"Roberto—what are you doing here?"

"I guess I could ask you the same thing. I came to see a certain F. Delgado. Ring a bell?"

"Can't say that it does. But maybe my aunt might know. I'm her attorney."

"Any chance I can talk to her?"

"What's this about Roberto? Are you with the police? That is so unbecoming of you."

"It's a bit complicated."

"I see. My aunt is very ill. She really can't see anyone right now."

"Maybe when she feels better?"

"Perhaps. But Roberto, excuse me, I'm late for an appointment. Can I give you a ride anywhere?"

"I'm on my way to Sixteenth and Valencia." It didn't faze her, which was a good sign. I wanted to see how she'd react to the fire scene. But I forgot all about that watching her drive, her profile like an Indian goddess, her eyes big and dark.

She drove a red roadster and moved smoothly into traffic headed down South Van Ness. "I hardly recognize you, Roberto. So, you're with the city?"

"Department of Building Inspection. I go after deadbeat landlords who don't provide habitable housing. And with rents so high, many landlords are ripping someone off. Especially in this barrio. And you—why such short hair?"

"I'm between men. Short hair makes me feel in control."

"Yes . . . and my girlfriend just left me."

"You mean you've lost your touch with women?"

"It happened when I lost you."

She looked at me hard and I wished I hadn't said that.

But she didn't slap me, so I changed the subject and took a crazy chance. "Say, there's a band playing tonight from Nueva York. You feel like maybe . . . ?"

She shook her head, in exasperation, I guess. "I can't

believe you asked me that. I guess I'm an idiot, but sure, why not? Haven't gone salsa dancing in years."

I bailed out at Sixteenth and Valencia. "Pick me up around 9:00, in front of the old can factory. Later, alligator."

I watched her drive away. My emotions were so tangled up knowing how dangerous it was to be involved with her. And yet, that was exactly what I was doing. It wasn't till later that I realized I'd forgotten to check her reaction to the smoldering remains of the Apache Hotel.

A chain-link fence surrounded the area. Two cops were guarding the site, looking bored. A big tractor inside the gates was headed for the burned-out walls. I whipped out my camera, but one of them jumped in my face.

"Morales—what the hell you want?"

"Photos of the site."

"For your scrapbook? Get outta here."

Then the tractor slammed into the building and knocked down half a wall.

"Hey, you're destroying evidence. Who gave you the right?"

"You're a day late. The D.A. has all the photos they need."

"How can he, if you're knocking down the building?"

"Are you doubting me, you flat-assed Mexican?"

"Look, Johnson, I know you hate my guts, but seven people died here. I want to know why."

"I bet you do. It's on your ass, isn't it? You're the one that overlooked the fire hazards. This is on your conscience. If liberals like you have a conscience."

"Have it your way, pin-head."

The word was already out on the street, the frame was on. The bulldozer had knocked down the side of the building facing Valencia Street, but the fire had started on the Sixteenth Street side. I stood in front of Esta Noche and shot a whole roll, clearly showing the charred side of the building where La Jessica claimed to have first seen the flames. It was obvious to me what had happened. Something had caught on fire in the passageway, right underneath the fire escape. The bastards could have spared the fire escape, giving those inside a chance to get out.

I saw Johnson on his walkie-talkie, so I made myself scarce.

I wanted to meet with La Jessica again. Show her the photos and have her mark where she saw the two men and the flames.

I went back to the bar on Twenty-fourth Street to drink a beer with the yellow dot on the neck and mull over the file. I went over my notes and wrote down everything that had happened. It was clear someone was trying to bury this thing, and quick. It was too messy for them. But who were they? Who was F. Delgado and the *et al*? They owned the Apache Hotel; their business address, the one on South Van Ness. I figured Sofia's aunt was part of the *et al*, and Sofia was lying to protect her. Or, Sofia didn't know anything about it—but as her aunt's attorney, that seemed far-fetched. As a precaution, I left my files, my notes, and my camera with Miss Mary, and just kept the empty briefcase.

I walked home to my loft in the deep gloom of evening. I was so absorbed that when I reached the gate that leads to the courtyard, I wasn't expecting the reception I got. Someone grabbed me from behind in a chokehold. I rammed an elbow in his gut to break free, but then something that felt like a brick smashed me across the face. *BLAM!* Stars, fireworks, nothing quite describes the sensation. I dropped my briefcase and stumbled to one knee, my head spinning. Far away, I heard thunder, then a flash of lightning that seemed like a spotlight; but it was a pair of headlights shining on me. I couldn't believe it was Sofia in her red roadster.

She helped me to my feet and I felt like a lame idiot. "I got jumped. They stole my briefcase."

"Come on. Tell me in the car."

As she slid behind the wheel, I couldn't help but notice how her dress fell between her legs in ruffles. *Not now*, I said to myself—*don't think about it now*. It started raining before she even pulled away from the curb.

The view from Sofia's apartment took in the wet palm trees of Dolores Park and the fragmented lights of downtown. The pale halo of a street lamp floated in a black puddle. Rain fell over the rooftops of the city and on the rows of Canary Island palms lining Dolores Street; the rain washed down the buildings and the cars, sloshed into the gutters. I stood looking out her window, haunted by that infinite nothing that is everything, that certain emptiness of every nameless second.

She switched on the light in the kitchen and the ochre-colored walls were covered with portraits of Frida Kahlo, the patron saint of pain. One had Frida with a necklace of thorns scratching out drops of blood. Another wall had Frida as the goddess Tlazoteotl, a bed sheet over her face, her legs spread, a dead baby half out her womb. And above the stove—Frida as a deer pierced by arrows. The kitchen looked like a monument to suffering, an apocalyptic gallery of pain and despair. I had a flash of Amanda—she liked to be tied to the bed— and shook it out of my head.

I rested on the living room couch while Sofia wiped the blood from my brow, and I told her what had happened. "I didn't get a chance to see their faces."

"The neighborhood is going downhill, getting so violent."

"I don't think it was that."

"Then . . . ?"

"Not sure yet."

"Men always bring trouble. That's for sure."

"I'll leave whenever you want."

She tried to light a cigarette, but her hand was trembling. I took the cigarette from her mouth, lit it, and put it back between her lips.

"Did the blood make you nervous . . . ?"

She shook her head. She was blushing now. I could see how needy she was, how desperate for something, I didn't know what. She turned on the radio. A jazz trumpet drifted arabesque notes that swirled around her cigarette smoke.

It hurt me to know a woman like her, so beautiful and so alone. I wanted to tell her she was beautiful, that I could be a good man to her. Instead, I told her the only thing I had ever kept secret from everyone, even myself. I told her so I could be close to her. In the candlelit room, the words seemed to take centuries to unfold. "I killed a man once." The silence was so thick it cut. "I was seventeen; it was a gang fight. I hit this vato with a pipe and kept hitting him till he was dead. *Muerto. Muertecito.*"

I could sense my words running through her like a hand-forged stiletto. Her eyes narrowed and she saw me for what I was, with all my flaws.

"Why do you tell me this?"

"I don't know; it bothers me sometimes. I never told that to anyone, ever. Can you be trusted?"

"Yes."

"Then that's why I told you."

Outside, the rain had eased and the faint rush of tires

reached me. After Amanda had jammed, I answered a few personal ads and hooked up with women who didn't care what I did to them as long as they felt something. Some scenes were sick, and when I started enjoying them I decided to quit. Since then I've more or less lived the social life of a monk.

I touched her shoulder and she turned to me. A pale vein in her throat pulsed wildly. She brushed her hair back from her face. The lamp light seemed like a witness to the crime. I reached to turn it off but she stopped my hand.

"I want to see your face."

"Wait." I held her hand. "So what's this about? Who is this Señora Lopez at whose house I met you . . . ?"

"Are you still thinking about that?"

"I don't know. It's all related. I can feel it."

"Everything is related, Roberto. After the last time I saw you . . ."

"The summer of Puerto Escondido. You were with Raymond then."

"We were engaged but we never married. It was my last year in law school. A weekend trip to Napa. We'd both over-done it. An accident along the side of the road. It was my fault Raymond was killed . . ."

"I'm sorry to hear that."

"You don't understand." Her voice was soft and pained in the shadows. ". . . If I trust you?"

"I'd do anything for you." I said that, but I didn't know for sure. In fact, I wasn't sure if I wanted her to go on. She didn't give me a choice.

"I'm being blackmailed. The classic story. A young, gullible, ambitious young woman sells her soul to stay out of jail. I was scared after the accident. In shock, really, for months. Clearly it was manslaughter, but she quietly cleaned it up. She has that sort of power. So instead of being a jail-bird, I'm an accomplice. She provides the fronts and I cook the contracts, make sure everything is legal."

"Your aunt?"

"Who else? Señora Lopez, when she comes out of the shadows. Oh, Roberto, I want out of her grip. It's like some-one is violating you every day. It never goes away." She took a long drag from the cigarette. "And she's Felicia Delgado. It's one of her pseudonyms. Her full name is Aura Felicia Delgado Lopez. I think she ordered the fire."

"Why do you say that?"

"It's an insurance scam. Plus, with the hotel down they can build something new, make a few extra million."

"I wouldn't bet on that. A fire like that will cause them lots of trouble, there'll be an investigation, and . . ."

"Who do you think you're dealing with?" Her eyes flashed with righteous anger. "My aunt is rich and powerful and evil. She has the mayor in one pocket and the chief of police, the next mayor, in the other. If you stand up to these people, if you mess with their plans, they'll hurt you. They'll hurt you bad, Roberto. There is lots and lots of money involved. The Builders Association? Their whole blueprint for the Mission?"

"I'm familiar with Callahan. I just had a relaxing chat with him last night. But look, it's a matter of conscience. You have to decide for yourself."

She was quiet for a minute. "I have the documents in my office."

"And I have a witness. Tomorrow I'll speak with La Jessica. Maybe all of us together can bring this *vieja* Lopez down."

She shook her head like she wasn't too convinced and lit

a row of votive candles on the mantlepiece. They lit up an eighteenth-century painting of *La Anima en Purgatorio*, the fires licking up her chained wrists. I couldn't help but comment.

"What's up with the burning lady?"

"Oh that? A gift from my aunt."

"You mean . . . ?"

"The very same . . ."

"Why do you keep it?"

"Purgatory. Where souls have their sins cleansed by fire."

She stared at me with those dark eyes that will stay with me a lifetime. Then she said something that changed my life.

"Did you love me then, Roberto? In Puerto Escondido?"

"I love you now."

"Would you really do anything for me?"

"Double back-flips on a high wire."

"I'm not joking," she hissed. Without breaking her lock on my eyes, she held the burning tip of the cigarette an inch from my skin. When I didn't pull back, she pressed the hot ember against my forearm and held it there for a quick second, just long enough to leave a red ring tinged with ashes. I didn't flinch.

"Do I pass the test?"

She sat back and took another hit of the cig. "Why don't we just leave? Turn over the evidence and get out of Dodge?"

"I don't have it on me. The photos are stashed on Twenty-fourth Street. I'm thinking that's what those thugs were after. And who would follow up on it? No, I have to stay."

"Then I'll stay with you."

I flicked away the ashes on my forearm and grabbed her hair. I knew this scene. Knew it very well.

"Now it's my turn, *cariño*."

I pulled her to me, and she was on fire. Our mouths kissed, hot and angry.

I finally let her up for air and she said, "I've never kissed a man with a mustache before."

Then I unzipped her dress, stopping my hand on the curve of her *nalgas*. She turned to face me and shrugged the top half of her dress off her body. She was naked above the waist, without a bra; a string of candlelight danced around her breasts, small as pomegranates. I placed one in my mouth and sucked the juice from it. We undressed each other before rolling onto the rug, the two of us twined together like serpents. I slipped my hand under her back and flipped her on her stomach, pulled her hair, and hissed in her ear—"I want you to be my *puta*."

She didn't hesitate in answering—"Make me do what you want."

And I did, over and over, all night long.

I woke up alone in her bed Sunday morning. I didn't have time to relish the night before. There was a note on the pillow and the morning paper. *Call me on my pager*—and her name scrawled in red. The headlines sent a shock through me: La Jessica had been found stabbed to death in her hotel room. The paper speculated that a john, angry at having discovered Jesus instead of Jessica under the wig, had taken out his rage with a twelve-inch blade. Somehow I was left unconvinced. La Jessica had struck me as flamboyant, a tease, maybe even a tramp, but not a whore.

I still had to wait for Miss Mary to open, so I went to the little hotel down the alley from Esta Noche. That's where La Jessica had lived, and I wanted to hear what the street had to say about her murder. There was an altar set up in the hallway and her friends were there, weeping and sobbing. They all knew me and they spoke frankly.

"Those *cabrones*, why did they have to kill her?"

"Because she saw too much. Everyone knows that building was torched. And that's why they killed her, Mr. Morales."

"She went home alone that night. Pobrecita. So there wasn't any john, that's just lies. *Puras mentiras.*"

I left the mourners to their grief and called Sofia but could only leave a message on her voice mail. "I turned up some interesting info. Meet me where I told you. Bring the documents."

I waited in a café till about 6 p.m., Miss Mary's opening time, and then hurried over to Twenty-fourth Street. As soon as I reached the bar I sensed something wrong. The door was ajar and the lights were off. I stepped in and Johnson and another cop were waiting for me. The place had been turned upside down and Miss Mary was in a corner, frightened to death.

"Lady's going to lose her license. Receiving stolen city property." Johnson had my camera and briefcase under his arm.

"The camera's my personal property, Johnson. You don't know what you're talking about."

"It's evidence now. Her license is gone. We're merely retrieving what belongs to the city. Boy, Morales, did you ever fuck up."

They left. I had just cost Miss Mary her gig. And I had a pretty good idea who had turned the cops on me.

I practically ran over to Dolores Street, and when I saw her roadster parked outside, I took the steps two at a time. I caught Sofia on her way out, with a little attaché case, all ready to go. I snapped. "You double-crossed me." SMACK! I bitch-slapped her hard as I could. She stood her ground.

"You think I would do that?"

"You did." And I let her have it again. SMACK!

"Then why did I bring you this?"

It was the señora's little black book, listing all the contributions, legal and illegal, to the mayor, the D.A., and the chief of police.

It wrenched my heart that I'd been so cruel to Sofia. "I'm sorry."

"Let's leave now, Roberto. Please, before anything else happens."

"Wait. There's something I don't understand. If you didn't tell them about Miss Mary . . . how did they know my files were there?"

I led her back inside and started throwing the cushions around, tearing out the stuffings. Nothing. She thought I was crazy. What was I looking for? The lamp? Yes. I tore off the shade. Nothing. Then I saw the painting, the gift from the aunt, *La Anima en Purgatorio.* And there it was in the frame. The wire I was looking for. I ripped it out.

"Your aunt bugged you. She heard everything we said last night. What do you think of that?"

"You mean *everything?* What a degenerate."

"We don't have a minute to lose."

"What should I pack?"

"Nothing but your lipstick. Leave no clues behind."

Night had already fallen as I took the roadster out Dolores Street and onto the freeway headed south. I knew a little cove out by Half Moon Bay, where a friend of mine ran a motel by the beach. We could hang there for a few days, gauge the fallout, figure out our next move. I took Highway

1 to Pacifica and right away we came upon fog. It was rolling in quick and thick, and as I started heading up Devil's Slide I could tell the ride over would be dangerous.

I put the fog lights on and looked in the rearview. Coming up behind me was a white SUV. I nudged the roadster and it rose like a bird. I lost them momentarily, but at the same time I couldn't risk hitting eighty or ninety on those twisting curves, blinded as I was by the fog. Headlights were creeping up again—it was the SUV and it didn't look like it wanted to pass me. It wanted to ram me.

We were going uphill but would soon come to a peak that flattened out before dropping again. With the SUV a few feet from my ass, I revved the roadster and flicked on the bright lights, creating a mirror effect, then snapped them off and did a hard brake onto the narrow right shoulder. The SUV had a choice: Pull over and smash into me, sending us both over the three hundred foot cliffs, or pass me by. It passed me by, but not without a burst from an Uzi. *Ra-ta-ta-ta-ta!*

"Duck!" I shouted, and pushed Sofia down. The windshield broke into spider webs, the impact of each round making the roadster tremble. Then I heard the SUV fade. I stayed down till several more cars had passed. In case there were more than one of them.

That's when I saw the blood. Sofia had been hit. The bullet had missed me but had found her right shoulder. She was bleeding in a bad way and her eyes were frightened.

"I'm going to get some help," I said through clenched teeth. I pulled out her little cell phone but there was no signal in this area, cut off by the sheer mountains. With my coat, I made her as comfortable as I could, but I knew she was in terrible danger.

I found a flare in her trunk and sparked it. Since the roadster was close to the cliff's edge, I walked back toward the oncoming traffic so I could be seen in the fog and drizzle. Then headlights approached, a car with two guys bullshitting instead of paying attention. And me out there swinging the flare at them in the middle of the road. Till at the last second, the driver saw me and swerved suddenly to the right, onto the shoulder; lost control, bounced fifty feet, and smashed broadside into the roadster. *KABONG!*

The rest of my life I'll remember that sound, metal against metal, heart against heart.

I ran to the edge and watched as the two cars went over the cliff, tumbling down together and bursting into a single fireball whose heat singed my face. I screamed, I howled, I don't know, it made no difference. I knew at that instant this would be the deciding moment of my life; the before and after that would scar whatever life I'd lived and whatever I have left of life now.

I started walking away. I didn't want to be around when the ambulance arrived. Didn't want to be anywhere near the scene. If someone figured that I'd been killed in the crash, so much the better. One day, those who did this would pay, and I wanted to be around to see it.

When I got back to La Mission I discovered my loft had been torched. A warning, I guess. The spray-painted graffiti, DIE YUPPY SCUM, didn't fool me. They would have liked a little wet work on me that night.

Obviously, I never went back to the job. I've stayed under the radar ever since. Gave up that whole other life to stay alive. But the circle scar on my forearm from Sofia's cigarette reminds me every day of the dead I carry.

The newspapers and the Fox Channel all played it another way. A niece of a prominent Mission district real estate matron killed in a tragic car accident with another vehicle on Devil's Slide. I guess the bullet holes on the roadster were caused by metal-eating termites.

Once the dust settled, so to speak, the Planning Commission approved the permit for the new building at Sixteenth and Valencia, and Callahan's outfit built it. That's what you see there now—that chrome shit glass monstrosity. But for a long time there was just a big gaping hole at the intersection, like when you have a tooth pulled. Arson as a cause for the fire at the Apache Hotel was in fact never investigated by the D.A.'s office, the Department of Building Inspections, or anyone else. But the word in the neighborhood is that the new building is haunted by the *animas*, the souls of the seven people who died that night.

And the big woman, Felicia Delgado, the one who profited from the insurance scam? She didn't fall. Just too many layers between the hirelings and herself. And too many people owed her. But she's old and sick, and her greedy heart can't last much longer, miserable with her bloody money . . . so it doesn't really matter. One way or the other, sooner or later, she'll get her ticket to the other barrio.

PART III

Neo-Noir

GENESIS TO REVELATION
BY PETER PLATE
Market Street

It was ninety-six degrees on Market Street the day before Christmas. Holiday decorations graced the windows of the check-cashing store at the corner. Weary junkies in goose-down parkas congregated around the Stevenson Alley methadone clinic. Teenaged hookers wearing rhinestone-trimmed spandex capris and halter tops loitered at the Donut Star coffee shop. Pigeons drunk on heatstroke were falling off the telephone lines.

In the 1940s, Market Street had been a constellation of movie houses. Blue-collar entertainment seekers flocked there for the vibrant nightlife. Nowadays the avenue was a forest of abandoned buildings. Under the old Strand Theater's marquee, homeless men and women had turned a fleet of shopping carts, suitcases, clothes, tarps, and strips of cardboard into a shanty fort.

A pale, unshaven twenty-four-year-old Slatts Calhoun, three days out of San Quentin Prison, stood near a pay phone at Seventh and Market. He was dressed in a Santa Claus suit stolen from a Salvation Army volunteer. To go along with the costume he had on a fake white beard and an ill-fitting stocking hat. A tarnished blue .357 Smith and Wesson revolver was stuck in his belt.

He reconnoitered the medical marijuana club up the street and cursed. Ever since weed became legal in the city, pot stores were everywhere. They were a venereal disease. It was impossible to get away from them. This one was squeezed in between a dentist's office and a sandwich shop. It had a brick façade and a single barred window emblazoned with graffiti. A bored surveillance camera was mounted above the security gate. The place resembled a police station.

Slatts limped over to the dope shop, stopped in front of the steel gate, posed for the camera, and buzzed the doorbell. Nothing happened. He waited a second and repeated the procedure. A thin Mexican hippie in paisley surfer shorts and a vintage Clash T-shirt came out to inspect him. "Hey, Santa, how the fuck you doing today?"

Keeping the gun concealed, Slatts said what came to mind. His first forty-eight hours out of the penitentiary had been a hassle. One night he slept in a garbage dumpster behind the new federal building. Then he got into a fight with a hooker and was jacked by her pimps. He didn't even have enough money to take the bus to the welfare office. As a bonus, the beard was making his skin itch. "I'm cool, homeboy. What's up with you?"

"The same bullshit. You got your ID for me?"

To gain entry into the club, a customer needed a physician-approved Department of Health identification card. Private doctors were handing them out at two hundred dollars a pop. Slatts didn't have a card, no place to live, or any food in his belly. He rasped, "Yeah, well, there's a problem, see? Can I come in and talk to you about it?"

The pot worker's smile faded into a cynical tic. He was prematurely aged by the needs of dope fiends. "Hell, no."

"C'mon, vato, give me a break."

"I can't do that, dude. It's against the law. You've got to have a card to get in."

"Listen to me, asshole, I want some fucking weed."

"Too bad, home slice. I don't give a shit."

"Fuck you, man. It's goddamn Christmas, you know what I'm saying?"

Slatts lost his cool in a delicious surge of adrenaline. It was time to introduce his revolver into the conversation. It would help move the dialogue along. He poked the gun's three-inch barrel through the gate's latticework and hooked the dealer in the nose with it. Reaching in, he yanked the lad forward. Then he groped the kid's shorts for the keys, found them, and unlocked the door.

Santa Claus was in the house.

Brandishing the heater, Slatts moseyed into the retail room. His mouth watered with excitement. This was better than the lottery. Cheap reefer was hard to find in the street. Plus, it was usually low-grade crap. Another worker, a lithe, tanned blond girl in patched denim overalls and Birkenstock sandals, approached him. Her oval face was a delicate flower, open and questioning. She asked, "May I assist you?"

Slatts produced a smile tempered by several missing teeth. "No, honey, Santa can help himself."

The store's damp walls were festooned with sepia-tinted concert posters from Bill Graham Productions. Two customers, an aged queen and a black guy with one leg, were getting loaded on a ratty divan. Ambient techno pulsed in the background. Slatts heard someone move and turned to confront a beefy longhair in tai chi clothes. It was the security guard.

"Hey, what are you doing with that gun?" The longhair had the attitude of a public rest room. "We're peaceful here."

"Shut the fuck up. Nobody talks to Santa Claus like that."

"Kiss my ass, motherfucker. I'm calling the police."

The cops loathed the pot clubs and didn't give a hoot if they were robbed. Slatts ignored the threat and examined the merchandise. The weed was in pastel-colored ceramic bowls on a counter top. The menu was listed on a chalkboard. Medium-quality green, mostly Oakland hydroponic, ran forty-five an eighth, same as in the streets. Stronger grades, like Canadian indica, were sixty for three and a half grams. Mexican syndicate pot was cheaper, but wasn't worth smoking. The stuff was first cousin to napalm. Mendocino boutique bud was four hundred and fifty dollars an ounce. Turdlike pot cookies were five bucks apiece. Slatts didn't see what was so medicinal about the prices.

Leaning over the counter, he probed the cash register. To his delight, a wad of twenties and fifties danced into view. He pocketed the cash and backpedaled out of the store into the ebb and flow of Market Street.

Columns of gold-colored sunshine haloed the roadbed at Seventh and Market. Panhandlers, speed freaks, and pickpockets milled at Carl's Jr. Bike messengers dodged cars and delivery trucks. A Muni bus seething with passengers lumbered toward Van Ness Avenue. Whirlwinds of leaves and empty nickel bags flirted in the gutter.

The heat outside was nauseating. The pavement was hotter than a match head. Making Slatts dizzy and ready to puke. Which was how he liked things. The gun dangled from his hand, muzzle pointed at the sidewalk. His beard and costume were drenched in perspiration. A homeless wino decked out in a garbage-bag poncho hailed him from an insurance office doorway. "Yo, Santa, yo, yo. Can you help me, brother man?"

Slatts flicked a sideways glance at the bum and smelled trouble. His voice was colder than his mother's pussy. "What the fuck do you want? I'm in a hurry."

"My partner is sick."

A white boy in an army jacket was slumped against the door frame. His tattered sneakers had holes in the soles. His cracked green eyes were intent on a faraway paradise. He didn't appear to be breathing. Slatts frowned and hissed, "What the hell is wrong with him?"

"I don't know," the wino said. "We were just sitting here and shit, and the pecker keeled over. Maybe he had a heart attack or something."

"You call an ambulance?"

"Yeah, it's on the way."

Nobody was coming out of the pot club. Slatts sighed. That was a good sign. He'd hate to have to shoot someone right now. Dropping to his knees, he placed a finger on the unconscious man's neck, feeling for a pulse. He didn't find it. Instead, an electrical charge zinged into his fingertip. He knew what it meant and jerked his hand away. Christ on a crutch. What a drag. The bastard had died on him. The electricity was his spirit, what was left of it. "It's nothing," he shrugged. "He's just resting."

"What should I do?"

"Keep waiting for the ambulance."

"Is he sick?"

All the interrogatives vexed Slatts. Like he wasn't tense enough already. "No, he isn't. So relax, okay?"

He hardly got the words out of his mouth when a black-and-white police van oozed to the curb. Three husky officers in midnight-blue combat overalls jumped out. Their scuffed riot helmets gleamed in the torpid sunlight. Slatts couldn't believe it. This was bad karma. The dope dealers had snitched on him. That wasn't kosher. It was disgusting. The wimps couldn't handle their own business. There was no honor among thieves.

Hefting the .357, he pressed the trigger. A lonely bullet flowered out of the revolver's barrel and sped forward in slow motion, burying itself in the pot store's window. The music of breaking glass rippled in the flat air. The cops scrambled for cover and returned the fire. A slug ricocheted off the pavement, catching Slatts in the wrist. The .357 went sailing into the bushes.

It was funny how things never worked out. Like he was falling through a mirror into a black hole. The cops dashed to the doorway, pushed aside the dead man, knocked Slatts onto his stomach, and handcuffed him in a pool of blood. An officer kneeled on the ex-con's legs and brayed, "Merry Christmas, baby," then shot him in the ear.

The blast loosened Slatts's bowels. A jet of warm shit trickled down his thigh. A pillar of unsavory steam rose from the Santa Claus suit. The ground was painted red and pink with bits of his earlobe. The pigeons on the phone lines shrieked with indignation. A moody cloud passed over the sun.

The gods of crime were not smiling on Market Street that afternoon.

DECEPTION OF THE THRUSH

BY WILL CHRISTOPHER BAER

The Castro

J ude opened her hand and the panic of blind horses seized her. The washcloth was marked with a bloody knot of red in the shape of a gouged eye. She sat naked on the edge of the bathtub and tried not to hyperventilate. She pushed from her head the uneasy idea that her blood on a white washcloth was the single source of primary color in a strange bathroom yawning black and white around her. She stared at the locked door across from her and counted to ten, and when the horses died away she took stock of her situation.

She was seventeen and it was a school night.

Her left arm was so bruised it looked like it belonged to someone else, the bruise running so deep she was sure she could smell it, as if the blood pooling in there had gone bad. Her legs were cold to the touch, her thighs rippled with goose bumps, and when she pulled her hands from her knees they left marks slow to fade. She wondered if it were true that fingerprints could be dusted from human skin, and made a mental note to look that up.

She had locked herself in this bathroom two minutes ago, not counting a few too rapid heartbeats, and by her estimation she could safely remain another four minutes more. Any longer and he might get suspicious and come to the door to ask in a soft threatening voice if she were all right, and she couldn't bear that. She needed to exit the bathroom without prompting.

Already it had taken her twenty-two seconds to pee, another thirty-six seconds to run water over the washcloth and bathe herself as instructed, and it sickened her to realize she had been staring at the knot of blood for nearly a minute, trying to organize her thoughts into any linear progression that made sense. She had a sudden overwhelming sense that had there been a window in the room, she would be scrambling with torn fingers for the roof, regardless of the screaming black vertigo in her stomach that said she was tucked away in a corner apartment on the nineteenth floor of a downtown tower with windows that were sealed shut and a sleepy doorman out front, where no one would ever think to look for her.

Nonsense.

The voice in her head was her father's, and she nearly glanced over her shoulder.

Animal urges, her father said.

Her father had often told her that some predators were comfortable only on familiar ground, and never strayed far from home. These were not the most skilled hunters, he said, but they were unpredictable, and dangerous as hell, because they hunted on impulse. Others followed the prey, shadowing the herd. But the smartest hunters roamed far from home, where the rabbits would not recognize them. He always laughed, telling her this. And he was right. It was more likely that she was still somewhere in the Castro, where she had been pretending to shop earlier in the day, because the man who waited for her on the other side of the bathroom door seemed the sort of predator who hunted near to home. And it didn't matter. She had to first get outside, then worry about where she was.

The bathtub was long and wide as a coffin.

Jude fought off the childish urge to crawl into the tub and shut her eyes and tell herself that if she couldn't see him, he would not see her. Her memory was splintered, so much so that she saw the landscape inside her head in the thousand and one reflections of a shattered mirror in the sun, and she had no idea how to sort the images, the sprawl of information. The first shall be last, she thought, and was briefly comforted to seize on something familiar, though she couldn't remember if that line came from the Book of Matthew or Mark, or what it meant.

The sisters would not be proud if they saw her now, she thought.

Jude was in her senior year at Sacred Heart, a private Catholic school for girls that was so old the halls smelled of raw earth and, according to her father, boasted tuition fees that could only be described as obscene. Jude had once calculated that, taking into account her spotty attendance record and history of expulsions, her education to this point had cost her father in the neighborhood of a thousand dollars per day. She was forever restless and bored to the edge of psychosis by the curriculum, and she had a tendency to get into fights. Two years ago, in a dispute over a borrowed jacket, she had hit a Brazilian girl named Noel much harder than she meant to, damaging the other girl's larynx. Only the fact that Noel threw the first punch had spared her father an expensive legal headache, but to be safe Jude had taught herself to be invisible ever after, to move through crowds of people without a ripple. She wished that a thousand people had noticed her today, but they hadn't. Because she had been practicing. She had been a shadow, her hand slipping in and out of their pockets.

She would regret being invisible if she woke up in a box tomorrow.

Jude lived with her parents in Pacific Heights, sixteen blocks from school. And though she left the house promptly at 7:00 each morning, she so rarely arrived at Sacred Heart it was unlikely that anyone would notice if she disappeared for a week. She still wore the uniform most days, because it prevented her mother from getting agitated. When her mother became agitated she tended to go overboard with her medication, a too generous cocktail of amphetamines and painkillers that pushed her into episodes of such extreme paranoia that she once nailed shut the door to her bedroom and burrowed into her walk-in closet with a hammer and small axe and tried to dig a tunnel to a neighboring room that existed only in her head.

Jude wore the uniform because it soothed her mother.

The sight of Jude in the familiar outfit gave her mother the temporary illusion that the inside of her head was in order. And because her mother was a near bottomless source of guilt for her, Jude wore the uniform.

But she would have worn it anyway, because it was so practical.

By the time she entered middle school, Jude had discovered that if she moved her hips just so and let the tiny blue-and-black skirt flutter at her thighs, the men and boys in her immediate vicinity became hushed, compliant. She crossed her legs and sneezed and the man nearest her trembled and handed her a tissue. She crouched on the sidewalk to dig through her purse with her knees pressed together and hair blowing in her mouth and her butt just touching the heels of her black Mary Janes, and even the stoned hustlers and street artists stopped to ask if she were lost. She twisted her white shirttails into a bow that exposed an inch of bare belly and a college boy would buy her a coffee. And if she tugged her socks up over her knees, cab drivers offered her cigarettes and took her wherever she wanted to go.

She would give anything to be in the back of a yellow cab right now. She would ask the driver to take her to the one place that felt like church to her, the ruined baths just up the hill from Ocean Beach. She would close her eyes as they sailed through the sunset, and thank God she wasn't on her feet, because she was so sore, so raw inside. The soft pink hidden flesh in what her mother perversely referred to as her *special prize* felt as if it had been flayed with a chunk of glass.

Again she looked at the washcloth, the smear of red against white.

This was not menstrual blood.

Jude had the altered internal clock of a long-distance runner and rarely had a regular period. She ran nearly seventy miles per week through the rain and mist in the Presidio, and trained with weights and worked out every other day with a tae-kwon-do master class, and this regimen combined with birth control pills and the amphetamines she skimmed from her mother's cave had pretty much cancelled her cycle. This was the blood of trauma, and now it struck her that she would never forgive herself if she left even a drop of it behind.

Jude pushed herself up from the edge of the tub and crossed unsteadily to the sink, where she turned on the hot water. She rinsed the cloth with liquid soap and scrubbed it with her fingernails until the water ran clear, trying not to glance at herself in the mirror, though not because she disliked her body.

The opposite, rather.

She was aware that most of the girls her age, the ones she ever bothered to talk to, suffered intense body-image issues and eating disorders that haunted and consumed them. Jude had never known what to say to them, though she had tried to feel what they did, thinking it would be a useful emotion or psychosis to access. Her own body was a product of conditioning that Bruce Lee would not have scoffed at, and the genetic gift of a Thai mother and Irish father speckled with Israeli blood. She was long and lean with fine yellow skin and small breasts with large brown nipples that paralyzed men and boys without fail. Her stomach was flat and hard, though not yet the washboard she coveted. Thousands upon thousands of pushups had brought out the shadow of definition in her arms and shoulders, and although she considered her ass to be on the smallish side, it was tight and curved and fit perfectly in the palm of the pool boy's hand, or so it had when she was twelve and shaped like a wisp of smoke and he was still unafraid to touch and pet and wrestle with her.

The pool boy was four years older than Jude, but small. He was just a whisper of bone and muscle. He had a pretty pink mouth and green eyes, long blond hair and the perfect sharp ears of an elf, and he seemed always to be tan, regardless of season. He was sweet and playful and Jude supposed she had suffered a temporary crush on him, and she used to hang around the pool in her red racing bikini and watch him while he worked. And sometimes she was able to lure him into the pool when he was done cleaning it, provided her father was not around. The pool boy was afraid of him, and rightly so. Jude's father had terrorized him often. But when her father was away on business, Jude and the pool boy wrestled and chased each other underwater, skin bright and flashing, and sometimes the pool boy retreated from her with a bulge in his swimsuit and a look on his face that she found fascinating. Jude was strong even at twelve. And one day, without meaning to, she held the pool boy under the surface too long, she held him down until he struggled and freaked out, and only when he scratched open her arms with his fingernails did she realize what she was doing. When she released him, the pool boy withdrew from her, pale and gasping, and ever after had avoided her.

Jude knew why she had done it.

Her father had thrown her into the swimming pool when she was five and not yet a confident swimmer. He stood watching from the pool's edge as she panicked and thrashed and finally went under. Her father had allowed her to drown, then revived her, and she was never sure if his intention was to teach her not to fear death or to remind her that he had the power of life over her. She had decided that it was both of these, and became wary of him. But aside from offering advice with math and soccer, her father left her alone until she was nine, when he drove her up the coast and made her hike through the woods in the dark until they reached the beach. He armed her with a knife and compass, then abandoned her there, telling her she had one hour to find her way back to the highway. He promised her that if it took her longer than an hour, the car would be gone.

And not long after her tenth birthday, he began teaching her to be a pickpocket. He allowed her to practice on him for exactly one day, in the relatively intimate space of his closet at home, before taking her for a ride on BART during the afternoon commute so she could try the real thing. He selected easy targets for her at first, then ever more challenging ones. The worst of these had been a burly, sweating man in a rumpled suit and tie with needle-bright eyes, who scratched at his arms and kept swiveling his head left and right. Jude had failed to come away with even a pack of cigarettes, but neither had she been caught with her hand in the twitching man's pocket. And when she returned with empty hands to her father's side, he gave a shiver of a smile and touched her face with one hand, and though she couldn't yet verbalize it, she comprehended that he was telling her to choose her targets with care, that the burly man had been a junkie day trader of some kind, chemically altered and paranoid and therefore not a suitable mark.

Her father was pathologically reserved with praise and affection. He touched her so rarely that Jude could number on one hand the times he had kissed her forehead or patted her knee. But when he wanted her to understand something important, he touched her face. He took her cheek and jaw in the hollow of his hand and the world fell away. So when she was thirteen, Jude had been surprised and curious to discover that the sudden proximity of her body made him uncomfortable. She first assumed this had to do with her resemblance to her mother and the natural spin of echoes and nostalgia that entailed, then she read Nabokov and understood.

And since then she watched herself through her father's eyes.

Jude looked into the mirror through his eyes and tried to grasp what it was about the curves and angles of her body that made her father uneasy. She stared at herself through the pool boy's eyes, through the eyes of men she passed on the street, studying her body for its strengths and weaknesses and trying to see precisely what these men saw, to access the rush of desire they felt when confronted with her flesh. She tried to conjure their secret, violent thoughts, staring at herself until she grew dizzy and her image wavered and she thought she might fall into the mirror and drown.

But this was not the mirror in her bedroom, where it was

safe to sink below the surface. She could not afford the chance that the image of herself naked and bruised in a strange bathroom would make her feel small, because when her four minutes expired she was going to kill the man in the next room, and she was afraid that if she felt small she might be unable to. Jude had to kill him not because he had so ravaged her with his hands and mouth that she bled, not because he had abruptly shoved her from the bed and told her in a soft cold voice that her pussy tasted of rot and to go wash herself, but because she knew he wasn't finished with her.

Drugged and disoriented though she had been, she had noticed the pink cell phone on the mantle, the rollerblades in the corner. The red cowboy boots on an end table, the baseball glove in a box, the tiny black T-shirt nailed to a wall. These were trophies of past kills. And there was a faint smell in his kitchen that made her think of maggots.

She calculated that two minutes remained.

The washcloth was white again. Jude turned away from the sink and gathered the remains of her clothes, the plaid skirt and thin white tank top. She had chosen not to wear a bra today, a move she made breezily in the rosy light of her room a half day ago that now felt like a lifetime stuck in amber, and while she remembered being satisfied this morning by how snugly the cotton tank fit her, she was less thrilled about it now. And as she pulled it over her head, she could smell him. She shrugged this away and concentrated on the task of fastening her skirt at her hips. She only wished she were wearing her shoes. Jude felt more vulnerable when barefoot, which she supposed qualified as irony. She hazily remembered kicking off her shoes upon entering the apartment, and knew she had done so because she was aware that men preferred that she appear small. A vaguely defined business associate of her father's had seized her and lifted her up once, without warning, in their kitchen when she was fifteen, his hands gripping her firmly and touching more of her chest than she liked, and he remarked that it was like holding a doll. His face had flushed brightly as he released her.

She had left her damp socks on the radiator by the window, and by then she had been truly dizzy, the room warped and turned sideways, the building tipping on an axis that wasn't there. Jude remembered the man had removed her underwear without her help, and without asking if she minded, after she sat down, or collapsed, in a leather arm-chair. He had pulled the pale pink boy shorts over her thighs and down with care, not ripping them as she expected but handling them as if they were a captured butterfly he was reluctant to crush. She thought it inaccurate to call that moment a memory because she had seen it happen from a faraway overhead view, as if she had briefly vacated her body and climbed to higher, safer ground. She had no idea what he had done with her shorts after that, whether he had stuffed them into his pocket for luck, or calmly eaten them.

Jude had seen but not touched her white shirt on her way to the bathroom, crushed at the base of a wall like rejected flowers, splashed with blood and one sleeve torn from the body. The blood had puzzled her, because she didn't remember spilling it. But now she saw another wide-angle bird's eye shot of herself on top of him, rising and falling in slow motion and underwater light, and remotely she was aware that he was inside her and she saw that her nose was bleeding, not because he hit her but because some critical piece of wiring had come unmoored in her head. The disconnected wiring and foreign, splintered memories that came with it were the result of an unknown drug in a cup of hot chocolate that she had lifted to her own lips. These broken memories and disturbing out-of-body images of herself were never intended for her, because the hot chocolate had not been hers. She had taken the cup in place of another, and as she drank she heard her father's voice telling her to be unafraid.

Jude had spent the day shopping, or hunting, in the Castro. The easiest pockets to pick were those belonging to tourists, and the easiest of these were the gay men in their fifties who came to San Francisco on vacation from Atlanta or Denver or anywhere that the same-sex culture was kept hidden from view. These men tended to be soft and unaware, with pink faces and eyes milky behind rose lenses. They were either very thin or shaped like pears and wore khakis or jeans that were too tight with new sneakers, and their T-shirts were always tucked in. They traveled in couples, one of them carrying a city guide, the other an umbrella, and sometimes they wore those Velcro travel wallets around their necks. They walked around the Castro with eyes so wide they might have been exploring the far side of the moon, and they were such easy targets that Jude generally made a game of it, following them for a block or two after she hit them and then slipping up to put their wallet or sunglasses back into their pockets. It had been raining today, but warm, and the streets smelled of urine.

And even though animal and human prey alike tended to huddle together and become more wary of others in adverse weather, and their pockets that much harder to reach, Jude had grown bored of her shadow practice and resolved to work the financial district the next day, where the men deserved to have their pockets emptied and where it was infinitely more difficult for her to be a shadow, especially wearing the uniform. And she had by now come to understand that her father had not taught her to lift wallets as a means of supplementing her allowance. The object had been to learn stealth.

Jude saw the man as she entered a coffeehouse called Last Drop, a long narrow place that had a cheerful plastic art deco–meets–*The Jetsons* feel, with Japanese nudes on the walls and funky details like barbers' chairs. He was in a booth with two white girls. Jude scanned them as she crossed the room. The man had blond hair that just fell in his eyes. Long nose and a crescent scar on one cheek, narrow red mouth. He was thin and looked British, but that might have been a false echo of his clothes, a mint-green teddy boy suit and boots with pointed toes. His hands flashed silver as he made a point and Jude saw he wore rings on both thumbs. He sat in the corner with his back against the wall. He kept his hands and mouth at a safe distance that posed no threat, then lunged forward as he said something that made the girls laugh, and Jude saw his thin lips pull back for a heartbeat to show his teeth, sharp and white, as he palmed and disappeared the plastic envelope and flicked the crystals into the blond girl's coffee cup while she laughed and wiped tears from her eyes.

The girls didn't seem to notice.

Jude marked them in the space of one breath as nineteen or twenty, second-year students at the art institute or New College, who lived in a flat with three other people in the Haight. They had come to California after boarding schools in New Hampshire, where they had gone into the city on weekends and listened to Velvet Underground in their rooms and done a lot of ecstasy and experimented with being bisexual, though both were straight. The one with the tainted cup was pale and blond with fragile cheekbones and black eye shadow, Sylvia Plath gone to heroin. The other was rich-girl punk with a pierced nose and shocked blue hair, and they were both perfect targets for the man because they thought of themselves as streetwise but were not. They were rabbits in dark woods, and one or both of them would be hanging upside down with her skin removed before morning.

Animal urges, she thought. She would be the thrush.

Jude made her decision with little deliberation. The man offended and fascinated her to equal degrees. That the college girls might be spared a blood-soaked washcloth was an afterthought. Jude was bored, and she thought she stood a better chance against him than they did. And she thought it would be interesting to try.

She went to the bar and ordered a cappuccino, walking with the shadow of a limp. He wouldn't bite if she was too obvious. It was only a sore ankle, and not even wrapped. She twisted it playing soccer, she fell off her skateboard. She paid for her drink and dropped a dollar in the tip jar for luck, watching the table out of the corner of her eye to be sure Sylvia didn't drink from her tainted cup. Jude hummed, waiting for her drink. When it arrived, she turned and limped across the café, her eyes skating left and right as if looking for just the right table. She held the cup to her face and blew on it with her lips curved into a bow, circling close to the table. Her one fear was that he had already made his choice, and would be reluctant to deviate.

But she could give him a push.

Jude stopped a dozen feet from their table, and winced. She crouched on one knee, her cup balanced precariously, and while she examined the sore ankle, her skirt slipped up her thigh just enough to flash the pink boy shorts.

Two heartbeats and he called her over to the table, insisting she join them. The college girls regarded her warily, then the one with shocked blue hair shrugged and slid over, and Jude sat down among them. She looked across the table at Sylvia and gave her a shy, nervous nod of hello, then turned her attention to the man. Jude looked first into the crosshairs of his eyes, and she had to admit the man had something, a hypnotic pull. The eyes were a shattering blue, the ghost of a smile in the crow's feet on either side, and now she saw his left eye was graced with a splash of brown and he was staring at her without blinking, staring into her as if he could stop her breath. Jude realized what he was doing, and she made a note of it. He was staring at her as if he loved her, as if he had lost her in the wilderness and found her again, and she imagined he had left a few bodies behind him in shreds with that look. Jude blushed and smiled, and sent Sylvia a telepathic smoke signal saying that if she ever laid eyes on her again, her soul would belong not to her, but to Jude.

Because she had made him deviate.

Jude took two sips from her cup and placed it on the table next to Sylvia's, so that they sat side by side like twins. Then it was a simple matter of redirecting the girls' attention with a trivia question about Elvis, one that had no answer, and reaching accidentally for Sylvia's cup, and drinking from it, and making sure that he noticed. And now she stood in his bathroom, seven hours later, exhausted and marking time by counting her heartbeats and wondering what she could use as a weapon, while blood ran down her thigh.

Jude was bleeding, still.

Maybe it was her period, she thought. Her cycle was altered, and almost nonexistent, but it did come around eventually. She was starting to hope that it was menstrual, after all, because the other choice was that he had ruptured something inside her and she was hemorrhaging.

Jude reckoned she had ninety seconds to act.

There was nothing under the sink. Nothing in the narrow closet but a few ratty towels and spare toilet paper. The medicine cabinet contained only the most essential toiletries. Mouthwash and hair gel, a blue toothbrush in a cup, a sliver of soap. She reached for the mouthwash, rinsed her mouth and spat. She looked left and right, listening to her heartbeat. This building was constructed in the 1920s, before there was plastic. The towel racks were slim pieces of iron bolted to the wall. She gave one a tug and imagined she could pry it loose without tools if she were locked in here for a week. The toilet tank lid was an option, but it wasn't very graceful, and she would need to surprise him. Jude turned to the tub and scanned the wall above it, her thoughts circling the concept of surprise.

She no longer knew where he was. He had been in bed when he dismissed her to the bathroom but now might be anywhere in the dark apartment, and the moment she walked out of the bathroom the advantage was his. Jude would call him to her, when she was ready. She would bring him into her nest. And now her eyes settled on a small round button set in the wall above the bathtub, and she was glad for the days before plastic, because that button was the end of a clothesline that she prayed was not rotten. She climbed into the tub and plucked the button from the wall, and the blood surged in her, for the clothesline was a sturdy nylon cord six feet long.

Jude pulled the line until she reached its end. She took a breath and gathered herself, then yanked it from the wall in a single violent twisting motion that burned both hands and showered her with plaster and dust. He might have heard that button pop, she knew. She needed to be faster than him, she needed to act at the speed of animal reflex. Jude prayed for her thoughts to race ahead of her body and let go of her. She would need to draw his eye when she called him to the bathroom, so without agonizing over it she changed her mind about leaving her blood behind. Jude pressed one hand to her bloody thigh, then slapped the wall, and now her handprint was the only source of primary color in the room. And as she stepped from the tub she heard in a back corner of her head not her father's voice but her own, rattling off a list of everything in the apartment that she had touched, that would need to be scoured for prints. Jude looked down and saw that she had already twisted the cord around one fist, and now the other. She coiled them around and around until she had an appropriate garrote, then unlocked the door and pulled it open with great care, as if she were peeling back the sky and expected a fury of angels to flood through the narrowest crack.

She called his name.

Jude called for help and stepped aside, and waited for him to come.

WEIGHT LESS THAN SHADOW

BY JIM NISBET

Golden Gate Bridge

> *Horatio: . . . think of it!*
> *The very place puts toys of desperation*
> *Without more motive, into every brain*
> *That looks so many fathoms to the sea*
> *And hears it roar beneath.*
> —William Shakespeare, *Hamlet*, I, iv

B aby and I were walking the bridge the day it happened. We had a beautiful afternoon—clear, breezy, plenty of sunshine, bright blue sky—though the traffic thrashed loudly. It was a Sunday, so we'd expected traffic, and all the pedestrians didn't seem unusual either, at first. Knots of them congregated here and there at the rail, mostly on the western or panoramic side of the bridge, the side that faces the ocean. They pointed and hollered at the sights and at each other, as most strollers on the bridge were wont to do; for the bridge is an exhilarating place, with its soaring height and the constant bluster of salt wind and automobiles.

What was unusual—so it seemed to us—was the range of interest or concern common to every face we were able to see, and, as we looked over the rail, the really extraordinary number of people already caught in the forcefield beyond. Among the latter many were yelling and gesturing at the people still on the sidewalk, as if daring or enticing them to jump. Some were squirming around, practicing their back-strokes midair, and some lay still, in a meditative pose, or cupped a roach against the wind, suspended and quiet.

I should diverge a bit here, as some of you may not be from around these parts. A little over one year ago this particular bridge was a favorite place to go if you were looking to kill yourself. Its central span arcs 254 feet above the sea's level, at which, because the bridge crosses the entrance to the bay at its most narrow stretch, there is always a powerful current, sometimes as swift as six knots, going one way or another with the tides through this natural venturi. Many bodies of jumpers were never recovered and, up until last year, out of some 700 recorded attempts, only twelve people had sur-vived the plunge.

Upon jumping—whether west, toward the ocean and into the sunset, or east, toward the bay and into a view that commands half the city—if a body didn't have a heart attack on the way down, the impact at sea level was almost certain to do the job; failing these, one could be swept out to sea and drowned, or die of exposure in the chill waters. Sharks, too, were known to lurk below. In any case, a suicide attempt from this bridge virtually contracted to be beautiful and deadly, a sure combination.

For some time there had been editorial campaigns, meetings, and committees about doing something to prevent these precipitous exits, but the taxpayer's good money being short, and other problems more pressing within the munici-pality, and the lack of any effective preventive technique hobbled and bogged down any real progress toward airbrushing this stain off the reputation of the city's most famous land-

JIM NISBET // 219

mark. The thrust of such prophylactic thinking some took to imply that any time Joe Blow so much as looked at the bridge, all other factors being equal, he must be nearly overwhelmed by an urge to kill himself. These people would have it that such malefic urges must occasionally torque at the breast of the most established citizen, as well as the least, and that such urges are an actual furniture of good citizenship. This eccentric opinion, unexpectedly amplified, moved those sensitive organs of citizenship, the newspapers, to reflect noisily that the citizen might prefer to be insured against the possible or at least facile realization of his own self-destructive impulses.

Further speculation indicated that this beleaguered citizen, if not himself untimely deceased, may have lost to the bridge someone intrinsic to his social circle, a person handy, for example, at conversation, which, though thought to be excruciatingly dull while its perpetrator was quick among his peers, has since by virtue of its absence been noticed as somehow essential to the arrangement of chairs at dinner. Such a host and the citizenry in general might like to be relieved of this sort of nuisance by the knowledge that when they do happen to rest their eyes upon the bridge, they will see it hung all bristling vigilant with nets, pincers, inner tubes, inflatable vests, lifeguards, searchlights, hooks, pikes, concertina wire, rubber sacks, plastic shields, helipads, etc., in order that unseasonable defection might be reasonably inhibited.

Personal motivation manifested itself only in the most ephemeral ways, as speculation printed and broadcast, editorials, political gambits, research-grant hustles, and social-maze theory, until two entirely unrelated events rendered it simultaneously germane and academic. The first was the unfortunate suicide committed by a young woman whose senseless body, plunging from the bridge at nearly ninety miles per hour, crashed through the foredeck and hull of a small boat as it sailed out from under the looming structure. The boat sank in an appalling three minutes, and constituted a significant loss to its captain who, alone on board at the time, was rescued by a passing fishing vessel. His cargo, however, was not saved. This ironic chattel consisted of little wooden replicas of the famous bridge itself, manufactured in various sizes, by hand, in cottages up and down the coast, regularly collected and shipped by the captain to the city for distribution and sale as souvenirs. The accident set these little bridges adrift by the hundreds. Whole and in pieces, left to the whims of the sea, they littered the beaches, inlets, piers, and marinas of bay and coast for months, as to all who might come by them grim, miniature reminders of the infamous utility of the giant original. This incident provoked much discussion, of the order that something—anything—be done about the bridge's ominous potential for death.

The second incident was the perfection and commercialization of a patented gravity forcefield. Within a year of its introduction, and less than six months after the dispersion of the little wooden bridges, the city government caused to be installed a forcefield network which controlled the entire length of the bridge. Along each side of the span, this marvel extended a sort of tube of weightlessness designed to catch and hold in suspension any individual or thing that might happen into its scope, until such time as the authorities might arrive to fish out the wayward article. Though in any case an effective deterrent, the collateral notion seemed to be that a potential suicide suspended in the invisible grasp of this device would be severely embarrassed by his public display, more or less as if he'd been clapped into the stocks in the town square with a large capital "S" painted on his forehead, and thus inhibited from renewing his attempt to end his life in so public a fashion. Accordingly, in a fit of legislated avuncularity, no penalty, beyond mandatory psychiatric counsel, was proscribed for a person chagrined in this manner.

From the very first day of construction and installation until well beyond the last, pickets who represented themselves as members of the "Right to Die Coalition" conducted peaceful demonstrations on or about the bridge. Their case was that suicide is a private act, over which no entity outside the individual can exercise judgment; that one should be as responsible to one's own person in a self-destructive mode as in a constructive one; that this particular bridge was as good a site at which to perpetrate this right as any other, and, in fact, being far more effective than most, was admirably suited for it; and, furthermore, to legislate public suicide out of the public eye was merely to sweep yet another fact of life under some sort of moral rug.

The nearly daily scenes of organized protest were marred only occasionally. A young man, haranguing workmen not to aid in depriving the world of one of its most useful manmade creations, was carried away by the emotion of his appeal and made what the newspapers impatiently dubbed a *salto da fe*— a leap of faith. As might have been expected, two or three people, each apparently acting on the assumption, perhaps cherishing the hope, that he might be the last on record as having done so, flung themselves from the bridge during the final hours of construction.

In the weeks following the completion of "Project: Wait!", much detritus collected in the two fields, for they were extremely sensitive, and just as indiscreet. The trash usually found along a freeway or sidewalk now floated alongside the bridge as well; this included the obvious beer cans, muffler clamps, and hubcaps—but the devices were so effective as to disallow the whimsical escape of so much as a cigarette butt, not to mention loose stones, newspapers, condoms, and rain, so that this famous bridge with its famous forcefields became even more famous for its asteroid belts of refuse.

At first the bridge authorities, publicly announcing that they were working on the problem, quietly turned off the fields once a week in the middle of the night at maximum flood, thereby plummeting the trash into the bay and sweeping it out to sea. But environmentalists and a couple of suicides soon got wind of this rather efficient practice and forced an injunction against it. Subsequently a special cleanup crew with unique machinery and techniques was designed and put into service.

As soon as the effect on roadside detritus achieved notice, individual humans began to experimentally, then playfully, throw themselves into the forcefields and squirm around in them, gleefully avoiding the especially contrived retrieval devices that were cast after these less than hapless and not particularly despondent victims. These people made the additional discovery that one could actually "swim" a full circle—vertically, or in any other direction—like a looping airplane. Reports varied, but one likened the experience to writhing in a large volume of transparent gelatin, excepting, of course, the degree of fluidity and the magnificent view. Firsthand testimonies were duly monkeyed in the tabloids (*CREEPS DOMINATE FIELDS* was one headline I remember) with the predictable results that the authorities spent more and more time and money skimming the adventurous out of the forcefields. These policing efforts were soon overwhelmed and, finally, so popular had "getting jumped" become, everybody but the newspapers realized that, although throwing oneself with abandon off the bridge into its forcefields may be vulgar, it certainly did no one any harm. Thus it came about that on any given sunny Sunday, as the bridge teemed with automobiles full of onlookers, any number of people might be found wriggling or sunbathing along either side of the entire length of it, with a population bias on the western or "sunset" side. And the police more or less looked the other way. To have spent an hour or so "jumped" or "suspended" on Sunday afternoon became a socially acceptable pastime, especially among the young, whose avant guard jumped while drunk or stoned. Certain lengths of the span soon became popular hangouts for the besotted, while other stretches were more popular with the stoned. It became not uncommon for a jumpee to find himself floating in company with a suspended quantity of vomit, or among a slowly dispersing nebula of stems and seeds.

It was into just such a Sunday scene that Baby and I had walked.

We hadn't gotten, nor had I intended to get, into this fad yet, but the time must have seemed right to Baby. She stopped walking before we'd gotten midspan.

Hey now, that looks like fun, she said, leaning over the rail.

It was true that under ordinary circumstances Baby would try anything, during which experiments I generally held her purse. We stood there, and as I tried to decipher the consternation evident on the features of all the faces around us—after all, I was thinking, if they don't like it, why don't they just move on?—Baby tugged at my sleeve and said, C'mon, Honey, let's do it too. Let's get jumped.

Don't be ridiculous, I said. What's in it for me?

Here, asshole, she said, and handed me her purse.

I held it and watched, still wondering about the appalled yet curiously fascinated expressions up and down the sidewalk, as she lifted a long leg up and straddled the wide rail. Once astride it, she hesitated. She could have been a little scared. After all, it certainly must have looked to Baby exactly as if she were about to kill herself. It looked that way to me. There were a bunch of happy people and a lot of trash floating out there, beyond the rail, but, even so, they looked very insubstantial against all that thin air and the tiny sailboats far below. Baby glanced sideways at me, and I couldn't resist a smile, as if to say, Yeah, so? and she frowned and pouted, then stood up on the railing, defiant; and holding her nose with one hand and pointing up with the other, she executed a kind of timid hop, backwards, over the side. She fell about eight feet, decelerating all the way, then oscillated, coming back up a couple of feet, then down a few inches, up an inch. And there she hovered, as if dangled from a spring or rubber strap whose coefficient perfectly understood her mass; giggling and squirming.

Hey, she shouted, come on! It *is* fun! and she waved at me, as if she'd just run into a line of surf that looked inviting but might have been thought too cold for immersion. In spite of myself, I gave a little wave in return.

She hung there, two hundred fifty feet above the glinting ocean, but not far from a disheveled, vacant-looking fellow who, observing Baby's classy entrance, rolled, wiggled, swam, and serpentined his way over to her, where he struck up a conversation. He must have been an old hand at getting jumped. The traffic was loud enough to prevent my overhearing their remarks, but as I stood there squinting, a very excited young woman came rushing down the sidewalk with one arm crooked under a clipboard. She wore a Right to Die armband just above her left elbow, its insignia a skeleton with one raised boney fist.

A great day, she effused, stopping next to me to make a mark on her papers. We've nearly made the quota.

I excused myself to her and inquired, What quota?

Why, we've nearly gotten it, she said, and held the clipboard under my nose. I could see that its papers were covered with figures and calculations, but they were meaningless to me. One number, written in digits larger than the rest, was circled heavily in red pencil.

Gotten what? I asked. What's this seven five nine?

That's how many we need, she bubbled. Seven hundred fifty-nine. And we're only a very few short.

Oh, said I. Is this a petition?

You mean you really don't know? It's . . . well. Now that you mention it, it is a sort of petition . . . Her voice, already closely contested by the noises of wind and traffic, was suddenly lost in a great roar that went up from the crowd milling about the rail further up the sidewalk, at the center of the span. These and some of the people already suspended began to chant the numbers *seven five nine, seven five nine, seven five nine*.

My goodness, I heard the girl say. She pushed past me and pointed. He must be the one. We've done it!

Following her gaze with my own, I saw a man standing alone on the railing. He bowed deeply to the crowd beneath him, who cheered him loudly. After several fancy adieus on his part, consisting of additional bows, florid salutations performed with the hands, the blowing of kisses, and even a curtsy, I'd begun to understand, and shoved the girl with the clipboard away from the guardrail. The young man with Baby had his arm tentatively about her shoulders, and smiled as if beatified. Baby's eyes, round and tense, caught mine. As another, louder cheer went up, her eyes smiled and she laughed outright at the consternation undoubtedly blatant on my own features. A third time the crowd cheered, and the man on the rail jumped. He fell as Baby had before him, and though his oscillations were more pronounced—he went down perhaps eight or ten yards, rebounded upwards two or three yards, went down again a couple of feet—his additional weight did not destroy the forcefield. The people suspended in its grip bobbed gently, like gulls on a swell. I made my decision. Glancing up the length of the bridge as I vaulted the railing, I saw that many of the bystanders, perhaps out of premeditation, perhaps spontaneously, had come to the same conclusion as myself. As we cleared the last bit of structure, I could see that the void was full of falling bodies, enough so that as Baby and I embraced, as I looked into her eyes—those lovely, mischievous eyes that did not retreat from the gaze of my own, oh, so foreverly—my fall was hardly interrupted. Our combined mass buckled the entire field on that side of the bridge and Baby and I, and nearly eight hundred others, minus the thirteen of us, survivors predicted by the harsh statistics of experience, fell toward our deaths.

And a victory, of sorts.

FIXED

BY JON LONGHI

The Haight-Ashbury

I used to buy drugs from Satan, a dealer who called himself *Hal Satan*. He was also a poet and performance artist, and Hal Satan was his stage name. He liked his stage name so much he decided to use it all the time. Besides, he eventually did so many drugs that the lines between reality and the creations of his own imagination blurred to the point where he couldn't tell the difference between them anyway.

"I've been going to some twelve-step meetings lately," Satan said. "With all the drugs and stuff, I've been feeling kinda broken and I just wanna get myself, you know . . . fixed. A lot of these people at these meetings may not be drinking or doing coke anymore, but they still have addictions of one kind or another. A lot of guys at these meetings are addicted to porn.

"Like this one guy who couldn't stay out of peep shows. His every extra cent went to magazines. One week, he was like, 'Well, I managed to get off the porn. I haven't been to a peep show or bought a magazine in two weeks. But now I find I can't keep myself from caulking parking meters.'

"'What do you mean, *caulking parking meters?*' I asked.

"'I mean just what I said,' he replied. He was taking a caulking gun and injecting it into parking meters. And I thought, *Jesus, how much more Freudian can you get than to take a phallic 'gun' and inject white goo into a little slot?*"

"You can see it on a lot of levels," I said. "It's like, in an attempt to stay out of peep shows, he had to go around sealing up all the coin slots."

"Just the whole thing," Satan said. "Well, a couple weeks later he's at the meeting again, and he says, 'Well, I managed to stop caulking parking meters but now I'm back on the porn again.'"

Although it was commendable that he was trying to clean up his act, the twelve-step meetings never seemed to help Satan. No matter how many he went to, he still managed to stay completely strung out. In fact, he frequently found himself doing drugs before he went to one, just to get through it. Eventually, he just stopped going to them altogether.

"I realized that twelve-step meetings had become just another addiction for me," Satan explained. "And since I'm trying to clean up my act and get rid of my addictions, I had to start somewhere."

Hal Satan was the only dealer I ever had who would deliver. A half hour, well, actually, forty-five minutes, sometimes an hour, after you called him, he'd bring by a quarter of generic green bud on his scooter. Just like Domino's Pizza.

Satan started out just dealing weed but he quickly diversified into all sorts of hard drugs. He wanted to be all things to all people. "Shouldn't Satan provide all vices?" he reasoned. But keeping up with such a complex line of distributed substances made his already crazy and chaotic life utterly schizophrenic. The biggest problem was that he couldn't stop sampling what he sold. "What's the fun of being Satan if you can't also enjoy the vices you hand out?" he once told me. The problem, though, with that line of reasoning is that Satan very rapidly became a total junkie. In fact, every time I scored drugs from him at his armpit of an apartment, I couldn't help feeling that he was a perfect illustration of what it must be like to be strung out in Hell.

Satan's apartment was right down from the corner of Haight and Ashbury. The address, appropriately enough, was 666 Ashbury, and this had been a contributing factor to him adopting the name *Satan*.

"Who else but Satan could live at 666?" he explained. It was hard to argue with that.

The apartment was a garbage dump where a few humans coexisted with the vermin. The kitchen sink was long lost in a fossilized stack of dirty pots. A huge heap of beer bottles, greasy pizza boxes, and other trash took over an entire corner of the living room.

"We clean the place once every three years, whether it needs it or not," one of the roommates once joked. In the bathroom, the toilet seat had stuck to the bowl due to a gluey growth of mold and it could no longer be put up. Sometimes when you got a bag from Satan you had to flick roaches and other little bugs out of your buds.

Nobody had washed the dishes at 666 in a long time. Very few of them were even still in the kitchen. Instead, they were on various surfaces around the living and bedrooms. Most of them looked like petri plates covered with medical experiments of mold and rotten food. The few plates that were still clean were used to consume drugs. The plates used to snort coke and speed off of, for example, were always licked spotlessly clean. Every piece of furniture in that apartment was so cratered with cigarette and burn holes that it looked like a map of the moon. The carpet was a grayish-black desert of ash. When you walked across it, little clouds of dust and ash rose up around your feet. There wasn't a square foot of the place that wasn't littered with garbage. The roaches in the place outnumbered the roommates ten million to four. In fact, me and some of Satan's other customers took to calling his place *The Roach Motel*.

Sometimes the Roach Motel looked like a scene out of *Night of the Living Dead.* Satan would get these drug zombies who'd camp out on his couch for two to three days at a time, not saying anything, only moving enough to keep themselves saturated with whatever drug they were consuming. There was a cannibalistic efficiency to their behavior. It was as if their humanity and personalities had been stripped away and all that remained was the mechanical core of their hungers and needs. What had once been human was now just a consuming machine, an engine designed only for eating. These zombie robots would stay with Satan until all the fuel he provided them was gone, and then they would shamble off into the night in search of more of the drugs that justified their existence.

"Lots of the people I know are just a combination of feeding and needing," Satan once commented.

One of the roommates was a guy named Rick. His father had been a congressman or something and had died about a year before and left Rick a lot of money. Rick took this new-found fortune and promptly became a coke addict. His dealer was Fat Carlo, a massive lump of a man who must have weighed close to four hundred pounds. Every now and then, Carlo would wear a white suit, and it seemed like all he'd ever done was sell the white powders. After a couple months, Carlo got along so well with Rick that he moved in with him. Can you imagine the parasitic relationship that ensued? Over the course of the next year, the dealer performed a steady, almost magical wealth transferal which kept half the household buried in snow. Hearts about to explode. We used to say about Rick: "I don't know what happened. One day my dad dies, and then I wake up a year later flat broke and without a nose."

Everyone from that household basically went insane. Take the case of the Human Waste. One night I was at a party and Satan was telling me about how squalid things were getting.

"It's so crowded and filthy," Satan said. "The sickest person there is just a loser. *Joey*'s his name. We call him the *Human Waste*. I can honestly say, I've never seen a more pathetic person in my life. This guy's thirty-five years old, grossly overweight, and fairly Neanderthal in appearance."

"Like someone moving backwards through evolution?" I asked.

"Believe me," Hal said, "he's already devolved. In fact, there are already primates higher than him on the genetic ladder. This guy walks around with six inches of butt crack showing out the back of his jeans at all times."

"He carries around a regulation-length ruler to make sure that six inches of butt crack is constantly maintained," I added. "If his pants start to hike up on him, he measures the butt crack and pulls them back down."

"Every afternoon, Joey the Human Waste comes home with a case of Rolling Rock, and by the end of the evening he has polished the whole thing off by himself," Satan continued. "He may give away one or two, but every day he drinks at least twenty or thirty beers. I did that a couple times in high school, but we're talking a thirty-five-year-old man here. And that happens seven days a week.

"It's not like he needs to relieve the stress from his job, because he's unemployed. For a couple years there, he was working in the family business, but Joey was such a fuck-up that eventually not even his family could put up with him and ended up giving him the axe. Now he just gets by on unemployment, food stamps, and the checks his parents still write him.

"On top of that, he never bathes. I've only seen him shower once or twice in the three years I've lived there. Every night when I walk into the apartment, he's plopped there on the couch, stinking the place up like a homeless person or a dead dog. Whenever anyone tells him he smells like a fresh turd, Joey just pretends he's not listening.

"Back when he was still working, it got so bad that one day his grandmother called our apartment. 'Can you get Joey to take a shower?' she asked us. 'He's really beginning to offend people down at the shop because he smells so bad.' And this from his own grandmother!

"But the most pathetic scene with Joey happened one night when everyone in the apartment was partying in the living room, which is his sole environment. Joey was shit-faced drunk as usual, and suddenly he gets up in front of everybody and says he has an announcement to make. Then he breaks down crying and admits right there in front of everyone that he's never had sex before. Not once in all his thirty-five years on the planet. Never even been in love. I don't think anyone's even touched him except his mother."

"Jesus," I said. "Somebody shared too much. Somebody committed an over-share."

"Maybe if he'd ever been laid," Satan speculated, "he'd only feel the need to drink ten or fifteen beers a day instead of twenty or thirty."

Hal Satan was the token troublemaker of the poetry scene. He caused a disruption at every reading he went to. That was his shtick. Hal took off his clothes, let off fireworks, bit other poets, anything he could do to interrupt things. At 666 Ashbury, Hal threw some outrageous parties with like ten bands, three to four hundred people, and marathon poetry readings. He used to let me do readings and throw together rock bands that performed at these things. I remember one night this band I was in played, and while we were setting up, Hal Satan came into the room with a bag of black beauties as big as my head and started handing them out. Hal must have downed a dozen of the things. He was always getting into epic trouble. He seemed to feel some kind of suicidal need to live up to his name. His crimes were many. And they were legendary. Like take the following, for example:

The local poetry readings are peopled by a number of eccentric personalities and even stranger acts. This one reading I went to at the Chameleon bar provides a good case in point. It was there that Dan Faller debuted his latest conceptual piece: "Interpretive Dance with Axe." It was a long parody of modern dance routines, which incorporated an actual industrial-sized lumberjack axe. Of course, Dan was drunk as a skunk when he performed it and many audience members gasped in real fear as he precariously swung the deadly device right in front of them. Sam Silent, who was MCing the reading, was tempted to give Dan the hook, but in the end his support for the First Amendment won out over public safety. Besides, he wasn't really in the mood to piss off a drunk guy with a big axe. All the same, when the owner of the bar heard about the incident the next day, she made a new policy that said all axes have to be checked at the door.

Dan Faller wrote and read stream-of-consciousness experimental poetry that he sometimes made up on the spot when he was standing on stage. He was also notorious for having introductory monologues that were longer than his actual poems. He frequently did back-flips on stage, usually while under the influence of large amounts of alcohol. I always hoped I wasn't there the day he snapped his neck. Dan had a voracious appetite for drugs that often steered toward the hard ones. One Saturday night at a party at 666 Ashbury, I saw him drop a hit and a half of acid and snort a quarter gram of speed at 2 a.m.

After his axe dance, Dan met up with Hal Satan, one of his partners in crime. Hal was already three sheets to the wind, and the two of them proceeded to get even drunker. They ended up closing the bar.

Hal decided to give Dan a ride home. They went out to Hal's monstrous white Cadillac and revved up the engine. Then Dan made a dare with Hal, knowing that Hal couldn't resist a dare, the more stupid and reckless the better. It was about forty blocks to Dan's house and Dan ended up driving. For most of the ride he went about eighty miles an hour and ignored the traffic lights. Hal rode on the hood. He was naked and swinging the axe around for the whole ride like some drunken Asgardian lumberjack. By some obscene miracle, Hal made it all the way to Dan's house without falling off and breaking his neck. Where's a cop when you need one? They were probably handing out tickets for minor traffic offenses while this naked madman on a white Cadillac drove right past them.

Hal Satan once told me this lost-weekend story about him and Fat Carlo:

"We used to play this game called 'blacks and whites'," Satan said. "It was where all weekend he'd freebase coke and I'd smoke black tar. Well, this game of blacks and whites had started around 3:00 Friday afternoon and now it was about 3:00 Sunday morning. The steep back slope of Saturday night. Everything was soft and fuzzy, but in a good way, and me and Fat Carlo were walking through the Mission around Twenty-fourth and Bartlett, right in the heart of gang country, but we didn't give a fuck because this was our town.

"Well, we're just walking down the street when this little punk starts running us a bunch of lip. And we're like, 'Fuck you! Fuck off! Don't give us any shit.' We're old-school barrio. So we think nothing of it and just keep walking.

"A couple blocks down I notice that something just isn't right. I had felt no pain for almost thirty-six hours, but now something had disturbed the fluid in my junky amniotic sac. I can't tell what's wrong with it, but my shoulder just feels like shit. Carlo finally checks it and there's blood all over the back of my leather jacket. Turns out, I've been shot!

"Now, I don't want to go to the hospital because that could lead to certain, ah, legal problems. So Carlo shows me all the finer points of digging a bullet out of your shoulder with a pair of needle-nose pliers. After that, he patches up the wound in a way that will kind of disguise the fact that it's a bullet hole. Then me and him go to the emergency room with some phony story about how I fell down in the kitchen or something."

I remember running into Satan at yet another party in the Haight. He was telling me about how things had gotten dramatically worse at 666.

"My three other roommates are just smoking crack all the time now. Like the other night, I came home from work and there were all these low-rent crack dealers, like the ones you see selling on the street at Sixteenth and Mission, hanging out in my room, sitting on my bed. My roommate Rick smokes rock all the time, and so does this couple, Ed and Julie, who have the other bedroom. Sometimes I can hear Ed and Julie in there scheming all night long. Plotting these weird crimes for hours. Sometimes they even talk about robbing me, even though I have nothing of value left.

"We were all going to get a warehouse space together, but I'm not so sure anymore. 'Cause I found out that these people have had a problem with coke before. In fact, that's why they're out here in San Francisco. Evidently, my roommates burned some coke dealers back in Michigan and are on the run from them. And I mean burned them for like big bucks. We're talking ruthless dudes, the kind who would kill them if they ever caught up with them."

"No good," I told him. "Some night these dudes in ski masks with AK-47s are going to kick in your front door and shoot everybody down." I pointed my finger at his forehead like I had a gun in my hand and pulled the invisible trigger. "They'll end up killing you just because you're a witness."

"That's what I'm afraid of," Hal said squeamishly. "I mean, these people are into some really shady stuff. Like the couple makes their living fucking over johns in the Tenderloin. Julie does a little whoring every now and then. But she usually doesn't actually have sex with the guys. Most of the time she gets them to give her the money first and just runs away with it. Her boyfriend Ed runs interference for her. He either slows the john down, or if need be, beats the crap out of the trick and steals his wallet. I mean, I liked these people at first, but they've turned out to be real criminals.

"Julie also gets money from a string of sugar daddies. Well, most of it comes from this one sorry-ass old guy who owns a chain of dry cleaners. He picked her up one night in the Tenderloin but he didn't want to fuck her. The old guy just wanted to befriend her. Julie was real happy to have a new friend, and over the months she's bilked him for thousands of dollars. Sometimes he gives her as much as fifty dollars a day for spending money. And he's not the only one. Like last week, some other old guy gave Julie a Cadillac El Dorado. It's too weird. I mean, this is how her and her boyfriend have been paying their rent.

"But now they're into crack. I already put everything I have of value into a storage locker. All I keep at 666 is a change of clothes and a couple of books, 'cause my roommates are really out there. Completely paranoid. I'm not allowed to answer the phone in my own house anymore, because they're afraid it might be those coke dealers tracking them down.

"And my roommate Rick has adopted all these weird projects. The other night he took all the doorknobs in the apartment apart with a screwdriver and then put them back together again."

The more strung out on drugs Hal Satan got, the more out there his poetry and performance-art pieces became. Everything he did in public grew increasingly confrontational and assaultive. He seemed to be committed to discovering the ultimate act of bad taste. Satan systematically attended and scandalized every poetry reading and open mike in the upper and lower Haight with the obsessive thoroughness of a psychopath hunting down every name he had randomly picked out of the phone book.

His performances were legendary debacles. One time Satan did a reading at the Holy Grounds Café in the lower Haight. He read a snuff porn poem called, "Manifesto: Why I Have the Moral Right to Rape Whoever I Choose." Even in a place as liberal as San Francisco you aren't going to find an audience where a piece like that goes over as anything but a Hiroshima-sized bomb. While he was screaming the poem above the boos and jeers of the audience, Satan stripped off all his clothes and proceeded to burn off his pubic hair with a Bic lighter. By the time all his man-fuzz had gone up in smoke, the room was filled with a miasmal cloud whose vapors were so foul it sent the entire audience staggering into the street, weeping and vomiting.

Dan Faller and Hal Satan used to go on drug binges that included crack, acid, and heroin, all in the same evening. The two had known each other for years, and when they were high, Dan and Hal were like brothers.

Well, one evening, Dan, Hal, and Sam Silent were drinking down in the lower Haight. It got toward closing time and Sam called it a night, saying he had a day job to go to the next morning. Faller and Satan sat there in the last-call haze, zoning out.

Then Hal turned to Dan and said, "Well, let's go. Let's go party."

"You can't be serious," Dan said.

"Yeah, I am. It'll be just like old times," Satan said. "Let's go."

They went down to the projects, scored some crack, and went back to Hal's apartment and smoked it. Then they went and got some more. And then some more. By 5 a.m., they had smoked a hundred and fifty dollars' worth.

"Let's go get some more," Satan said impatiently.

Dan was lying on the couch.

"No way, man," he said. "It's late. I'm fucked up. There's no way we're going to get any higher. I don't want any more. You can go if you want, but I'm not leaving this couch."

So Hal got up and left.

He came back about forty-five minutes later. Faller noticed he was covered in blood.

"Goddamn it, the motherfuckers stabbed me!" Hal Satan screamed out.

Somebody had knifed him in a bad crack deal. But Hal had still managed to score the goods. They had stabbed him, but he got away with his drugs and money.

Dan and Hal tried to stop the bleeding by applying direct pressure and holding rags on the wound, but the blood just kept gushing.

"This bleeding isn't stopping, we've got to get you to a hospital," Dan said.

"Okay," Satan agreed. "But let's smoke some more crack before we go."

So they smoke some more crack, which of course just makes Hal Satan's heart beat much faster, pumping the blood through his veins, and the wound just starts spraying blood. Red jets are squirting out all over the living room. It looks like a scene from *Life of Brian*, some kind of gory Monty Python skit. By the time they get to the hospital, there's blood all over the inside of Dan Faller's truck.

Satan doesn't have health insurance, so the only place to take him is General Hospital. General is like a cattle pen of urban horror. In a fetid waiting room reeking of feces and urine, skeletal patients huddle, wasted by illness and drug overdoses, along with bleeding homeless people and the victims of gang shootings. The place looks like a Red Cross triage tent from the Vietnam War. The nurse at the front desk is like, "Oh, you have to go over there and wait for three or four hours because you've only lost a hand, and this gentleman over here, who has lost his whole head, has been sitting here for an hour and a half before you arrived."

By the time Satan's sewn up and they get out of there, it's like 10 or 11 in the morning. The sun is up and shining, stinging their eyes, as Dan gives Hal a ride home in his truck. The blood stains all over the upholstery are already turning brown.

"Well, don't take me home yet," Hal says. "Here, pull over at the Safeway."

"Why?" Dan asks as he turns into the parking lot.

"So I can go by the money machine and take out more money to score more crack with," Satan says.

Two years later, Dan Faller told me what finally happened to Satan. Dan kept in touch with Satan all through his long decline, till almost the bitter end. Other details he managed to cobble together from a motley assortment of street connections, junkies, and local dealers. No one knows exactly what happened but it probably went down something like this:

Evidently, Satan's trajectory remained relentlessly downward. Over time, his various species of addiction had consolidated themselves into one overly gigantic monkey: heroin. It was the apex predator of the whole wild kingdom of drugs. Black tar took over Satan's body and soul to a degree that put all the previous controlled substances to shame. Pretty soon smack was more important to him than oxygen or food. This was a town of burned bridges for him—no friends left, no doors opened to Satan. Homeless again, he got by on petty thefts and robbery. His habit ate away any scum of humanity that still clung to him. Everything went into the spoon.

Satan ended up delivering heroin to street buyers. In exchange for a hit he worked as a gofer, a mule transporting black tar from pushers to loyal customers. Satan's monkey was so big that his arms were covered with abscesses and staph infections. And that monkey got greedy, started dipping into the stashes it was carrying. Sometimes Hal Satan didn't show up at all and shot up every bit of what he was supposed to deliver. Other times he just took the junkie's money and ran. Any dealer will tell you: Angry customers aren't good for business. Whenever he hit rock bottom, Satan displayed a rare talent for finding a trap door that led even lower.

Over time he had burned a lot of dealers, and eventually his junkie karma caught up with him. Couple of heavies cornered him in an alley and shot him up with a combination of battery acid and PCP. That foul mix got Satan so delirious he wandered around Mission Street completely naked and smeared with his own excrement. Was totally out of it for over forty-eight hours. Had no idea of where he was. Eventually he crawled into a dumpster for shelter, passed out, and almost died. By the time some kids found him and brought him to the hospital, Satan's arms were so gangrenous that the doctors had to amputate them.

When he woke up in the hospital, it took him awhile to figure out what had happened. Fresh amputees experience ghost sensations of their lost limbs, feels like they're still there, so he didn't immediately notice that his arms were gone. What tipped him off was when he went to scratch himself. Couldn't get his hand to reach the itch. First he thought they had restrained him. Maybe when the paramedics brought him in, he had been delirious and thrashing around so they'd strapped him to the bed. But when repeated attempts failed to eliminate the itch, Satan finally looked down and saw his gaping absence. His arms were history.

Oh my God, oh my God, Satan thought. *How am I going to wipe my ass? How am I going to pick my nose?* And then, with an even more sinking horror, *How am I going to fix myself?*

He'd been in the hospital a long time and the with-drawal and junk sickness was already coming on. In a junkie, the hunger for heroin can bring about feats of strength and determination not often seen in mortal men. Less than three hours after regaining consciousness, Satan managed to escape from the hospital.

He ran straight down to Sixteenth and Mission and scored a fat bag of junk on credit and his last few dollars. The dealer looked like a pickpocket as he reached the crumpled bills out of the junkie's pants, then Hal Satan ran off with the baggie clenched in his teeth.

He made a beeline to a flophouse hotel about a half-block away and looked up Vampire Annie. They called her that because she could find a vein even in a pitch-black night. Knew how to locate the elusive opening in old junkie arms that were nothing but scar tissue. Annie had given more shots than a nurse, and for a little fee she cooked and shot up the disabled junkies and the ones whose hands shook too much to fix themselves.

Vampire Annie did it right there in the gloomy second-floor hallway which stank of dirty underwear. Cooked that tar and shot up Satan in the neck. As soon as the rush came on, the amputee knew she'd given him way too much. That was Annie's plan. Why bother to share a bag when you could have it all to yourself? All it took was a simple O.D. Who'd miss a broken-down scumbag like Satan? Some of the dealers he'd burned would probably even reward her. Give her free hits of black tar or a line of credit. Besides, Satan had asked for it. He wanted a fix, so she fixed him. Fixed him good.

Euphoria burned out the crippled man's head like a matchstick. Satan collapsed, and since he had no arms to break his fall, his head smashed into the hard floor with the full force of gravity, breaking his jaw and knocking out three teeth.

Five minutes later he was dead. Vampire Annie had closed and locked her door and was already shooting up the rest of his bag. And it was a big bag. She knew the cops wouldn't even bother to ask any questions. Things like that happened all the time around there. The junkies had a saying: "If you overdose at Sixteenth and Mission, they don't call an ambulance, they call a garbage truck."

Satan's corpse was as blue as a healthy vein. But he died with a smile on his face. Because Vampire Annie had fixed him. Right in the jugular. He'd gotten that shot he wanted, needed, so bad. It's the only thing that gives even a dead junkie peace. Satan may have been fixed, but now he was permanently broken.

PART IV

FLOWERS OF ROMANCE

BRILEY BOY

BY ROBERT MAILER ANDERSON
The Richmond

The first time Briley had his nose broken, he just laughed. And then, bracing himself for another surge of blood, dizziness, and memory, he let the skuzzy little bitch hit him again. Why not? He had been dodging his old man's blows since he was old enough to see them coming, developed a tic as a toddler, twitched at birth, flinched in the womb. "That's why the scrape doctor missed you," Pop said, catching the flesh of his cheek, chin, side of neck, or temple. "Stand still and take it like a man!" But Briley never did. Bobbing and weaving. Skit. He had learned to become elusive, especially to himself. He didn't stand in front of a mirror long enough to see his own reflection. It helped when he was stealing cars, scouting houses for a B&E, scoring drugs. Living with women who had only heard the word *blow* used as a figure of speech. Nobody got a good look at him. Not the slightest slanted-eye contact from his Chinese and white Russian neighbors in the outer Richmond or nod of recognition while grazing chips at Tommy's Food and Yucatan, swiping day-old sweets from the biddies at Tbilisi Bakery, having a happy-hour heave-ho at Trad'r Sam's in a backbooth marked *Pago Pago*. So now that the bridge of his nose had collapsed under the weight of her flattened palm, all he could do was spit blood and laugh.

He was happy she was the one. God knows she deserved

the honor. He had hit her too many times to count, cuffings and jabs, sometimes straight on, knuckles tingling up the length of his arm into his teeth a metal taste that told him *one more and you better ice them down—otherwise, you won't be able to hold a crowbar tomorrow.* Then he'd unzip his pants. Sometimes she would be unconscious. That made it better. Nothing to prove. Often he satisfied himself, wiping clean on the curve of her cleavage. Ripped her panties to feel the silk tear between his fingers. It kept her guessing when she came to. Deep down they both knew it didn't make a difference either way. They weren't the first. It would happen again. Nobody ever got it right. He couldn't remember the last time they had embraced without a bruise. You can't kiss a shadow or a memory, he had been told. It was hard enough to stare someone in the eyes and wish them dead.

Her eyes were like tunnels. No train coming. They had been blue once, but the beatings had darkened them as if they really were windows of the soul. And the speed they shot together sunk them into her head like a couple of billiard balls in the side pockets of a worn and tattered table. He didn't enjoy looking at her. Nobody did. But when they had met, anonymous men at the Market Street Cinema stuffed money into her garter hoping to get a glimpse. She'd purse her lips and lean forward, bump and grind, making them feel special until the meter in her mind ran to zero, then it was onto the next toupee, leering Chinaman, aluminum-siding salesman. Twenty bought a Polaroid with her on your lap spreading herself, c-note for a nuzzle and a handjob, two and she flatbacked on a Murphy bed in her dressing room. Lately, there were no cash transactions.

Briley's neck snapped back and his head hit the wall a double blow. Just like her to get something for nothing.

Vision blurred. But he could see a flash of brass pulling away. She had loaded up for her Briley Boy—something more than a fistful of fingers. Fine. Let her have her fun. He was enjoying himself too. He spit a piece of his tongue onto the carpet in front of her like a cat offering up a gift from the garden. He continued laughing. Nothing was funnier. Not even their wedding.

She had said "I do" so many times nobody doubted her, regardless of the question. Saint Monica's on Twenty-third and Geary wouldn't take them. Neither would the Holy Virgin Cathedral, Joy of All Who Sorrow. No money for Vegas. So, Reno was obviously the place. Where else could she wear white? A ruffled rented tux, soon to be smeared lipstick. No veil. They stayed seven days at the Lucky Horseshoe until they were down to their last dime. Then she spun cherries for silver dollars in the parking lot. Hard luck. Jackpot. Enough for bus fare back to San Francisco. But she had developed a thing for a customer, some Detroit blizzard pimp giving her a tryout in the backseat of his snow-chained El Dorado. She didn't want to leave. Briley convinced her. First with his fists, then with a hanger he heated over a Sterno can. Just like Dad used to do, across the ass so nobody could see the scars. She couldn't sit still anyway. He bought two decks of playing cards and they each flipped solitaire in silence as drought-brown hills passed outside like legless camels. They rented a room above a nail salon on a treeless block back in the Richmond. Crumbling stucco and mold. They ate fog. The honeymoon was over.

Briley felt his leg splinter as she brought down her heel onto the inside of his knee. There was a strange pop, and it went goofy like a chicken leg. Wing Chun. He had paid for the lessons. Sammy Wong's: laundry and self-defense.

Dragon, tiger, lotus, monkey. Shirts: $1.29. Six kids and an amphetamine addict. He was certain she fucked them all; dragon, tiger, lotus, monkey, any way they wanted, pocketed the money and practiced evenings when he wasn't around. Parlor tricks. If he could grab hold of her, he'd show her some real chop-socky. Not some Hong-Kong four-star double-bill. Americans had invented the bitch-slap. She wouldn't forget it. Size is what mattered. Who wore the pants. Who swung the belt.

But Briley couldn't move, and didn't want to. He waved an arm in feeble defense of a lamp crashing across his shoulder. Ceramic explosion. Shards of clay cutting into his eyes, lids running red. Blood, not anger. Tiny helpless bursts. Just like the hamsters he'd had as a boy. Father foraging through the wire enclosure, hand full of shit and gnawed newspaper, coming up with a Vida Blue kick and a fur fastball. *Splat.* "That was because of you! Next time you'll do as you're told!" his old man would shout. Not likely. And the rodents multiplied like guilt, bad report cards, pornography, dirt under his fingernails. Dad left two alone: male and female. Breeding. He called their crap-covered coop the *Garden of Eden*, less like the Bible location and more like the strip club cross town where his mother was a "waitress." Finally, Briley took the vermin to the toilet tank and watched them drown, whirlpooling away with a sudden suck. The stains stayed behind, above the bed, closet doors, wild ceiling caroms. Reminding him what he had done. No amount of scrubbing could make them come clean. Late at night, awake with one hand working his cock, he would stare at certain spots for hours, forming their faces, making sounds, having them do tricks. That's when they became his pets. That's when he named them.

Briley tried to focus on his current situation and surroundings, but all he could see was a square of static encased in cheap plastic with the word Zenith below a row of busted knobs. At first, the poor reception had appeared as a woman's face, a beautiful woman with a complexion clear as milk, eyes bluer than a breezeless sky, contented smile, mouthing the phrase, Fresh from the start. She stood in a living room of an impossibly clean house, something out of Pac Heights, not Briley's plaster and pressboard roach trap. The ashtrays were empty too, magazines stacked, couch crammed with fluffy cushions, and although everything seemed immaculate and impeccable, the woman was vacuuming. Then electricity. It came down like a thunderbolt. Briley's head gave way with a sick crack and he jerked spastically amongst the wires and shattered tube. He wanted to say something, not an apology, perhaps an epitaph. Something more than the cackle caught crushed in his throat. She stood above him screaming, replacing the other woman, replacing the static and white noise. Replacing himself. Waiting. He heard sirens in the distance racing toward him as if there was something left to save. No need. The best thing to do was quit moving. He knew that now. Take their best shot. Don't cry. Go to sleep. Be still.

KID'S LAST FIGHT

BY EDDIE MULLER

South of Market

Danh woke up that morning excited. Today he was finally going to use the pruning shears. He'd learned about the technique at a lineup the previous week. Some guy was bragging how he'd done it to his ex-fiancée when she wouldn't give back his engagement ring. Ever since, Danh had wanted to give it a try. Grab some rich bitch by the wrist and snip her clean, like a butcher scissoring a duck. There'd be lots of blood and screaming, but he'd just calmly pocket her fingers with the fat-ass jewels and be gone, quick as a hummingbird. Later, at Li Po, when it was his turn to buy, he'd toss a finger on the bar and say something funny, just for the reaction. After that, he'd be known as the craziest fucker in the crew. What to say when he threw down the finger? He hadn't figured that part out yet, but it would come to him.

Hanna hiked up the shoulder strap on the briefcase and checked her wristwatch as she blew through the doors of the Jewelry Mart. She wasn't going to make the 2 o'clock briefing with the caterers. She'd driven all the way across town to get a deal on the earrings for Katie's birthday, and for a second she regretted it. But only for a second, since nothing made Hanna happier than buying wholesale. At the foot of the stairs, she hesitated. It took her a couple of seconds to remember where she'd parked.

Bud couldn't remember why he was on this street. He was headed someplace, had something important to do. Back a couple of blocks he'd remembered, and his shuffle shifted into a determined stride. But then he started looking at buildings and street signs, recognizing places from long ago, and his head began filling with pictures and sounds from the old days and pretty soon he couldn't recall what was obvious only minutes before. *Damn it.* Anger welled up in him, making it harder to hold onto a thought.

Bud turned around and looked back. Maybe he'd dropped the answer on the sidewalk. Had he come this way? Maybe Joan had given him a note, to remind him what to do. From his jacket pocket he pulled a wad of paper.

A hundred-dollar bill. Had she put it there? *Yes, Joan put it there.* He remembered that now. She'd told him he needed to go somewhere—*where?* The money was for when he got there.

I'm supposed to buy something. Goddamn if he could recall what it was. *I had eggs this morning,* he thought. He could still taste the yolks, that's how he knew.

Hanna was almost to her car when the Asian kid appeared. She barely had time to gasp. He ripped the briefcase off her shoulder, but instead of running away with it, he trapped her arm between his ribs and biceps and grabbed her wrist. She started screaming when she saw the pruning shears. Instinctively, she made fists of both hands.

"Open!" Danh shrieked. "Open!"

Something slammed Danh's left ear, hard and heavy as brick. To protect himself, he had to let the woman go.

Another blow banged his skull. He swung the shears blindly, then took a third blow on the jaw, just below his mouth. Down Danh went, dropping the shears when his hands reached out to break the fall.

That last right hand was the best one Bud had thrown since he decked Lyle Cooley at the Cow Palace in 1958. He'd set that up with a left hook, which missed high but made Cooley bend at the waist. Bud came over the top with a punch that had every ounce of his shoulders, hips, and legs behind it—Cooley was lights-out for three minutes. Every second of that fight was clear as a bell to Bud, to this day.

The final punch in the flurry had hurt like hell; his knuckles had hit flush on the kid's jawbone. Something might have busted. Bud instinctively flexed his right hand a few times, already feeling the swelling. His whole body vibrated. The fight had lasted about six seconds—the cleanest six seconds he'd experienced in a long time. He stood over the kid, left cocked, just in case the little fuck had some guts and wanted to fight. Of course he didn't—he mugged women, for chrissakes. The kid scooped something off the sidewalk and ran like hell, never looking back.

Bud turned, expecting to see his manager, Joe Herman, smiling at him.

"You saved my life," Hanna said, trying to compose herself. "Or at least my fingers."

Bud stared at her, trying to piece things together.

Hanna could tell right off the guy wasn't all there. His clothes were neat and clean and his white hair was cut short, so she didn't figure him for a street person. A line of blood had dried on his throat where he'd cut himself shaving. He was strongly built, handsome, seventy-something years old. But his eyes were glazed and suspicious.

"Were you a boxer?" Hanna asked.

"I still am." Bud smiled, because he felt *good*.

"Yeah, I guess you are."

She was already inexcusably late, but it would have been too rude to brush the old guy off—as if what just happened was merely one more example of life's daily irritations, nothing more than a speed bump in her busy schedule.

"My name's Hanna," she said, extending her hand. "I can't thank you enough for stepping in like that. Not many people would have done it—or known what to do."

"Bud Callum." Her hand felt like a leaf in his. "Good to meet you."

"Should we stand here?" Hanna asked, looking around nervously. "Maybe he'll come back."

"Let him."

Bud's adrenaline was still pumping, making him feel twice his size. He'd rescued this beautiful girl and she appreciated it. She had gorgeous skin and a lopsided smile and everything about her said *money*. He may not have known where he was, but Bud didn't need any extra clues to know this woman was loaded.

"What was your name again?" he asked.

"Hanna. Eastman." She walked toward her car. "Can I drop you somewhere, Mr. Callum? It's the least I can do."

Bud couldn't remember the last time he'd been driven in a car.

"Yeah, that'd be good. 'Preciate it."

It made her uncomfortable, the way he stared as she called the caterer to reschedule. Maybe he didn't like people talking and driving at the same time.

"That's one of those special ones, huh?" he said, after

she'd tucked the phone back in her purse. "It goes up to some satellite or something, right? Not through wires, not like a normal phone."

"Right." She felt a twinge of fright: Had this guy been *away* for the past twenty years? Just out of prison, or a mental hospital? How could you live in this city, today, and not have a cell phone?

"When I was growing up we had one phone in the whole 'partment building, in the hall at the top of the stairs. All the families used it, that one phone, if somebody was sick or needed to call the butcher or his bookie. Now everybody's got a phone. Little kids got phones. This morning I seen a kid talking on one."

Bud's eyes lit up—he'd remembered something from that morning. Through his brain he chased the young girl with the tiny phone, hoping she'd lead him to wherever he was supposed to be. But, like the rest of day, she slipped away into a bunch of dim fragments.

"Are you from here?" Hanna asked.

"Yeah, I was born south of the Slot. Used to fight here professionally," he said, marshalling thoughts into a familiar pattern, one that made sense. "Middleweight. I'm heavier now but not by much. I was right in the thick of it back then, fought all kinds of main events. The Civic, Oakland Auditorium. I was on the undercard when Joey Maxim fought Ezzard Charles here for the title. I fought in L.A. a bunch of times, but never back east. Here in this town, I was a big draw. I gave *value*—that's what the promoters used to say. Those were the days. My days."

He watched the city glide by outside the window. Every street seemed to be under construction, like the whole town was being rebuilt. Nothing looked familiar. Inside, the car was as silent as a tomb; he couldn't even hear the engine running.

"Where can I drop you?" she said.

He felt defensive, like he was being backed into a corner. His mind raced, but didn't get beyond the usual place.

"I fought Ray Robinson one time, can you top that? I beat him, too. Right up here at the Civic. Knocked him out in the sixth round. Set him up with a hook, made him bend at the waist. Then over the top I came with a big right cross. *Bang!* Just like that. The crowd went nuts. Local guy knocking out Sugar Ray, can you top that? I fought 'em all, one time or another. What a life I led."

It went on like that for blocks. A litany of Bud Callum's ring accomplishments, each opponent growing in stature, each bout becoming a greater life-or-death battle. Hanna didn't know anything about boxing, but she knew she wasn't hearing the truth. It sounded too much like the lies Uncle Bob told the other residents at the retirement home, before they'd had to move him to the assisted-living facility. Before they dared even speak the dreaded A-word.

Bud took his eyes off the street and peered at the woman. In profile, she looked like Nora. Same angular nose, same strong jaw. He was suddenly back in the apartment they had on Jerrold Street. He saw the kitchen curtains that she'd made and the ugly pink-and-brown speckled linoleum they both hated, and for a split second he smelled the burning remnants of the dinner he'd tried to make for her twenty-fifth birthday, when he had no money to take her out.

"You look like my wife," Bud said.

Hanna blushed. "How long have you been married?"

"She's dead."

"I'm sorry," she said, cheeks reddening. "Was it recently? That she died?"

"Tell you the truth, I can't remember. I think it was a long time ago. She was beautiful, I remember that." They fell quiet as traffic on Ninth Street surrounded them.

"Where can I drop you?" she asked, delicately.

"I guess I should go home. Can you take me?"

"Sure. Where's home?"

"You know, where I live."

"Well, actually, I don't know. What's the address?"

"I can't remember right now. It's around here somewhere."

She drove back and forth on the grid of one-way streets South of Market for the next half hour, while he searched for a landmark he recognized. The problem was, he recognized everything as it was sixty years ago, and delivered a running commentary about what *used* to be there: the bakery where the homeless shelter now was, a nightclub that had been the glass works, the office building that replaced Coliseum Bowl, the combination boxing arena and roller-skating rink. *He knows exactly where he lives,* Hanna suspected. *He just wants somebody to talk to.* Like Uncle Bob. She wondered if Bud Callum knew there was something wrong with him.

"Mr. Callum," she said, tentatively. "Are you seeing a doctor?"

Doctor. Medicine. Prescription. Drugstore. That's where he was supposed to go: the drugstore. Joan had gotten him a prescription for some kind of medicine she wanted him to take. Oh Christ, he could hear her now, bitching about how long it took to arrange that appointment at the free clinic. They had a huge fight when he refused to go. *There's nothing the matter with me!* he yelled. But he went. Joan was unstoppable; she always won in the end.

Bud dug into his pants pocket. He still had the slip for the prescription. What about the money? She'd given him cash. A bill, one big bill—a hundred dollars. He couldn't find it. Joan would kill him. Where had the money gone? It was right in his hand, he could see it.

"Did you lose something?" Hanna asked.

Suddenly, Bud was afraid. He wanted to go home.

"Sixth. I live on Sixth Street," he said.

Bud didn't want Nora to leave. He could tell she didn't believe all the things he'd said, the stories he'd told her about what he'd made of himself, and how close he'd come to fighting for a title. She needed to know. Nora needed to know.

"Please," he said, looking at her behind the wheel of the expensive automobile. "Come up just for a minute. I've got something I want to show you. Please. It's been a long time, and I just—please."

What's the proper payback for someone who's saved your life? Certainly more than she'd given so far.

"I'd love to, but—there's no place to park." It was automatic, the quintessential San Francisco excuse.

"There's a space right there," he said, pointing.

She'd never been inside squalor, only driven past. Everything about the building scared her: the creaking of the old warped floors, the stains and graffiti all over the walls, the neglect that hung in the dingy corridor, the misery she imagined behind every door. When she heard the muffled screaming of a baby, she thought she'd be sick. And the worst part was, she knew this wasn't the bottom.

Bud lived at the far end of the second floor. One bedroom, a bathroom with a shitty shower. A hot plate, no stove. He kept it clean as a whistle.

Uncle Bob had four rooms, an ocean view from each, and

a staff of nurses 'round-the-clock: eight thousand dollars a month.

"Wait here," he told her. "You can sit right there if you like. I can make tea or coffee."

"That's okay. I can't stay long."

She sat at a small Formica-topped table while he went into the next room and rummaged around. A narrow band of sunlight cut through the window, slicing between buildings across the alley. Bud Callum came back with a scrapbook, which he set in front of her.

"Just look at it for a minute," he said. "So you'll know. You'll know I wasn't making that stuff up. You think there's something wrong with me, that I'm ready for the nut house. But I did all that. Here, look. It's real."

She slowly turned the black pages, scanning a procession of brittle clippings that told the tale of Bud Callum's rise. It was a hell of a life, a lot more dramatic than anything Uncle Bob had ever done. Looking at a big halftone of Bud throwing a punch, Hanna had to laugh. "My lucky day," she said, tapping the picture. "At precisely the right moment, *this* guy came into my life."

Bud smiled and went back to the other room. From the top shelf of the closet he pulled down his old foot locker and flung it on the bed. He started digging through it. Nora's pictures were in there. Weren't they? This is where he kept them, where they'd always been. She'd see the resemblance, once he showed her. *Nora.* He hadn't looked at those pictures in ages. *Or had he?* They'd better be here. Joan better not have moved them, or thrown them out.

Hanna opened an envelope that had been set inside the scrapbook and slid out the contents: photographs of a dark-haired woman with shining eyes and sharp, pretty features. In some of the pictures she was dressed in a bridal gown. Bud was right—they did look alike. He was in a lot of the photos, too. After flipping through them for a moment, Hanna put them aside. She felt she was violating an intimacy. Also in the envelope was a section of newspaper, quartered. The *San Francisco Examiner,* dated June 11, 1951. An article gave details of a fire on Jerrold Street that claimed the life of Nora Callum.

Hanna quickly put everything back in the envelope, then placed it carefully in the scrapbook.

"Why are you crying?" Bud asked as he stepped into the room.

"Just looking at all this. You've had quite a life."

"Stop crying," he said. He hated it when people cried. He could understand crying at beautiful music or the finish of a great ballgame or a terrific fight, but he couldn't stand it when people cried out of sadness or regret. It made no sense. Crying solved nothing. If something hurt, you stowed the pain and kept on punching. You just banged your way through it, that's all. You banged your way through to the end.

"I have to go," Hanna said, standing up. "My daughter's having a birthday party and I'm supposed to be getting everything ready." She couldn't stop the tears. "My God, I must look a mess. I'm sorry."

"Here, hold on." From the rear pocket of his trousers Bud pulled a folded white handkerchief, perfectly fresh.

Hanna laughed, which made her cry more. *Nobody carries a clean handkerchief,* she thought.

She drew in a sharp breath, almost a gasp, as he cupped the back of her head in his huge hand. "Don't cry," he said. He dabbed the black streaks from her cheeks and she forced herself to look into his eyes.

"I'll walk you down," he said. "This isn't the best building."

Out front, as they approached her car, he said, "Thanks for listening before. I go on sometimes. And the ride, thanks for the ride."

Before she knew what she was doing, she kissed him, half on the cheek, half on the mouth. Maybe she knew what she was doing. She wasn't sure. "Thanks again," Hanna said. "I'm glad I met you."

She buckled herself into the Lexus and drove away. Bud went back upstairs to the room at the end of the hall.

He was re-stowing the footlocker when he heard the front door open.

"Who was that woman?" Joan called out.

He hated how she'd walk in and start talking, not even knowing if he was there. Loud, so loud.

"What woman?"

"Don't start with me," she said, entering the bedroom. "I saw her kissing you on the street. What's been going on?" She eyed the mussed-up bed, which he always kept obsessively neat.

"Did you go in my foot locker?" Bud asked. "Did you take things out of my foot locker? I'm missing some important papers."

"Bud, you hid those pictures yourself. Don't change the subject. Who was that woman? Why was she in here?"

He hated her accusing tone, making him feel like a child being chastised. But she was all he had; without her he could barely negotiate a single day.

"I saved her," Bud explained. "This guy was gonna rob her and I was across the street and ran over and I nailed him—three good shots, all right on the button, and she was so grateful that she gave me a ride home and then she came up and we talked for a long time, maybe an hour, about all kinds of things." Bud brushed past Joan, reaching for the scrapbook. Had to put it away, before something happened to it. "She wanted to see my book, 'cause of the way I knocked that guy out."

"Uh-huh. And did you remember to go to the drugstore? Bud? Did you remember to get the medicine? Look at me when I'm talking to you."

Bud just stood there, holding the scrapbook, keeping his back to her. His face burned. When he didn't answer, Joan came up behind him and reached into his trouser pockets. His knuckles bled white as he clutched the pebbled leather book.

"Goddamn it! You still got the prescription, Bud! What have you been doing! Where's the goddamn money? You gave it to that whore, didn't you? Saved her, my ass! You bought yourself a fucking blowjob, you son of a bitch! With money I gave you. Goddamn it! Is that how little you think of me? Is it? Look at me, you fucking idiot!"

Bud turned around. Joan was crying. Crying solved *nothing*. If something hurt, you stowed the pain and kept on punching. You just banged your way through it, that's all. You banged your way through to the end.

"Budweiser, all 'round!" Danh shouted.

Even if he drank ten more he'd never tell anybody what happened that morning. Shit. Sucker-punched by an old fuck. He nursed his jaw, tossed the hundred he'd rescued off the sidewalk onto the bar, and chuckled to himself.

It was like his mother used to say, back home: *Sometimes, Fortune doesn't need a reason to smile.*

CONFESSIONS OF A SEX MANIAC

BY DAVID HENRY STERRY

Polk Gulch

Eleven o'clock Monday night I was standing in the nasty skank stink of a body-fluid-scented room trying not to pant as I basked in the glow of the Snow Leopard. She was decked out in black jacket and sleek black boots, the long of her straight black hair leading directly to the short of her barely-there black skirt that hid little of the loveliest legs I'd had the pleasure to gander in God knows how long. Coal eyes with glowing embers in the center made my breath synchopate, and I could almost feel her long red claws at the end of her paws digging into the small of my back.

I couldn't quite pin down exactly what she was. Asian? African? Mexican? Italian? Spanish? She seemed to shapeshift as she sized me up from the lone chair in room 211 of Felipe's Massage Parlor. There was no Felipe. No one was there for a massage. Behind her the wall was stained with what looked like splattered brain, and if you listened hard enough, you could hear the ghosts of ho's past screaming.

My eyes enjoyed their tour of the Snow Leopard. The race-car curve of her neck. The flesh bulging out of her bra under the tight black shirt under the black leather jacket. The cocoa-butter brown of all that smooth silk skin. The smile that was so tiny I couldn't even tell if it was really a smile.

I was falling under the Snow Leopard's spell, I could feel her Black Magic working on me, and I couldn't stop seeing her straddling me, those thick red lips contorted with mad passion as she ravaged me like a crazy jungle cat.

Being a sex maniac has a way of clouding a man's judgment. The doctor said I was a *problematic hypersexualist*. I said, "Doc, that takes all the romance out of it. Can't I just be a sex maniac?" He told me I needed to see him three times a week. I never went back.

People have many misconceptions about what it's really like to be a sex maniac. They think just because you'll rut with any old skunkhumper when the hunger's upon you, that you don't crave the crème de la crème. I was the junky who was after the finest China-white high. Only, of course, I was a junky of love. And at 11 o'clock on Monday night, the Snow Leopard looked like the greatest score in a lifetime of scores.

Keep your mind on the job, my mind reminded me. I was a distribution specialist in the illegal goods and services industry. A master courier. A bagman. Not to be confused with a bag lady, who keeps all her possessions in a shopping cart and screams about how the aliens won't stop probing her. There are, in fact, female bagmen. Being a postmodern sexualist myself, I don't have a problem with the gender blurring. I was basically a high-end black-market messenger boy. I picked shit up. I dropped shit off.

People often assume that just because you're a sex maniac, you can't have a life. Wrong again. As with anything, there are all levels of function among sex addicts. I was never one of those grab-a-kid-from-the-schoolyard-and-keep-her-in-my-basement sex maniacs. I was a very high-functioning sex maniac. An ethical sex maniac. I was all about consent. I had rules. I didn't mix business with pleasure. I took pride in my work. Being the best distribution specialist I could be. That's just how Mother raised me. So when I was on the job, I showed up on time, I got my package, and I was on my merry way.

That night was supposed to be no different. Show up, get package, deliver. My boss, Chinese Willy, had made a big point of saying that he was giving this job special attention, like: *If you don't mook this job up, you just might get invited into the club to play some of our little reindeer games.* All I had to do was get the package back to Willie's by midnight. Cake.

That was before the Snow Leopard. When Shiva Shiv said the name, I laughed out loud. I stopped laughing when Shiva Shiv said, "What the fuck you laughin' at?" in a voice dripping of curry and murder. The name rattled around in my brain the whole day. Naturally, that night the Snow Leopard invaded my dreams. She was half-cat, half-woman. I could smell the fertile sex as she kept changing back and forth, from cat to woman and back: whiskers and lips, fangs and fur, that rough tongue, claws and paws, breasts and wet flesh, all hungry jungle feline in-heat heat. She was tearing me to shreds, guts ripped open, and blood, my God, she was pounding me, eating my flesh and taking me right to the corner of Ecstasy and Death. I woke up in a cold sweat with a curtain rod for a johnson. I should have known right then and there. Dreams never lie.

So there I was, staring at the Snow Leopard, with her incredible flesh and her sex-red lips, and I could smell that smell from my dream. That in-heat smell. Or was that just in my head? Being a sex maniac has a way of blurring the fine line between reality and what you'd like reality to be.

Shut up! I scolded myself. Get your package, take care of your business, and be on yer merry way. I fondled the fifty Large screaming in my secret jacket pocket. Why doesn't she say something? my mind asked me. She got up and paced like, well, like a big dangerous hungry cat. And I could hear the beat of the jungle drum. Or maybe it was just Busta Rhymes booming from the next room. Money, danger, and the distinct whiff of Snow Leopard shivered me from eyeballs to nut-balls to foot-balls: Adrenaline pumping furiously, I was jacked to the max and stone-cold sober.

I loved my job. I used to try to explain to people who'd never been in the illegal goods and services industry why it's such a fun and rewarding line of work. Often when I was on the job I got what I can only describe as an evangelical feeling. Like this is what God wanted me to do. And on that Monday night, I felt like He, or She (I'm not gender-restrictive when it comes to my deities), had brought me to the Snow Leopard to change my life. I can't explain it, really, except to say I was sitting there thinking that this job felt like one of those jobs where you look back from the future and you say, *Wow, that was the greatest job in the history of jobs!* But then I started thinking, No, maybe this is one of those jobs you look back on and say, *I let myself drift, and that's how I got this scar.*

The more we didn't talk, the more electromagnetic the air got, like two saturated clouds bumping and rubbing, the rumbling building as the lightning gathers. I wanted to get a good look at her, fix the constellation of her features in my head so at least I could have her star in my fantasies later. I reached for the light. This is what prompted the first word she ever spoke to me. Naturally, inevitably that word was:

"No."

Spoken in the chilled voice of a seasoned predator.

It hung there in the air:

"No."

I did not turn the light on. So we stood there in the dark.

"Are you in, or out?" she purred.

This was not in the script. When Chinese Willy is expecting delivery of his package at midnight, and it's 11:13 p.m. and fifty Gs are flaming in your secret jacket pocket, you need to keep your priorities straight. My dance card was full. Or was this the call of the wild? That's the problem with being a sex maniac. You can never really be sure.

"I like to know what I'm getting into before I get into something—"

"Look," she shot back, those coal eyes glowing, "any minute now two big guys with automatic weapons are gonna bust through that door, and if you're not in, you should get out."

"I like to know what the stakes are before I go all in," I said.

"You play your cards right, I'll make sure lady luck blows on your dice." She licked her whiskers.

"What's the game?" I asked.

"Look, all I need is an ace in the hole," she hissed, "and if you're it, I guarantee the pot'll be very sweet. But tic-toc, we're on the clock."

"How do I know you're not bluffing?" I asked, ready to crawl through broken glass for her, but trying not to show it. "Trying to set me up for a big fall?"

"Tic-toc, tic-toc." She blazed those cat eyes at me.

I folded with a sigh: "I'm all in."

"I just hope you got enough hand—"

Before she could even get through the sentence, two *very*

big guys with *very* automatic weapons busted through the door. She dropped straight down, behind the bed frame, while pulling out a petite little pistol. I unholstered and duck-n-rolled under the bed, firing as fast as my fingers'll fly, taking down the very big guy on the left. First shot: right shoulder. Second shot: belly-blast. Third shot: left kneecap. As he fell he fired his Glock, bullets spraying around the room like his gun was prematurely ejaculating. When he hit the floor, eye level with me, I got off the shot I'm truly proud of, as I plugged a slug right over the mug's noseholes. That's when the big guy's lights went out.

The Snow Leopard fired one quiet dainty shot from her petite little pistol. It slid with the greatest of ease through the left eyeball of the very big guy on the right. And that was all she wrote for him.

In the calm-after-the-storm aftermath, all I could hear was her cool kitty breath, hot on my neck, as we huddled under the bed, two very big guys sprawled dead on the floor in front of us in spatters of assassin-red blood.

Panicked screams from fleeing Felipe freaks now careened into the room. In a flash I turned, my gun at her temple, and I was face-to-face with the Snow Leopard, eye-to-eye with all that coal and fire, breathing her, that in-heat dream smell making me swell, and I knew I was losing myself in her.

Something hard poking into my ribs brought me back. Lo and behold, it was her little pistol. Suddenly I was love-drunk no more, smack-dab in the middle of an old-fashioned Mexican stand-off.

Maybe it was being under the bed. Maybe it was the red on the floor like a blood Rorschach. Maybe it was the thrill of the kill. Maybe it was just the Snow Leopard paying her debt. All I know is that those ecstasy-red lips were moving into mine, and suddenly hands were under shirts and skin was scorching under fingers. Before I knew what was what, she had me in hand, as cold metal pressed into my testicles. Made my nuts do the bunnyhop. As she worked me over, she dug those long sharp red claws into my chest, opening my flesh. Yes, there was pain, but it was good, as an animal-wild growl rose from way deep inside her throat, and there was much bumping and grinding.

I reached down to reciprocate. Surprise, surprise. There was something down there. Between her legs. Wait a minute, it's my package, my mind said in surprise. I slipped it out and into my pocket. As I pulled the cash out of my secret jacket pocket, and as I slid the money into her hand, I moved her scanties aside with my gun and gave her the tiniest taste of all of me.

Right away she wanted more. Tried to shove me further in. But I wouldn't let her have any more. I wanted to make her work for it. Which she did: teeth into my shoulder, claws into my back, this krazy kat was actually drawing blood. She quickly got me pinned on my back and started to have me for a late-night supper. Then she put her pistol tip on my lip and she sucked on both at the same time.

I confess, as a sex addict, the most gratifying aspect of the whole Snow Leopard experience was how she kept maneuvering me around so she could get at me better, bucking and howling, growling and grunting, groaning and moaning, fast, cuz she knew that bigger and larger trouble was most certainly going to walk right through that door at any second.

This is religious, I was thinking, it's superhuman, interstellar, transcendental. Time was no more. The mind was no more. There was nothing else in the world, even as the universe rushed through me and into her, then back again.

Estrogen shockwaved through my central nervous system and my johnson was transformed into a lightning rod that shot bolts as we skydived together off the top of the Golden Gate Bridge and floated, shaking and speaking in tongues together, landing back under the bed at Felipe's, panting and radioactive in the afterrapture.

Like a stop-action movie she:

Stood

Rearranged

Cat-stretched

Walked toward the door to leave.

I struggled up and stood paralyzed, like a life-sized action-figure of myself, watched each event transpire, but somehow missed all the connecting moves, how she got from point A to B to C to D.

"Hey, wait a minute," spurted out of my mouth with a disturbing level of desperation. "How can I get ahold of you?"

"You can't," she purred, just loud enough for me to hear, as she approached the door.

"Hold on a second, I wanna—" I didn't say that I wanted to have her again, right away, and for the rest of my life.

"Yeah, I know." She gave me this devastating, bored-on-jaded Cheshire half-grin, and I knew she was going to just disappear any second as her hand fingered the knob of the door and she was inches away from being gone.

"Hey, look, I just saved your life here." I hated how limp and lame and tame my voice sounded. "I was your ace-in-the-hole."

"Why do you think I blew on your dice?" She nodded ever-so-slightly, the door was opening now and she'd almost slipped all the way through it.

"I thought it was my boyish good looks and my winning

personality," I cracked back, hoping a laugh would buy me another minute.

"That's why I didn't kill you."

The Snow Leopard's grin spread, and after she left, it lingered for several moments before it slowly faded away.

Suddenly everything went back to regular speed, and the sounds of all the freaked-out Felipe habitues had a new sound added to them. Cop sounds. Sirens and intercoms and heavy steps headed hard down the hall, capital-T trouble, and I was out the window, escaping down the fire escape, and *boom!* walking up Geary, breathing the cool yet fetid air of Polk Gulch, the taste of Snow Leopard wet on my lips.

I tucked in. Took a breath. Checked the time. 11:38. How can that be? I was biblical with the Snow Leopard for all of eight minutes. Why did it feel like eight lifetimes?

Chinese Willie's was five minutes away, and walking up Geary toward Van Ness, the deep peace of a job well done, combined with the high of scoring all that pure Snow Leopard, caused a highly satisfied sigh to slide out of me. In front of Frenchy's Adult Emporium, where they're always *HIRING*, Rasta Hat Man was taking a wee late-night nap on his sidewalk bed. I admire a man who can just curl up right there on Geary and catch a few winks. No pillow, no blankets: That's discipline. An old blind brother in a ratty-tatty shabby old overcoat held a blindman cane, only it was all duct-taped together. I couldn't help it, when I saw the old blind brother with his busted, taped-up cane, it really got to me. So I went over to the guy and I slipped him a sawbuck.

"It's a ten-spot," I said low, and the guy came over all humble and happy.

"Thank ya, sir, God bless ya, thank ya, sir, God bless ya."

I like that in a bum. Gratitude. I hate these bums, you

give 'em coin and they look at you like they're doing you a big favor by taking your money. No, I want some genuine thank-you from my bum.

By the way, *bum* is the word of choice down here. Once I was talking to one of these superindustrious bums, you know the type, always hustling around a hundred miles an hour, busting their bony butts, they have a whole circuit worked out, cashing in hundreds of bottles a day. I love this guy, he's always got a line of bottle-loaded shopping carts all tied together like he's riding herd over a bum wagon train. I called him James Brown, seeings how he's the hardest working man in show business. He got a kick out of that. So one time I was talking to James Brown about homeless-this and homeless-that, and the brother went off:

"Don't call me no *homeless*, mutherfucker! I'm a bum! I don't work but when I wanna work, I don't kiss no bawsman's ass, I take my own vacation, I make my own rules, I'm a bum, mutherfucker, and I'm proud. Hallelujah, I'm a bum!"

Okay, you're a bum, Hallelujah. And every time I saw James Brown, there was some shoeless loser, some lower-class riffraff bum railing on this superindustrious brother from another mother, sticking a raw, puffy-bum hand out, screaming: "Why you don't you give me some love? You owe me, you sell-out mutherfucker!"

It happens all the way from the outhouse to the penthouse. Some citizens work their noses to the bone, and some jealous leaching ne'er-do-wells are always there to knock them down a peg. Sweet misery loves her company, from Nob Hill to Polk Gulch.

People dis the Gulch, but as far as I'm concerned, it's the only neighborhood if you're really serious about being a sex maniac. The Haight's too full of gentrified Gap-heads, gone-to-seed hippy hopheads, and runaway urchin thieves. The Richmond is a great place to go if you're lookin' for the slowest, most boring death imaginable. SoMa? Please! Those dot-con pseudo-hipsters deserve every scrap of misery they've heaped on themselves. I do enjoy North Beach on a sunny afternoon, but in the end there's too many clueless tourists clogging up the arteries. Nob Hill is a travesty, teaming with all those vaginally challenged fashion victims. Hell, even the poodles get botoxed up there. And there's nothing tender in the Tenderloin. The only loin in the TL is crawling with nasty maggots. I once saw some toothless loon cap his running mate over a Q-tip. Hey, I like Q-tips as much as the next guy, but only in the TL can you get terminated over one.

Because of its equidistant location between the Tenderloin and Nob Hill, you will hear the sisters sometimes call Polk Gulch the *Tender Knob*, which I quite enjoy. Here's a little known fact: The word *gulch* comes from an Anglicization of *gulchen*, which means *to gulp*. When you consider how much has been guzzled and gulped in the Gulch over the years, it seems a perfect fit, doesn't it? Don't get me wrong, the Gulch is not for the feebleminded or the weak-willed. The Gulch will chew you up and spit you out if you let it. But if you have Game, you can get anything any-time in the Gulch. And you can get it for cheap.

The Gulch is where rough trade goes for a vacation. So you can bag a nasty little bit of fluff, like this girly hanging out-side Koko's, with the hiphuggers revealing pretty pink panties and *FOXY* plastered in cheap lettering across the seat of her jeans stuffed full of all that fine white flesh, she's positively spilling out her too-small pleather jacket, and for twenty-five dollars and unlimited meth, chances are she'll let you have an unlimited all-access pass to her hidden treasures until she's not high anymore. And with the connoisseur-quality meth I kept on hand for specifically this purpose, that could last days at a stretch. Yes, she was rough, but sometimes I liked it rough.

But the true glory of the Gulch is that the very next second you'll spot two touristy girlies shivering in shorts walking by with beautiful pale goosebumping gams, swathed in big *I ♥ SF* sweatshirts they had to buy cuz nobody told them how freezing cold it is in SF. You'd be shocked how easy it is to sidle up to these corn-fed beauties (who are most of them looking to take a walk on the wild side in Baghdad-by-the-Bay, by the way) and take them for some paella at the Spanish joint on the corner, then end up back at my lovepad for some wine and some weed if they're into it, which they almost always are, and all of a sudden they're on my big round bed begging for one more to make it an even ten so they can go back and tell their cheesehead friends about how they ♥ SF.

Across the street heading toward Polk, three of the loud brothers congregated around a lost-looking white man in a too-expensive jacket, they were waving DVDs in his face, screaming about how they could get any title he wanted. Then suddenly eight or nine of the loud brothers crawled out of Godknowswhere, surrounded the lost-looking jacket like a giant black widow spider, and swallowed it and its owner whole.

A tattooed post-teen with a hunk of metal through her lip and one stuck through her eyebrow clunked by next. I found myself wondering where else she was pierced. Sometimes those tattooed pierced freaky females enjoy a bit of punishment with their pain and that can be fun, riding that line between angel and devil.

More local color, Gulch-style, sashayed past in a ridiculous micro-mini and huge balloon breasts. She was one of these tiny passable Thai trannies. Very tidy. Truthfully, as a sex addict, I enjoy a passable trannie. Take it from one who knows, a hotty tranny'll rattle your bones and make yer cahones dance like a couple of Mexican jumping beans. Because she wants to be a *she* more than any female. But I could only go to Trannie Land if she stayed a she. That's just me. Maybe I was just not evolved enough to be comfortable with man-love. I wish I could've. I tried, believe me. My life would have been so much easier if I could've gotten off on men, cuz you can have man 25/8. Shake a tree in the Gulch and a ton of love-ready man falls out. Woman, even faux-woman, even bad woman, even the nastiest skagmeister skunkkunt, is often so hard to come by. I mean, obviously there are women everywhere, but it takes so much effort just getting in most of the really exceptional woman, it's exhausting.

Next up on the Gulch hit parade was a disaffected arty sweet-sixteeny, all gangly angles and long colt legs, hoody ripped so her bra strap showed over the softness of all that untouched skin underneath, with all that attitude heaped on top. I just loved going up to one of these flouncing clomping angry grrrrls and saying, Hey, I know how it is, your parents suck, your school sucks, your teacher sucks, your friends suck, the whole world sucks, but I can show you how to escape into ecstasy, lose yourself to the pleasures of the flesh, primal scream all that bopper angst right out. You have all the equipment you need, but you have no clue how to use it, I can show you the whole thing in a couple of hours. Plus, you cannot believe how jealous your stupid sucking friends'll be, and just how much this will piss your stupid sucking parents off.

Oh, I love this guy: He never wears a shirt, even in the

freezing rain, he's so wired and wiry, you can see every bone in his body, he's like a skeleton wearing a skin tarp stretched too tight. He loves to run right in front of speeding cars. That's his thing. And he never gets hit. I saw him cause three separate accidents, one of them a three-car fiasco. But he never gets so much as a scratch. 'Course, he is lean and lithe and wiry as hell, like I said, so he's very hard to hit. But as I walked past and watched him, I wondered what he might've been, like maybe an Olympic hurdler or an NFL scatback or a Hollywood stuntman, instead of a death-defying crack casualty.

As I turned down Chinese Willy's alley, the animal cried out inside me: *I need more Snow Leopard!* The pictures flashed back: those throat moans, cold steel on my boys, her squirming so she could have all of me. My open chest skin was stinging in the chill of the night, and I could still feel her digging into me.

It's so gratifying when reality actually turns out better than fantasy. Chinese Willy, who's actually Mexican but really looks, I kid you not, Chinese, was even fatter and happier than I'd imagined he'd be. If there's one thing he likes more than getting his money, it's getting his money early. So he was practically jovial as he counted all those potatoes at 11:52, instead of midnight. I watched him touching and fondling his cabbage, and suddenly I understood: This is his thing. The man is a cash addict.

Chinese Willy is an old-school gangster, which has its ups and downs. On the one hand, he's hooked up with everybody and nobody can touch him, which meant nobody could touch me. On the other hand, he's prone to irrational outbursts of ultra-violence that can really wreak havoc on a person's skull. He loves all that vendetta malarkey, and he's very big on LOYALTY and RESPECT. And he loves to break balls. His whole social hierarchy is based on the breaking of other people's balls. It's his way of saying he likes you. When Chinese Willy stops breaking your balls, that's when it's time to watch your back.

One of the odder things about Chinese Willy is that even though he's actually Mexican, he surrounds himself with Chinamen, and he's always bankrolling these high-end Chinese honeys so they'll hang with him, and he even kind of talks like one of those old-timey Chinamen. It's like somehow because he looks Chinese, he's become a Chinaman.

"So," he mumbled through a huge mouthful of egg salad, "how you like Snow Leopard?" He glanced sideways at Crack Harry, Shiva Shiv, and Knuckles, and when he did that insinuating vulgar guttural chuckle, that was their cue to do the same. Like they were all in on some secret that I wasn't, the object being to make me feel like a big steaming heap of shit. But the beauty of being a sex maniac is that you could just not care less about any of this. It was just so much water off the back of my duck, while I maneuvered my way toward my next fix.

"Yeah, she was a real piece of work—"

"You say *mouthful* there." Assorted grunts and belches and chortles erupted from Crack Harry and Shiva Shiv and Knuckles.

"Yeah, I was just wondering if I could get her digits, cuz I gotta proposition I wanna—"

Chinese Willy shut me down like I was the clap and he was penicillin: "No! You thank me for this. I tell now, you listen: You not wanna make fuckeefuck wit' this clazy bitch! Right, boys?"

They nodded and grunted like the chunks of muscle they are.

"Naw, you don't understand," I plodded on, "I have an unresolved situation on my hands vis-à-vi—"

"Now you watch my lip: No!" Egg salad sprayed from the Mexican lips of Chinese Willy. "Stay fuck away from this clazy bitch!"

"With all due respect"—Willy loves all that all-due-respect business, you could feel his sphincter unpinch—"I've been working for you for five years, I'm always straight, I bring you a steady stream of new business, and I have never asked you for one single thing. This is all I ask. I need to talk to the Snow Leopard. With all due respect—"

I couldn't even get the last due-respects out on account of the veins that were popping up on that huge Chinese-looking head, as "NO! FUCK DAMN YOU!" thundered from Willy, along with another fusillade of egg salad, a small particle of which flew all the way over the desk and landed on my vintage Warriors warm-up.

This always signals the end of any dispute involving Chinese Willy. It is a well-known fact that after the third "No!" from Chinese Willy, you continue a dispute at your own risk, as an irrational outburst will most likely result. Since I did not wish to have my cheek pierced by a staple gun, or my nose broken with Chinese Willy's Ugly Billy (his billyclub of choice, a slender twenty-four inches of hardened metal, conventionally used for bashing fish in the head until they're dead after you've reeled them in), I dropped the topic.

But just when I was ready to write Chinese Willy off as a classless thug, he peeled off five Large and handed them to me, even though he only owed me a G, and with great pomp and ceremony, he proclaimed:

"Okay, maybe you right. You don't never fuck up. Not never. So maybe Chinese Willy take you for granted. But I do you favor here. Snow Leopard, she take no prisoner. This for you own good. You understand I no want to see this clazy bitch fuck you shit up?"

"Thank you for taking the time to help me, and I appreciate your generosity, which I am not even deserving of, but what the hell, I'll take it."

I pocketed the five Gs with a flourish, and they ate it up, loved that I was giving a tiny little shot to the man himself, as he laughed: "He got brass monkey balls, don't he?"

Everybody made little grunty snorty sounds, and Chinese Willy continued: "I got pickup for you, noon tomorrow, Sophia's, Butterball, he got thing for you, you take to Sweetmeat, he got thing for you, I need back here by 1:00."

"You got it, bawss." I smiled wide, and as I sidled out, Chinese Willy shoved a huge hunk of egg salad into his fat, happy Mexican face.

I practically skipped down the alley to Polk: It was barely midnight, I had four free Gs itching to be scratched in my secret jacket pocket, I didn't have to work again for twelve hours, I was still throbbing from the Snow Leopard work-over, I could feel the cool air soothing the open love-wounds inflicted by the saucy minx I wanted to have every day for the rest of my life, and as I smelled her again, she jolted me to the bone.

Next stop: Eyeball. The queerest of queer ducks. He's as tall as he is wide, somewhere between thirty and six hundred years old. Possibly the hairiest man on the planet, he's got one of these Fabulous Furry Freak Brothers 'dos, slate-colored hair flying everywhere, flowing over the shoulders, burying the ears, drooping in front of the eyes, and avalanching uncontrollably down the front and the back. At a certain point the head hair meets and joins the beard hair, and it looks thick enough to contain entire meals. Which, at times, it does. Thicket of brambled monobrow. Hair sprouting out of knuckles, pouring out of shirt collar and sleeve, pant leg bottom. You could make braids out of the hair coming out of his nose. I've never seen Eyeball's eyeballs. I don't know that he actually has eyes. But here's the weird thing: Eyeball's the guy you go to in the Gulch when you want to know where to find somebody, and he never travels more than the fifty feet between his flophouse hellhole on Larkin, and Hung Wang's, the filthy greasy-spoon dim sum joint he frequents on O'Farrell. It's one of the great mysteries of life how this human hairball who can barely see, hardly walk, and never goes anywhere, knows everything there is to know about everyone in the Gulch. If you didn't see it with your own eyes, you wouldn't believe it. But this is how Eyeball makes bank. People pay him to tell them where to find what they're looking for. It makes you think about miracles, how they're everywhere, only nobody's paying attention.

The thing about Eyeball is, he's a cantankerous troll, and whimsical in the worst sense of the word. For example, one time you'll come to him with the simplest piece of information, and he'll charge you a grand for it. Another time he'll give you the Governator's cell digits for a buck. So I was a tad apprehensive about what he was going to charge me, but at the same time, I had four free Gs pulsating in my secret pocket, and with four Large I was confident I could find the Snow Leopard.

So sure enough, there he was, as advertised, Eyeball, buried somewhere under all that hair, stuffing his piehole with vile dim sum. Before him sat three plates pregnant with rancid rolls and skuzzy buns, grizzly gray meat and dumplings lying there like stillborn dog fetuses, and rice with little things that looked like dead insects sprinkled in it. Crumbs spread out in a half-moon on the floor around him, his hair/beard layered deep with bits of chow from meals present to years-gone-by. I loved to watch the man attack and subdue his dim sum. As I watched him ravage his food, it became clear: This is Eyeball's thing. This is what he lives for. The man is a chow junky.

I didn't want to interrupt him when he was in the middle of a big feed, he can be cranky as a mother bear when you threaten her cubs, he'll take your head clean off if you're not careful. I waited till he came up for air, then moved in, gentle but firm: "Hello, Eyeball, how's life treating ya?"

"I got gout. Ain't that sump'n'? Gout." Eyeball shook his head, which made his hair ripple in waves of frayed gray.

Eyeball's a mumbler. I always forgot that. Actually, it's not that he mumbles so much as the fact that the food he's constantly stuffing into his mouth serves as a natural muffler, making it difficult to hear more than about forty percent of what he says.

"Sorry to hear that," I said, as I tried to figure out exactly what he had. Bout? Doubt? Gout?

"Gout!" Eyeball shouted, dim sum flying as if from a volcano. "Ain't that a kick in the ass?"

Ah, gout! I didn't even know what gout was. But it sounded like one of those things you definitely don't want, like you never hear anyone say: *Hey, everybody, congratulate me, I got gout!*

I leaned as close as I could without invading his personal space, as my ears adjusted to his volume.

"Do you even know what gout is?" Eyeball snapped, cranky.

I wanted to chill his wig as quickly as possible, so I

jumped right in: "No, I don't, but it sounds bad. Can I get you anything for it?"

Yes, I did want to soften him, but I was sincere about getting him some meds if he needed them. That's just how Mother raised me.

"Thank you, very kind of you to offer," came out from under Eyeball's hair. "Either my liver is producing more uric acid than I can excrete urinarily, or I have more uric acid in my bloodstream than my kidneys can filter. Apparently, the uric acid has crystallized in my feet, and it feels like Satan is punishing me for my sins by shoving white-hot knitting needles into my big toes."

"Sorry to hear that," I empathized with my feminine side.

"How's Chinese Willy?" Eyeball grunted as he stuffed an entire dumpling into his mouth and swallowed it whole like a snake sucking down an egg.

"He's fat and happy. So, listen, I'm looking for someone, she's—"

"The Snow Leopard," he said without missing a beat.

"Eyeball, you never cease to amaze me, how did you know that?" I was actually flabbergasted, although in retrospect I should've seen it coming.

"There was some nastiness at Felipe's, no? Several brutes bought the farm at the hands of a coupla very talented individuals, one of whom is the Snow Leopard. The police are quite interested, by the way, so if you know anyone who might've been involved, I would advise them to lay low." Insinuation oozed out from under that hair so hard you'd've had to be in a coma not to feel it.

"Thanks, Eyeball, I appreciate your concern. If I run into any such individuals, I'll pass on that valuable information. So, where do I find her?" I tried not to betray too much of the ill and all-consuming lust madness that burned in me. I'm afraid I was not quite successful.

"You don't," he snorted matter-of-fact.

"No, you don't understand, I have some unfinished business with her, this is a once-in-a-lifetime opportunity, and—"

"This is not a person you want to find." Eyeball said it like he was telling me without question that the earth is round and revolves around the sun.

"No, I do, I really do, see—"

"I don't feel comfortable dispensing this particular information," he said, as he wiped his mouth with his stain-besotted sleeve, "as I'm quite sure it will be extremely hazardous to your health."

"Do you know where she is?" I asked.

"What kinda question is that?" Eyeball came over all insulted: "Of course I know where she is. I know where *everyone* is. What I'm saying is that I do not want to be responsible for the shitstorm that will rain down upon you."

I got very serious now, and tried to find Eyeball's eyes in all that hairy chaos. "Look, I appreciate what you're saying, I really do, but I don't care what a dangerous psychopath she is, I have got to get ahold of her. I'll be responsible for the consequences. Trust me, I need this."

Nothing came out of him. More dim sum went in.

"How much?" I persisted.

"Not for sale," he insisted.

"Everything's for sale." I was the dog with a bone that wouldn't let go.

"You can't afford it," Eyeball mumbled.

"How much, Eyeball, seriously."

"Five grand," he said, knowing I'd never come across.

I felt like the star of my own movie as I reached inside my secret pocket, extracted the five Large, and handed them to the stunned Eyeball, who had no choice but to say: "Over the tarot joint on O'Farrell, she owns the building, lives on the top floor."

With a five-grand spring in my step, I headed happily to the Snow Leopard's pad. I was really looking forward to breaking into her place. I was born blessed. Ever since I was a kid, there was no place I couldn't break into when I put my mind to it. As a child I was always sneaking into people's houses when they weren't home. I loved being inside their lives. Snooping through their drawers. Rifling around in the back of their closet where they hide everything they didn't want anyone to find. I was always drawn to the unmentionables. And I loved seeing one of these pillar-of-society types walking around town like they're the head of the Committee for Moral Decency, and knowing that they have dirty magazines full of schoolgirls and Great Danes at home just waiting in their closets.

So when I walked up to the tarot joint on O'Farrell, I was thinking: *Cake.* It was almost 1:00 in the morning, so there was still quite a bit of street action. Stumpy Charlie and Tripod, his three-legged dog, teetered by. That chick I saw before with the tattoos stumbled by, she'd clearly found a fix and was happily self-medicated. Well, maybe not happily. A behemoth with a three-foot orange mohawk and chains connecting various parts of his anatomy like they were holding him together stopped in front of me, looked me right in the eye, and said with malicious intent: "What the fuck are you starin' at?"

I love these guys that get themselves decked out in some outrageous Halloween-looking costume so everybody has to stare at them, and then when you stare at them, they want to rearrange your face. The begging-for-a-fight boys.

But me, I just could not have cared less, particularly not tonight. So I smiled easy-as-you-please and said: "I was just admiring your hair, my man."

Because I was so easy with it, all the piss and vinegar drained right out of him, and he said, "Oh, uh . . . thanks . . ."

Then he clomped off to find someone weaker and more feeble to smack around.

There was a door next to the tarot joint that led into her building. Too obvious. The building next door was clearly the way to go, so I skeleton-keyed in lickety spilt, shot up two flights of stairs, out the back window at the landing, and grabbing a drainpipe, I swung around so I landed on the Snow Leopard's roof, quiet as a love-monkey making a house call. I hopped down onto the fire escape and leaned way out so I could see inside the window of the Snow Leopard. Sadly, drawn drapes stopped me from staring into her lair.

A nobody's-home vibe radiated through the walls and I could barely stand it, so close to being inside her cave, sniffing around her unmentionables, uncovering her underbelly, unearthing the sweet secrets that make the Snow Leopard tick. One foot on the fire escape railing, the other on her sill, I jimmied my handmade fenestrator in, guided the lock to the disengaged position, slid the window up, and slithered in like an oiled snake.

Surveying the place with my penlight, I couldn't quite wrap my eyes around it. It was as elusive as she was. One huge room, the whole floor of the building. I could see what was probably the front door, around 150 feet away. Only the moon through two skylights provided light, and that came and went as nightclouds drifted by. Another door on the west wall. Closed. One more door on the east wall. Closed. In the back corner, one giant bed with four posts was covered in carved cats chasing each other up and down. Fur blankets piled high. No chairs. No table. No kitchen. No garbage can. No TV. No computer. No, wait. Next to the bed, growing up the wall, was a ten-foot bookcase with a ladder next to it. *And what, pray tell, does the Snow Leopard read?* my mind wondered to itself. You can tell everything about a person by their library. Or lack thereof. *The Jungle Book. The Cat in the Hat. How the Leopard Got His Spots. Why Cats Paint. Taming the Tiger Within. How Large Cats Kill. The Leopard Hunts in Darkness.* I smiled.

Inside one door: bathroom. Or rather a shell of a bathroom. A toilet. A standing sink. A claw-foot tub. A bar of soap. No beauty products. No medicine cabinet. No medicine. It's like she was not quite human.

Behind door number 2: walk-in closet. Outfits hang on rods. All black. Hump-me pumps, kick-yer-ass boots, gouge-yer-eye-out stiletto heels, thin Chinese slippers, and one pair of spiffy spats. One dresser. Three drawers. Bras. Panties. Stockings. One pair of black panties. I picked them up. Wrapped them around my face like a gas mask and breathed in the secret scent of the Snow Leopard. Pavlov was laughing in his grave as that smell invaded my central nervous system and zapped my boys while blood pumped automatically toward them. I considered stealing them, but I didn't want to piss the Goddess off. I'll ask the Snow Leopard for them after I re-sex her, I thought.

Snap your fingers. Do it now.

The time it takes you to think about snapping your fingers is how long it took for her to have the muzzle of her petite little pistol in my earhole as I left her walk-in closet.

My first thought was: How did she do that? That's *my* thing. Nobody gets the drop on me.

And yet there it was, her cold metal stub at the tip of my earhole.

The next thing was smell. That in-heat scent, that aural-sense memory that made my thing sing as the breath drained out of me in a long warm sigh.

And suddenly her face was in mine. Those burning-coal eyes sucked me into the sunspots in the middle and I remember thinking: How did I get to be the deer in the headlights? The monkey in the middle?

She just stared. Looked like a smile was hiding under her quicksilver face, but there wasn't enough light in the room to tell, just little flashes of moon through the skylights. I kept waiting for her to ask: What are you doing here? Or: How did you get in so easy? Or: What is wrong with you? But nothing. While freakydeaky cracklyscary estrogen-testosterone-saturated atoms careened around her huge empty cat cave.

She leaned in sooooo slow. Just kept leaning. Closer and closer. A picture popped into my head: She'd bitten my lower lip off and it was hanging out of her bloody mouth and she slurped it in between her teeth with a hungry happy growl.

Her lips were right at the tip of my lips and the heat of her breath made it feel like there was a furnace inside her pumping vaporized sex into my mouth and down my throat, filling my lungs and pulsating into my chest, then spreading all the way down to my hips, which began humpdancing unconsciously into her, and the chemicals were changing in my brain, synapses firing, my heart rate erupting through the roof of my mouth, the flow of blood altered, redirected by the Snow Leopard.

I wanted to say: How the hell did you sneak up on me like that? Or: Are you mad that I'm here? Or: Who are you, anyway? But the cat got my tongue. The tense intense antic-ipation was killing me, and all the while I was madly aware of her metal rod flirting with my earhole. I simply cannot emphasize enough how this added to the life-n-death of the whole thing, knowing I was one itchy trigger finger away from having my brains turned into wallpaper.

The tip of my lip got the softest lick from her rough cat tongue as her other hand grabbed my package hard, knock-ing the air right out of me, while she shoved me back into the wall with a *thud*, her claws digging into my boys.

And then I understood. This is her thing: Getting guys by the balls. Literally. Her grind finding mine, she dug in, yes it did hurt, but at the same time, pleasure shot to all my centers, all at the same time. Pleasure. Pain. Pain. Pleasure. I couldn't tell anymore where one ended and the other began. She dragged me back and forth fiercely, and I had never felt more alive in my entire life. She squeezeboxed me like a rhythm queen working overtime, working me over but good.

I was now waiting to wake up overheated and covered in cold sweat from this dream.

But no.

She pushed me hard, my back literally up against the wall. She shoved me down onto the floor, and plopped down on me, she had me pinned, straddling one boot on either side of my thighs, black skirt up over her hips, sucking on my tongue so it shivered me with freezing heat, and that little prick of a gun was always there, hard and cold in my earhole, my death at her whim a whisper away.

The Snow Leopard started making crazy growly hissing sounds, I could feel the pull of the moon from inside her, and I knew I never wanted to leave there.

She maneuvered herself open, pulled back her head and looked into my eyes, inviting me inside to ride her Ferris wheel to the stars. She took a deep breath, and a sweetness came over her face, it filled me up, everything softened and she melted me in places I didn't even know I had places.

Then she grabbed me behind the neck with her free hand and gathered herself like a hurricane off the coast.

And then *BOOM!* she shoved down with all her might, with all those muscles, with all that leverage, all that wet and that swell, sliding down deepdeepdeep into the depth of her holiness, all the way to the bottom of the well, splitting her open like an atom, an explosion of heat blowing my mushroom-cloud heart all the way up.

More crazy roar big cat scratch fever screams as she rocked slowly, flexing in rhythm with the tide, tugging and grinding, pressing flesh on flesh, sweat beading out now, the sound of squishing liquid wet, ecstasy crawling from pleasure center to pleasure center up and down my tingling spine as she pulled me up higher and higher, while ripping into my skin. *Is that sweat or blood trickling down my neck?* my brain asked. *Yes, it is*, my body answered.

She was back in my face again, the Snow Leopard. I could finally see her, as a strip of moon filtered through her skylights, and she poured herself through my windows, and this is what took me to the edge of Lover's Leap.

She nodded at me ever so tiny, she wanted to know if I was ready to jump off with her, to take the great plunge, and into her eyes I nodded, *Yes, I'm ready, jump off and I'll jump with you.*

Funny what a person can get used to. When the muzzle of her petite little pistol first nuzzled my earhole, everything else in the entire world faded away, and there was nothing but the cold steel feel of that gun, death at the tip of her finger.

But by the time I heard the click of the trigger, I had quite forgotten, in all the excitement, that her petite little pistol was there at all. It took me a moment to realize what that sound was, to remember that her gun was indeed in my earhole.

How long was it between the time I heard that click and the time that bullet ripped down the tiny barrel of her pistol, barreled through the hole of my ear and into the fishy tissue of my brain? Couldn't be more than a flicker of a blink, right? A heartbeat? At what point during its passage through my skull did the bullet take me from orgasm to death? I cannot accurately answer that question.

But as a sex maniac, I couldn't have asked for a better death: coming and going in the same moment, at the hands of the Snow Leopard.

Acknowledgments

The editor wishes to thank the following for their encouragement and support: Andy Bellows, Sona Avakian, Jennifer Joseph, Paul Yamazaki, Miriam Hodgman, The Matlock Brothers, Ashish & Janaki Ranpura, Daphne Gottlieb, Alan Goldstein, Tasha Keppler, Daniel Mandel, Jane Ganahl, Cheryll Eddy, Jeffrey Chan, Justin Chin, Mattilda, Johnny Strike, Nichelle Tramble, Michael Disend, Alan Black, Jill Tracy, Charles Gatewood, Marta Koehne, Stacey Lewis, Melissa Wagner, Jon Bradford, John Hurtado, Richard Poccia, Sherry Olsen, Lawrence Ferlinghetti, Nancy J. Peters, Elaine Katzenberger, the gang at City Lights, and to Chris & Alex for logistical support; past, present, and future.

ABOUT THE CONTRIBUTORS:

ROBERT MAILER ANDERSON was born in San Francisco in 1968. He finished his first novel, *Boonville*, in a hotel room in North Beach while jocking coffee at Caffe Trieste. He now lives with his wife and three children in Pacific Heights above a robot, and is a board member of SFJAZZ and the S.F. Opera Association.

WILL CHRISTOPHER BAER is the author of the Phineas Poe trilogy: *Kiss Me, Judas, Penny Dreadful,* and *Hell's Half Acre,* to be released in omnibus edition fall 2005 by MacAdam/Cage. He lives in California. For more, see willchristopherbaer.com.

KATE BRAVERMAN first came to San Francisco as a runaway in 1965. She has written four novels (including *Lithium for Medea* and *Palm Latitudes),* four books of poetry, and two collections of short stories, mostly set in a California that doesn't appear on the postcards. She is the recipient of many awards and fellowships for both her fiction and nonfiction. Braverman currently lives in Russian Hill with her husband.

DAVID CORBETT was an operative for the San Francisco private investigation firm of Palladino & Sutherland for fifteen years. His first book, *The Devil's Redhead,* was nominated for the Barry and Anthony Awards for Best First Novel of 2002, and his second, *Done for a Dime,* was nominated for the Macavity Award for Best Novel of 2003 and was named a *New York Times* Notable Book. He lives in dismay.

BARRY GIFFORD, a novelist *(Wild at Heart, Wyoming),* poet *(Back in America),* and screenwriter *(Lost Highway, City of Ghosts)* has resided in or around San Francisco for thirty-five years. "After Hours at La Chinita" is an excerpt from his forthcoming book, *The Stars Above Veracruz.* For more information please visit www.BarryGifford.com.

JON LONGHI is the author of five books: *Bricks and Anchors, The Rise and Fall of Third Leg, Everyone at the Funeral Was Slam Dancing, Flashbacks and Premonitions,* and *Wake Up and Smell the Beer.* He has been published in numerous anthologies and has performed his work throughout the United States in cafés, bookstores, libraries, and nightclubs. He lives in San Francisco.

J Joseph

ALVIN LU was born in San Francisco. He wrote the "City God" column for the *San Francisco Bay Guardian* for several years and is also the author of a novel, *The Hell Screens,* published by Four Walls Eight Windows.

Unknown

PETER MARAVELIS has been a bookseller for over fifteen years. He is currently the events coordinator for City Lights Bookstore. He was born and raised in San Francisco where he currently lives.

Perry Matlock

EDDIE MULLER is a native San Franciscan and author of three popular studies of noir: *Dark City, Dark City Dames,* and *The Art of Noir.* He is a multiple Edgar and Anthony Award nominee, and the recipient of the Shamus Award for Best First Novel *(The Distance).* He is founder and president of the Film Noir Foundation, a nonprofit dedicated to the rescue and preservation of "lost" and damaged noir films.

Ron Rinaldi

ALEJANDRO MURGUÍA is the author of *Southern Front,* a short story collection about the Chicano internationalists in Nicaragua, which received an American Book Award in 1991. *This War Called Love, Nine Stories* was also honored with an American Book Award in 2002. He is working on a new collection of short stories, *Tropic Noir.*

Luis Delgado

©Philippe Matsas

JIM NISBET has published eight novels and five volumes of poetry. His novels include *The Gourmet (aka The Damned Don't Die)*, *Lethal Injection*, *Death Puppet*, *Prelude to a Scream*, *The Price of the Ticket*, and his latest, *The Syracuse Codex*. He lives in San Francisco where he operates the design firm Electronics Furniture.

Nina Glaser

PETER PLATE is a self-taught fiction writer and former squatter in the Mission district of San Francisco. His books address the history and geography of inner-city life. His latest novel is *Fogtown*.

t. gimmick

SIN SORACCO was born at St. Luke's Hospital in the Mission district of San Francisco. She makes up her life from whatever's around—if there's nothing handy, she goes somewhere else. The center remains steady: the intense visceral pleasure of stories. She says, "One day our stories will bring the bastards down."

Gillian Conoley

DOMENIC STANSBERRY is known for his dark, innovative crime novels, including his award-winning North Beach mysteries, *The Last Days of Il Duce* and *Chasing the Dragon*. Stansberry is also the author of *The Confession*, a "modern noir shocker" that has been hailed as the vanguard of the neo-pulp renaissance. He has been nominated three times for the Edgar Allan Poe Award.

Phyllis Christopher

DAVID HENRY STERRY is both writer of and performer in a one-man show based on his memoir *Chicken: Self-Portrait of a Young Man for Rent*. His next book will be *Putting Your Passion into Print*. He has worked as a chicken, chicken fryer, a Hollywood screenwriter, a cherry picker, a sitcom actor, a poet, a stand-up comic (at Holy City Zoo, Cobb's, and Sutro Bathhouse), a barker (at the Garden of Eden on Broadway in San Francisco), and a marriage counselor.

Kelly Davidson

MICHELLE TEA is cofounder of the legendary all-girl spoken word road show known as Sister Spit. She has contributed to many fiction anthologies and written several acclaimed novels, the most recent of which was a collaboration with illustrator Laurenn McCubbin, titled *Rent Girl*. Her first collection of poetry, *The Beautiful*, was released in 2004 by Manic D Press and she curates a reading series called SF Radar at the San Francisco Main Library.

Also available from Akashic Books

BROOKLYN NOIR
edited by Tim McLoughlin
350 pages, a trade paperback original, $15.95, ISBN: 1-888451-58-0
*Finalist stories for EDGAR AWARD, PUSHCART PRIZE, and SHAMUS AWARD

Twenty brand new crime stories from New York's punchiest borough. Contributors include: Pete Hamill, Arthur Nersesian, Maggie Estep, Nelson George, Neal Pollack, Sidney Offit, Ken Bruen, and others.

"*Brooklyn Noir* is such a stunningly perfect combination that you can't believe you haven't read an anthology like this before. But trust me—you haven't. Story after story is a revelation, filled with the requisite sense of place, but also the perfect twists that crime stories demand. The writing is flat-out superb, filled with lines that will sing in your head for a long time to come."
—Laura Lippman, winner of the Edgar, Agatha, and Shamus awards

BROOKLYN NOIR 2: THE CLASSICS
edited by Tim McLoughlin
309 pages, trade paperback, $15.95, ISBN: 1-888451-76-9

Brooklyn Noir is back with a vengeance, this time with masters of yore mixing with the young blood: H.P. Lovecraft, Lawrence Block, Donald Westlake, Pete Hamill, Jonathan Lethem, Colson Whitehead, Irwin Shaw, Carolyn Wheat, Thomas Wolfe, Hubert Selby, Stanley Ellin, Gilbert Sorrentino, Maggie Estep, and Salvatore La Puma.

CHICAGO NOIR
edited by Neal Pollack
252 pages, a trade paperback original, $14.95, ISBN: 1-888451-89-0

Chicago Noir is populated by hired killers and jazzmen, drunks and dreamers, corrupt cops and ticket scalpers and junkies. It's the Chicago that the Department of Tourism doesn't want you to see, a place where hard cases face their sad fates, and pay for their sins in blood. This isn't someone's dream of Chicago. It's not even a nightmare. It's just the real city, unfiltered. *Chicago Noir.*

Brand new stories by: Neal Pollack, Achy Obejas, Alexai Galaviz-Budziszewski, Adam Langer, Joe Meno, Peter Orner, Kevin Guilfoile, Bayo Ojikutu, Jeff Allen, Luciano Guerriero, Claire Zulkey, Andrew Ervin, M.K. Meyers, Todd Dills, C.J. Sullivan, Daniel Buckman, Amy Sayre-Roberts, and Jim Arndorfer.

SOUTHLAND by Nina Revoyr
348 pages, a trade paperback original, $15.95, ISBN: 1-888451-41-6
*Winner of a LAMBDA LITERARY AWARD & FERRO-GRUMLEY AWARD
*EDGAR AWARD finalist

"If Oprah still had her book club, this novel likely would be at the top of her list . . . With prose that is beautiful, precise, but never pretentious . . ."

—*Booklist*

"*Southland* merges elements of literature and social history with the propulsive drive of a mystery, while evoking Southern California as a character, a key player in the tale. Such aesthetics have motivated other Southland writers, most notably Walter Mosley."

—*Los Angeles Times*

ADIOS MUCHACHOS by Daniel Chavarría
245 pages, a trade paperback original, $13.95, ISBN: 1-888451-16-5
*Winner of the EDGAR AWARD

"Out of the mystery wrapped in an enigma that, over the last forty years, has been Cuba for the U.S., comes a Uruguayan voice so cheerful, a face so laughing, and a mind so deviously optimistic that we can only hope this is but the beginning of a flood of Latin America's indomitable novelists, playwrights, storytellers. Welcome, Daniel Chavarría."

—Donald Westlake, author of *Trust Me on This*

HAIRSTYLES OF THE DAMNED
by Joe Meno
290 pages, a trade paperback original, $13.95, ISBN: 1-888451-70-X
*PUNK PLANET BOOKS, a BARNES & NOBLE DISCOVER PROGRAM selection

"Joe Meno writes with the energy, honesty, and emotional impact of the best punk rock. From the opening sentence to the very last word, *Hairstyles of the Damned* held me in his grip."

—Jim DeRogatis, pop music critic, *Chicago Sun-Times*

These books are available at local bookstores.
They can also be purchased with a credit card online through www.akashicbooks.com.
To order by mail send a check or money order to:

AKASHIC BOOKS
PO Box 1456, New York, NY 10009
www.akashicbooks.com, Akashic7@aol.com

(Prices include shipping. Outside the U.S., add $8 to each book ordered.)